www.kristinsample.com

ISBN: 9798632059749

STAGECRAFT
by Kristin Sample

Lovingly dedicated to my mother and father who sat through
So. Many. Recitals.

And for the Preston Players who taught me more
than I taught them.

I was raised to be charming, not sincere.
INTO THE WOODS
»----»

She has more hair than she needs;
In the sun 'tis a woe to me!
And her voice is a string of colored beads,
Or steps leading into the sea.

"Witch-Wife" by Edna St. Vincent Millay

Prologue
Harrison Hospital
Westchester County, NY

Zoe needed to stay in her coma, dreams induced by medicine. A life-giving cocktail that kept her body alive even if her mind would never be the same.

I hope she stays here the rest of her life, Hannah wished then immediately felt shameful.

There's too much to lose.

"So, what's your big plan?" Skylar began. Her voice wavered just a bit. It unnerved Hannah. She was never the one with a plan. She'd always been the lieutenant in this relationship, a dynamic duo since freshmen year at Whispering Hills Country Day School.

Hannah tried to sound strong, "Her sister said that Zoe showed signs of waking. We are going to talk to Zoe. Remind her how we are all best friends. Tell her that she doesn't know who was driving the other car. Convince her that we had nothing to do with it. If we talk to her enough…"

As soon as she started speaking, Hannah felt like an idiot. *Fall in line, Lieutenant Cross,* she said to herself.

Skylar pulled Hannah into the bathroom with new roughness. Then she whispered. A darkness ensconcing her face despite the fluorescent light flickering to life.

"That's the plan?" Skylar's face burned, "God, you're an idiot. You want to talk Zoe out of what she already knows?"

"I've heard that coma patients can hear you. I think…if we talk to her…maybe come back a few times…she'll believe us…at least she'll be confused when she gets up."

Skylar put her hands on the counter and clicked her tongue. Her shock of brown waves fell forward. *I failed her. I failed us. I thought it was a good plan. It sounded good in my head.*

—

"It's worth a shot. According to the websites I've been reading, you're supposed to talk to loved ones, tell them about your day. Some people wake up having heard everything that happened around them while they were asleep." But Skylar's face was unconvinced. *This plan is quickly unraveling.*

"Fine," Skylar wagged her head in disgust.

She thinks this is a waste of time. That I'm a waste of time. Hannah simmered with frustration. *We're here because of her!* Hannah thought about theatre camp last summer. *Once again, I'm with Skylar. Doing bad things.*

The two girls surrounded Zoe's bed. Hannah took the patient's limp hand. It felt old and spent. She looked over Zoe's blanketed body, her sunken cheeks, her pale neck.

"Zoe," Hannah began. "It's Hannah and Skylar. We've come to visit you again. We miss you so much at school."

Hannah went on, voice mellifluous, chatting idly about school, the show. *Ignore Skylar.* Skylar, who stared at Hannah across the body with death in her eyes.

Hannah went on, "Your little sister is so good, Zoe. I can't believe she's only a sophomore. Her ankle is healing well. I think she will be back by hell week." After a few minutes it didn't seem weird anymore, just like talking to a friend.

"This is never going to work. *We* have to make sure she doesn't wake up. We have to do it."

Hannah's rib cage contracted. *What did Skylar just say? Did I hear her right?*

"We can't make sure of anything. She could never wake up or wake up after we leave. That's why we have to play the long game," Hannah pleaded.

"I was never one for patience," Skylar grinned.

"What are you doing?"

Skylar bent down behind the hospital bed and fiddled with wires, "Looking for where to unplug Princess Vegetable."

"What?" Hannah's voice caught in her throat and cracked.

"You heard me. It would be a mercy."

"What?!"

Hannah glanced toward the door then the clock. The nurse wouldn't be around for another seven minutes. Skylar knew them, knew their schedule. She could be so charming. It terrified Hannah.

Skylar's head popped up, "A mercy for you. You're pathetic right now, Hannah. We aren't going to come here every night and con Zoe into thinking that the accident didn't happen."

Hannah desperately searched for something to say that would derail Skylar. *She's a maniac. I can't believe I let it go this far.*

"Found it," Her voice was almost small from behind the bed.

Hannah rushed around to see Skylar contorted, hands following wires to their homes.

"Found what?"

Skylar kept fiddling and adjusting her body at different angles. The lulling beeps of the machines now sounded like ticking bombs. And Skylar was Jack Bauer from 24, diffusing the explosion that would ruin Hannah's life. Was she grateful for Skylar in some dark recess of her soul?

"Found what?" Hannah choked. *I could let her do this. Right now. I could be free of this.* The blackness filled her chest — like cabernet spilled on a creamy white tablecloth.

Skylar lifted her body up and sighed, "You know nothing, Jon Snow." She dusted off her Lululemon leggings. "All you have to do is unplug the ventilator. The patient loses oxygen and dies. That's how easy it is."

"How do you know that?" Hannah's stomach lurched. *How fast can I get back to the bathroom?*

11

Skylar twirled her hair flippantly, "One of the perks of sitting through countless boring dinners with my dad and his friends. See, my dad is on the board of Harrison Hospital. And one time, this young doctor—another board member brought him along, I guess, for colorful conversation—well, he went on and on about the need to lock down the plugs. While he was in residency, a janitor unplugged a patient by accident, and they lost him."

The information sank in. Horrifying. *But it would be so easy. And then this would be over. I can't believe I'm trying to rationalize this.* After a deep breath, she appealed to reason, "If you unplug one of these machines, they will beep like crazy. Surely there is some, I don't know, mechanism, that tells the nurses in the hallway what's going on."

Skylar stepped over to one of the machines and flipped a switch. And just like that…the machine kept nagging the body to be alive…but in silence. "Silence button," She flipped it back on. And the device began its song again. "My mom was in hospice forever, remember?"

"We can't do this. I won't let you kill her."

"She's already dead. I don't know what the hell those doctors are telling her family."

"How many coma patients do you know?" Hannah snapped.

"It's in the pamphlets out in the hall, stupid. If she didn't wake in the first month, the chances of Zoe waking are slim."

Skylar ducked under the bed once more.

Hannah grabbed her friend, "Skylar. No!" But Skylar swatted Hannah away and scratched her face.

"Ow!" Hannah cried. A little too loudly. *She can be vicious sometimes.* Hannah touched her cheek tenderly. *I guess this is because of me though. We are here because of me.*

Just then, the machines around Zoe started beeping with more urgency. Sentient beings protecting their ward from these evil spirits around her.

Zoe's eyelids fluttered. *Was she moving? No, she was still. Shit, she moved.*

Then shouting out in the hallway. Then footsteps.

With ninja speed, Skylar grabbed Hannah's arm and pulled her back in the bathroom. Finger to mouth, Skylar motioned to be absolutely still.

Chapter One
The Moment Before
Six weeks earlier

AUDITIONS for Spring Musical

STAGECRAFT

Date: Saturday March 7th for Vocal Auditions at 9 am.
Dance Auditions will follow at 1 pm.
Call backs at 3 pm.

Bring sheet music to Vocal Auditions and be ready to sing either a Broadway show tune or an American Standard.
No *Rent*. No *Spring Awakening*.

Bring dance shoes and wear comfortable clothes for dance auditions. Bring tap shoes if you have them.

Be prepared to be at auditions ALL DAY.
DO NOT ARRIVE LATE.

"Well, this sucks. Hashtag TheatreKidProblems!" Greg Tate slapped down the audition flyer and plopped his lanky body into the orange plastic composite chair. The screech of the chair legs on the linoleum jarred Hannah from her daydream. *Brody again.* Hannah read the flyer. *Why did we change musicals? I thought we were doing Fame. Now, we're putting up Stagecraft?*

"This is bullshit. I've been practicing 'Dancin' on the Sidewalk' with my coach for like *four* weeks now."

"Because you were def going to get Tyrone. Hashtag delusional," Cynthia raised an eyebrow. *Hmph, she's right.* Greg Tate, long and lean and completely gay, was never going to play Tyrone in Fame, the street kid who raps in the first act. *But I'll never publicly agree with the likes of Cynthia Wolcott.*

Hannah Cross chuckled thinking of Greg rapping on the porch of his Lakeside Manor home while his cook made rice and beans at his request. *I need to be in character*, Hannah thought in Greg's voice.

Greg snapped, "Hashtag bitch."

Cynthia slouched and pretended to check her phone. Hannah sipped her Diet Coke and waited. *Better not get involved with these two.* Greg Tate came out last year after breaking up with Cynthia. *So...hashtag awkward?*

Besides their cattiness was low on Hannah Cross's list of priorities. The flyer posed a huge problem for all theatre geeks at Whispering Hills. Their senior year musical was supposed to be Fame — the old director told them so. Just waiting for librettos. Great choice for their age group. Lots of different roles. The whole show wouldn't be about one person.

Like it usually was.

Whispering Hills Country Day School was a far cry from LaGuardia HS in the NYC where Fame actually takes place. Not much public transportation in Whispering Hills. No Section 8 housing either. And nobody was waiting for a performing arts school to save her from her miserable existence.

Besides, if you had a miserable existence at Whispering Hills, it wasn't because you had to take three buses on your commute and play nanny to your younger siblings. If your life was miserable at Whispering Hills, it was probably because your mom did coke. Or you did coke. Or you did coke with your mom.

Hannah looked down at her monstrous fake Louis Vuitton tote. It was spring of senior year and she was hands-down the most believable as a character from Fame.

Everyone else was a Gossip Girl.

Hannah leaned back in her chair, taking in Cynthia and Greg, some of her best friends. Greg diligently ate his usual lunch—a Caesar salad, no dressing. So, yes, he basically ate romaine lettuce and diet soda. He got thinner every week. Hannah smirked and thought of Greg shopping in the children's section of American Apparel. But when she looked at her own sandwich, she pushed it away.

Greg chatted idly about Fame. "And doesn't every girl love leg warmers? And Hannah, you would look killer in that chevron stripe leotard. I love a high cut leg."

Hannah smiled and reread the audition flyer.

Interesting. The flyer is pretty standard Mr. Jacobsen. He loathed anything late 90s Broadway, so students were never allowed to sing a piece from *Rent*. Who wants to listen to the torch song about how many cups of coffee are in someone's lifetime? Hannah gagged every time "Seasons of Love" came on Spotify.

Cynthia snatched the flyer, "Stagecraft? That's the show? It ran all of 100 performances. I heard the producer was dating Blair Solomon and that's how she got the part. And when you cast some TV actress who's more famous for showing her boobs on HBO than she is for her singing voice, you only run 100 shows."

Stagecraft was a backstage musical about a young ingénue from a small town come to the big city to make it on Broadway. Between the hackneyed plot and poor casting, the original cast barely made out of previews. Hannah never saw it. And she sees almost every show. Most of the time she goes with Skylar Clarke, her bestie and the resident queen at Whispering Hills. If there's no invite from Skylar, Hannah scrounges together her paltry allowance, birthday money from grandma, and babysitting money.

Cynthia and Greg continued whining about changing their audition songs. Hannah planned on "Maybe This Time" from Cabaret. It was her sad clown song, full of vitriol but also wonderfully expectant. Great belt at the end. You need a great belt for a vocal audition. No chance of a callback without one.

Hannah stared blankly around the cafeteria. It was the only room not touched by the school's renovation, furniture from bygone days and food that tasted decades old to match. But the cafeteria had the best view. The lake. Some days the water beckoned. Expansive and crystalline. It made Hannah question why she bent toward performing arts and not crew team.

"Hannah. Hannah! Girlfriend, you zoned out," Greg snapped his long fingers.

Shit. How long have I been zoned out? Reliving my whole existence on this lake. Hannah flushed — did they know the envy that resided in her heart?

"Sorry. What?"

Greg's rolled his eyes dramatically, "Where is Skylar? Is she coming to lunch? I mean, you can't throw up your lunch if you don't eat it first." Feigning nonchalance as he looked over his shoulder. *What a coward. Greg, you stand a full foot over petite Skylar. But you would never (never!) say that to Skylar's face.*

Not that Greg was making stuff up.

Skylar started purging about four months after her mother passed. Maybe it was earlier, but that was the first time Hannah cringed at awful sound of the vomit. When you're not actually sick, vomiting is different. There's hoarseness in the sound, like your stomach saying 'I need that.' Self-inflicted gasps for air. Fingers exploring further down the throat.

Hannah knew about getting rid of unwanted calories too. In middle school, she attended a summer intensive down at American Ballet Academy. All the older girls were binging and purging. So, she joined in—amused and horrified at how easy it was. Who wouldn't like eating whatever you want at Pizza Mia on East 77th and then not worrying about how you looked in the skintight leotard and unforgiving pink tights?

When Hannah's mother found out, Gillian Cross cursed out the academy's director, effectively ending Hannah's ballet career. Hannah still remembers her mother's eyes—angry but terrified.

Hannah didn't stop hurting herself right away though. She'd worked three years for ABA. But by the end of the summer, it was time to end her foray into eating disorders. Stop punishing her mom. Time to stop acting like an ass, like Hannah's father.

When Hannah discovered Skylar in her bathroom—that massive pink and cream marbled asylum—she tried the same look—the self-blaming look Hannah's mother used. Naively, Hannah believed her love for Skylar would be the cure. Make Skylar see that she was hurting herself.

But the cell phone just missed Hannah's head. And then Skylar charged. With a swiftness so cold, she whipped her hand across Hannah's face. Astonishing strength.

Fist curled around Hannah's ponytail, Skylar threw her friend up against a wall. Picture frames crashed down. A picture of Mrs. Clarke on vacation in Sun Valley reeled to the floor. The glass shattered and Skylar dropped her friend's defeated body.

"Now look what you've done! Clean it up!"

Hannah sat on the floor crying for the better part of an hour, panties damp with urine. Skylar texted three hours later with a half-hearted apology and an invite for a sleepover.

The two never spoke of it again. In the vault. Just like what they did to Katie Greco at theatre camp.

"Boo! You scared Sky is going to catch you talking shit, Greg?" Cynthia sneered. *You wish Skylar would catch Greg. So desperate.* In middle school, it was always Cynthia and Skylar. But that changed when Hannah came.

"She's here," Hannah whispered as her friends squabbled pathetically. Then their eyes fixed on the double doors of the cafeteria. *Is she actually entering this scene in slow motion or is it me?* Hannah imagined wind machines blowing Skylar's brunette waves.

She was flanked by two new beaus. A Lacrosse no-name with hairy legs. And the brooding, aloof Derrick from auto shop class. *All he cares about was getting laid and fixing cars.* Derrick Sullivan. A weird blotch on the Whispering Hills class pictures. The clichéd outsider.

Ugh, Derrick Sullivan. Gross. And why the hell does Whispering Hills still have a shop class? Like anyone actually wants to learn how to change the fluids on their BMWs. But then a pang jolted Hannah's chest. She had more in common with Derrick than any of her friends.

No doubt the entrance was a show for Will Bartlett. *Show him what he's missing, Sky.* Skylar's ex was now dating Zoe Kellogg—the go-to girl for musical leads. And Skylar's calm and easy acceptance of the new couple was downright sociopathic. But she hibernated, her body resting and her mind planning their absolute misery. She would wait all of senior year if she had to. Pull Zoe closer. Earn forgiveness from Will. Skylar would blame her mother's passing and rise like a phoenix from the ashes of unrequited love. It was already happening. Hannah watched with a mix of pride and excitement and horror.

Skylar laughed and threw her head back like wild horse. Chocolate-colored mane tossed back and forth. She had their complete attention. And then, without ceremony, Skylar cantered away, leaving both of them holding their proverbial limp dicks.

Her petite frame loomed large over their chairs, dwarfing even Greg. He and Cynthia were still overusing hashtags.

"Hashtag shut the hell up with the hashtags," Skylar cocked an eyebrow. "How about that? Go ahead. Tweet something passive aggressive about me"

Both stared blankly. The salty greeting from Skylar was fuzzy.

Skylar laughed hard and kissed Cynthia on the cheek, "I'm joking, bitch. Don't be so basic." Cynthia finally released the breath she'd been holding.

"What's this? More prom stuff?"

"We're not doing Fame. We're doing Stagecraft. Everyone is freaking out," Hannah handed Skylar the flyer. She tried to keep her reply nonchalant, like a mafia underboss.

Skylar reapplied lip-gloss, "I knew that already. Got any *actual* news?"

"Well *I* didn't know. And now I have to change my vocal audition. I was going for Tyrone."

Skylar regarded Greg with chilling sincerity, "You totally had a shot at Tyrone."

He basked in the light of the compliment as Cynthia growled.

"I think we have a different director. Mr. Jacobsen would never waste money on rights to a show and then not do it," Hannah offered.

"Yes, we have a new director. And don't worry about the money, Hannah. Clearly Whispering Hills can afford to eat the money for the rights," Skylar looked up momentarily from her texting then added sarcastically, "The school will just take more out of our cafeteria budget. Fish sticks are cheap. You don't mind eating those, right?"

The remark could've been a gripe about the state of the lunchroom, but Hannah couldn't help but register it more pointedly than that. She ate school lunch every day. She got it for free because her mom worked at Whispering Hills. Most students brought lunch from home—a meal prepared by their housekeepers or bought from a gourmet deli. Some ate from the overpriced vending machines. Skylar didn't eat at all.

Still Hannah laughed hard.

Skylar went on about the transition of power. A new director was major variable for a pack of skittish theatre kids. Greg and Cynthia were already ejaculating their 'I can't evens' and 'Literally can't evens' in rondo. Besides, Mr. Jacobsen was a good man, a good teacher, and a passionate director. He always made the people with smaller roles (Hannah) feel just as important as the leads. Hannah sighed deeply—she thought for sure that Mr. Jacobsen would reward her past work with a bigger role this year, her senior year. She'd given up so much at her dance studio for this.

With a new director, who knows? This guy could come in and cast a damn freshman as the lead. Upperclassmen would be pissed. The freshman would feel the wrath of the older kids and in turn, suck. Rehearsals would be misery. Skylar would wreak havoc because the pecking order was screwed up.

Skylar slid her phone under her thigh as the cafeteria monitor strolled by. "Sorry guys. So, as I was saying, Mr. Jacobsen is long gone. And thank God for that."

"I know, right?" Cynthia concurred.

Oh, Cynthia, you moldy sponge. What do you truly think about anything? Ridiculous.

Skylar contemplated aloud, "I mean, Mr. Jacobsen was…so…mediocre. And now he finally got a Broadway tour. A tour, mind you. Years of auditioning for shows and he gets the *Footloose* tour that stars some loser from *American Idol*."

The biology teacher, Mr. Pollix, appeared at the table and scolded Skylar for having her phone out in school. If you got caught, the teacher could take the phone away and give it to your class dean. Dean Feldman was a colossal mouth-breather. Hannah never abused the phone rule. The rule posed a problem for Skylar Clarke who texted everyone constantly and *always* expected prompt responses.

Mr. Pollix eyed Skylar, ready to spar. Hannah already pitied him. "Put away your phone or I'm taking it, Ms. Clarke."

"I don't have my phone out," her voice downright saintly.

"No one stares at their crotch and smiles *that* much. Put it away," Mr. Pollix parried. He still lived at home with his mother and worked as a security guard at the mall right outside the Bath & Body Works, so he always smelled of jasmine and cucumbers.

And he was clinically depressed. Hannah's own diagnosis.

Skylar leaned forward so that her full breasts nearly sat on the lunch table. Then deliberately and quietly, "You look at my crotch and smile."

If another teacher were present, Skylar would've been suspended. But alas, Mr. Pollix was alone, like he was for most of his wretched life. Pollix turned the color of Dorothy's ruby slippers and skulked away.

Skylar continued texting. The school paid a hefty dowry for the Brooks Clarke endowment. The headmaster seemed to enjoy his new office courtesy of Clarke money. The librarian liked her new first edition collection. And the science teachers really had to shut up and take it from Skylar. Her dad was the reason they had state-of-art labs—next level NASA stuff. And then, of course, there was the Clarke Theatre.

Skylar draped her arm around Hannah, "Are you going to tell mommy that I mouthed off to Pollix?"

"Nope," Hannah smiled wide and raised an eyebrow, "I'm fine with you mouthing off to Pollix. That way, when he goes postal, I'll know that he'll shoot your snotty ass and not mine."

Skylar giggled, placed her hands on the table dramatically, and looked at her minions coyly, "Okay, so do you bitches want to know who the new director is?"

"Umm, yes!" Greg sang vibrato, both jazz hands raised to his cheeks.

Before Skylar could announce the news, Zoe Kellogg walked over, "Hey guys. What's up?"

A flash of hatred crossed Skylar's face. But instantaneously, Skylar was collected, "There you are, pretty girl. I've been asking for you. Where have you been all lunch period?"

Zoe sighed, "AP Calc extra help. I still have no idea why I created the worst senior schedule known to man."

"Well, you got out of boring math just in time. We have a new director for our musical." "I know. I met him last week at Will's Student Council thing."

———

23

Another flash of rage. The queen took a deep, cleansing breath this time.

Zoe started to talk when Skylar's voice interrupted. She leered at her squad, "I was about to say, that our new director is Aaron Samuels. I met him last night at the board meeting. I was there with Daddy. They said I couldn't stay for the boring budget stuff, but I was allowed in the reception after. Cheap champagne and cheese cubes from Costco for the win!"

Zoe tried to enter the conversation again. *Does she really not see that Skylar will eat her alive? Skylar probably ate her own twin en utero...out of boredom.*

Now there was only three minutes till the bell.

"Okay...Aaron, I mean, Mr. Samuels is bringing his friend who choreographs Broadway shows to do a big group tap number. That's why the audition flyer says to bring tap shoes if you have them. His friend is legit too. Has a Tony award."

Greg nearly jumped out of his seat, "A Tony award? Who is it?"

"No idea," Skylar's lip curled.

She knows. She just gets off on being withholding.

"Are you guys worried? I'm a little freaked out," Zoe interjected, hopelessly earnest. Zoe played Sara in Guys and Dolls as a junior and Glinda in The Wiz as a sophomore. Furthermore, she was impossibly beautiful and nauseatingly humble.

Zoe. The perfect storm of audition competition. The lead in Stagecraft? In the bag.

Gosh, the sincerity is grating. Was she from Oklahoma or something? Hannah gritted her teeth and thought of how much work she'd put in over the years. *It's my last show at WHCD too. But of course, Zoe will get the part. The lead – again.*

A wicked thought popped into Hannah's head, but she shoved it down somewhere dark.

"Like you have anything to worry about?" Skylar's words curved through the air and petted Zoe like a puppy. Zoe smiled back. Cynthia was about to agree profusely but the bell rang.

Greg scurried off, shoving his chemistry lab work in his messenger bag and nearly knocking over a freshman to get to class early. He left his garbage on the table. A cafeteria monitor ordered Cynthia to clear it. She sighed melodramatically.

As Cynthia went one way to the garbage pails, Skylar laced her arm through Hannah's and hurried toward the doors. Hannah felt the thrill of triumph. Cynthia would see the twosome walking arm-in-arm, like some ladies strolling in some huge 18th century novel that her mom reads. Hannah felt lighter.

When you were with Skylar Clarke, you were the only person in the world.

As they joined the cattle exiting slowly through the double doors, Skylar leaned in close, "Can you keep a secret?"

"Of course! What is it?" Hannah whispered, half aroused and half terrified. It could be that she just went down on Derrick and the Lacrosse boy. Or got a teacher fired.

Hannah swallowed hard, hoping it was about the show but prepared to be equally dazzled by anything Skylar had to reveal.

"I know who the Broadway choreographer is." Skylar ducked her head lower and a few mahogany strands tickled her tiny nose. She spied Will Bartlett.

"He can't hear us. It's too loud in this hallway," Hannah assured her.

Will grinned slightly. But not at Skylar. Or Hannah. Zoe was by his side, giving him a peck on the cheek. Skylar stared menacingly at the couple but spoke to Hannah, "The choreographer was at camp this year. The week before you came. He taught a tap workshop and loved me. I mean, it was almost creepy. He really liked me. I talked to him afterward and he said I was every bit a star. In fact, he couldn't believe that I wasn't a lead at Whispering Hills yet. I was clearly the most mature student in the workshop."

They entered the chemistry lab.

"So, who is he?"

Skylar flared her nostrils, "And I told him about perfect Miss Zoe Kellogg. He knows her mom. Thinks Zoe's mom is a joke. And he nearly fell over when I said that Zoe was top dog last year. Fell over. Like I could've poked him in the arm, and he would have tumbled to the ground, Hannah."

The bell rang, and Skylar stopped abruptly. She sat up tall and began copying directions from the board, her books and lab report placed on the desk with neurotic precision.

Hannah checked out completely during the lecture. *Who was this Broadway guy? Of course, he came the week before I got to camp.* Hannah only could afford one week of theatre camp to Skylar's three. *Did she say his name?*

Skylar leaned in, "I'm friends with him on Facebook too."

"What's his name?" Hannah murmured.

"I told you already. And shhh." Skylar folded her hands primly.

Hannah sighed. *I wish this didn't matter so much. Why does it matter so much?*

But if this choreographer would be at auditions…
If I just knew his name…
If I knew the director too…

A wave of nerves washed over her chest and neck. Blood pricked her cheeks. *I'm going bomb auditions this year.*

After a few spinning moments, Hannah rallied. She knew her audition song. And the lead didn't matter anyway. *I do every show this school put on from the fall drama to the holiday Nutcracker, to the spring musical and the May follies. Getting the lead never mattered before. Why should it matter now?*

Hannah did community theatre in the summer. She worked at the local dinner theatre while Greg traveled down to NYC for dance classes and Skylar took voice lessons from a retired Met Opera prima donna.

Hannah felt a clear sense of resolve—she didn't need this rich people one-upmanship.

A light from the backpack at her feet. Skylar texted. *Texted? We're literally sitting next to each other.* Hannah placed her new iPhone (a birthday gift from you know who) gingerly on her right thigh.

> SC: singing maybe this time for auditions. what r u singing?

Was she kidding? Like acid after a spicy meal, the rage rose up in Hannah's stomach. Hannah was using "Maybe This Time."

> HC: no idea.

Hannah stared at the board.

> SC: what the hell r u singing? don't be coy with me, bi-otch.

Shoot. What do I say here? You never sing the audition same song as your friend. Maybe you do at a school where the performing arts suck, but not at Whispering Hills. Unless you are singing something from the show the school was producing. But even then…

Usually, Skylar announces what she's singing and then everyone else chooses around it.

Hannah texted back — bravely.

> HC: maybe
> this time. been
> practicing it for
> weeks

Skylar laughed out loud when the text came through. The teacher noticed that one, "Something funny, Ms. Clarke?"

"Nothing. So sorry," her body straight like a spear.

Ms. Connors continued lecturing about the properties of acids and bases. Hannah tried to ignore the steam rising off Skylar's body.

> SC: whatever.
> a soprano
> doing a mezzo
> song?! ur
> funeral.

Now Hannah was pissed. *Why can't Skylar just deal with it? Who gives a shit?* But the anger quickly gave way to worry. Hannah breathed deeply — the way one pulls on a cigarette. A deep drag of anxiety and umbrage.

And Skylar was right. Hannah understudied last year for Zoe. Her character's songs were in the rafters. Only Zoe and Hannah could hit the notes consistently without cracking. *Maybe Skylar is right.* The thought poked into Hannah's train of thought again, like a car cutting over two lanes on a busy highway. *I'm not a belter.* This big torch song was much better on Skylar's raspy, storied voice. She would kill it and Hannah would look like crap by comparison.

It would be a repeat of freshmen year. Hannah made the colossal mistake of singing the same song as Zoe at auditions. She sounded terrible. Zoe crushed it. Hannah cried like a colic newborn in the last stall of the girl's room. Skylar comforted her. "That's Zoe Kellogg," she had said. "Her mom used to be on Broadway. Everyone sounds like shit compared to her. You were great. Really."

"Hannah. Earth to Hannah," Skylar's index finger crept up into Hannah's face. She put on an alien voice and giggled softly. "Come on, girl! Ms. Connors told us to start and you're just staring into outer space."

"Sorry. I just…have a lot to do when I get home," Hannah apologized meekly and organized some beakers on the table.

"Yes, you do. Like pick a new audition song. That was a joke, right? I mean, you knew I was singing 'Maybe This Time.' Been talking about it since auditions for *Midsummer* in September. I was even humming it when we were supposed to be practicing lines," Skylar pulled her goggles down to her eyes and then made a silly face.

The pair recorded measurements and wrote down hypotheses so Ms. Connor could check when she came lurking. But Hannah found herself replaying call back day for *Midsummer Nights' Dream*, the fall drama this year.

Sweat pooled on the small of her back. Her thigh twitched a little where her phone sat and vibrated with all those text alerts. Hannah flexed her quad by pulling up her kneecap to make the twitching stop, take control of the muscle.

Skylar worked diligently—a change from her usual letting Hannah do all the work and then copying the answers. Skylar only used science to cross check the interactions between Adderall and Oxy.

"Don't worry. I'll help you pick something. Or you could always use something from *Guys & Dolls*. You won't sound as good as Zoe, but you'll be okay for a call back."

"I'll figure it out myself," Hannah replied as nastily as she could manage. Nasty considering she was replying to Skylar, the most powerful student at Whispering Hills.

The unexpected reticence brought color to Skylar's face. She was about to say something cutting when Will Bartlett entered the room. Something about leaving his copy of Death of a Salesman. He was probably coming from Hannah's mom's class. She talked just last night of how good he was at playing Biff Loman.

Will peered around lab tables. Skylar froze when he walked by, living in her own version of Fatal Attraction. Will tiptoed around, careful not to upset the panopticon that was Ms. Connors.

"Hi Will," Skylar gave a dazzling grin and put on her most mellifluous voice. The words hung in the air. Even Hannah was lured in—the trap not even for her.

Will nodded quickly, "Skylar." Gave her nothing. Barely an acknowledgement and within seconds he swooped down on his book.

She will need to punish someone for this rejection. Cynthia isn't around. Guess I'll get the abuse. While Skylar's wrath never came, Hannah spent the rest of the period like a dog about to get hit. Ears back, tail down.

After the final bell, Hannah trudged up to the faculty lounge looking for Miss Brewster, a new hire this year. Right out of grad school and ready to change the world, one rich kid at a time. She totally belonged in some charter school in the city. Miss Brewster's passion for the intersection of great literature and young people would be squelched by helicopter parents. But she'd be married and pregnant in a few years anyway. At least Miss Brewster could say that she made an excellent salary at Whispering Hills. One thing Whispering Hills didn't do — underpay the staff. When Hannah's mom got English Department Head, she was able to stop working the whole summer. It was nice to have her around more.

Hannah knocked tentatively on the faculty lounge door.

"Hi Hannah!" another teacher answered, "Here for your mom? Come in."

"Actually, I needed to ask Miss Brewster something. I have a few questions about my essay."

Gillian Cross chimed in anyway, awkwardly joking about how her daughter wouldn't need any assistance with writing.

Then, as Hannah stepped out with Miss Brewster, her mom added, "I'll be off at four today. Go to the library or computer lab. I don't want to go looking for you. We have to pick up your brother at 4:30 from soccer practice."

"Okay, mom."

"Hannah! Pizza's here! Come downstairs," Gillian called from the first floor. Hannah was surfing YouTube for new audition songs. *Something from Funny Girl? Too predictable.* Elbows on her desk with chin in her hands, Hannah watched the eighth video of some teenage girl belting out "Don't Rain on My Parade" through the shitty sound system of her high school's auditorium. The grit in the speakers and the ill-placed body mics were exhausting to listen to. And the iPhone video was nauseating.

"I'm doing my homework!"

Another voice. This time from upstairs. "No, she's not, Mom. Unless you count watching some douchey theatre nerds on YouTube." Then Ricky sang off-key, "My life has no meaning!"

Hannah popped out of her room and startled her little brother. *Jerk.* He discovered his wit recently. Hannah flicked his ear and slammed her bedroom door. She sighed — no pizza for dinner. She would make herself a smoothie. Hopefully that Greek yogurt she spied in the fridge this morning wasn't past its prime.

Another few calls from the first floor. All oddly sing-songy for bookish Gillian Cross. *Why is she so interested in feeding me?* Post-separation from Mr. Cross, the remaining three usually just fend for themselves. Sometimes they attempt a family dinner at the local diner. But Gillian doesn't cook. Hannah's father never needed her to. Joshua Cross lived on cigarettes and wine and self-loathing. Amazing how satisfying that last one can be. You can be full for days on righteous hatred.

Hannah cracked open her Chemistry textbook, but her fingers made their way to the school-issued laptop keyboard. A brand-new MacBook Air she was allowed to take home, even on weekends. Perks of being a teacher's daughter, she guessed.

soprano audition songs

The bedroom door opened noiselessly, and Gillian slipped in. *What is up? Is dad here? No, that would never happen.*

"Hannah, come down and at least have salad if you don't want pizza."

"You made salad?"

"Downstairs. Now. I want you to meet someone." As she padded down the stairs Hannah heard, "Oh, Aaron, she's coming. Just finishing something for chemistry class. Have you met Colleen yet? Great teacher. Been at WH for years."

Why does that name sound familiar?

Holy shit! Aaron Samuels! The new director was at Hannah's house. And the way her mother used her scolding whisper voice could only suggest one thing—Gillian Cross had a new love interest.

Hannah paced around the room. *What do I do with this new information? Is mom dating the director? Are they just friends?* Of course, Mom would say so. "Oh, just friends, Hannah. And don't make a big deal to Ricky."

Hannah racked her brain. *Wait, was that Aaron Samuels mom gushed about last night? I heard her on the phone with Ms. Panzini. Why do I eavesdrop when I need to?*

Then Hannah remembered her mom going out two nights ago. *Or was it three?* It didn't matter. *Wow!* Hannah twirled her hair around her fingers until it almost knotted. She should text Skylar. *No.* Hannah threw her phone down. *Not after that bullshit in chem.*

Hannah got downstairs to see her mom and Mr. Samuels sitting side by side at the dining room table, waiting for her. Almost tableau. Hannah smirked. The duo sitting there waiting, just like the salt and pepper shakers. Like it's always been this way.

He's hot too. Younger than mom.

"So that's what the surface of our dining room table looks like," Hannah plopped down on a chair and started serving herself salad. *Play it cool. Don't ask the three hundred questions you have about Stagecraft auditions.*

"Hannah, please." Mom raised her eyebrows. The dining room table was used for anything but eating. Just this morning it was piled with books, sundry office items, two dead laptops, and an old fish tank from Ricky's room.

Mr. Samuels poured Hannah some water and smiled, "I don't believe we've met. I'm Aaron Samuels. I'm directing the show this year. And I'll be filling in for your music teacher once she goes on maternity leave. Hannah, right?"

Hannah stared. Her mom nudged her. Mr. Samuels tried again, "Your mom tells me that you've been in every production at school since your freshmen year."

"I have."

Gillian Cross piped up. Maybe an explanation would help. A new man at their newly cleaned dining room table. Must be awkward. "Mr. Samuels has a meeting with the nice dad who builds the sets for the play. It's tonight at 7:30 so I invited him here for dinner." Then they shared an oozy smile exchange. "Too much to go all the to the city only to come back up to Westchester."

"How's chemistry going, Hannah?" Mr. Samuels took a big bite of pizza. *Like nothing. Like he eats dinner with us family all the time. This was weird. I kind of wish Skylar was here. She'd know what to do.*

"Chemistry is not as hard as music theory, Mr. Samuels."

"You can call me Aaron," his voice dripped with false assurance. He beamed at Gillian. For a split-second Hannah thought she heard him say "dad" instead of "Aaron." Hannah pinched her thigh till she winced. She wanted to jump over the table and slap him across his clean-shaven face. Smiling politely, Hannah reminded herself that her mother dating was a good thing.

Hannah prayed every night that some gazillionaire-Jesus-dad would walk into her life, sweep her mom off her feet, and move them all to the hamlet of Whispering Hills and out of shitty Oakbrook. Hannah could attend Whispering Hills Country Day on her own money. And Hannah would stop turning cherry red every time someone at school mentioned that Oakbrook was allowed to remain in the affluent township of Lakeside because "the help" needed to live close by.

Oakbrook. The name doesn't even sound like it belongs. Oakbrook is indeed where you'll find housekeepers, landscapers, pool caretakers, and all the staff that work for the folks in Whispering Hills, Lakeside Manor, and Lake Hills. It's also where most of the people who work at the recycling plant in Pembroke live.

Mr. Samuels explained his ideas about sets to mom and Hannah listened intently. Good stuff for lunch time intel swap tomorrow. Gillian was fascinated, of course. Ricky swiped a fourth piece of pizza.

Hannah's phone vibrated the waistband of her yoga pants.

> SC: just did a
> drive by. you
> guys actually
> eat at the
> table????

Hannah was careful to keep her phone under the table.

> HC: u stalking
> me?

Ricky was about to rat when Hannah eyed the pizza emphatically. Then she puffed out her cheeks. *Keep eating and shut up, fat boy.*

SC: always
stalking u.
[heart emoji]
[eyes emoji] is
there a man
there too or
did ur brother
suddenly turn
35? tell ur
mom we have
2 study and
i'm coming
over.

Hannah stalled a few minutes, replaying the conversation before chemistry. *Of course, Skylar has a crush on Mr. Samuels. Mid-thirties. Good looking. And he can probably sing his tight little ass off.* What more could a theatre-obsessed hormonal teen want in a masturbation image?

HC: i'm going
to bed. totes
exhausted.

"Hannah, we don't use our phones at the table."
Why are "we" were even at the freaking table? But every time Hannah gets angry with her mother, Hannah feels an ulcer open up. *All the crap Mom put up with. I have to be better.* Gillian Cross spent seven years married to a failed alcoholic poet.
Skylar never wrote back. Hannah looked around fruitlessly — expecting to see Skylar hiding in the bushes outside.
"Mr. Samuels…err…Aaron," she started.
"Yes, Hannah." His eyes were bright blue and clear.
"I don't know if you can discuss this since auditions are so close. But I don't have a song yet for vocals."

He looked genuinely baffled, "You don't have a piece prepared? Chemistry must be harder than we thought, Gillian." Their guffaws sounded like a sitcom laugh track. *Everybody Loves Hannah. Tuesdays at 8 on ABC Family.*

Hannah started to explain when her mom intervened, "I thought you were singing that song from Cabaret?"

Hannah glared at her, the anger about summer ballet intensive opening up like a wound. Gillian Cross would never understand her daughter's addiction to Broadway because it wasn't literature.

"I was going to sing that song. But I don't think it's right now. 'Maybe This Time' is too much of a belt for me."

Mr. Samuels hummed the melody a little. "Yes, I know that one. Your mom tells me that you've been working on your belt though. Why the change up?"

"Well, uhh," Hannah debated, "Skylar is singing it and I don't want to sing the same song."

Gillian gritted her teeth, protective mama lion that she was. Of course, Skylar was singing "Maybe This Time" and told Hannah not too. Mr. Samuels could sense the tension.

"Hannah, I think it's fine to sing the same song as another auditionee. I met Skylar and the dance teacher tells me she's a good dancer." Then after a beat, "But we know that musicals are built on singers, not dancers. And your mom tells me your voice is quite good."

Hannah offered a feeble smile.

In the small foyer of the Cross's home, they said their goodbyes. Ricky and Hannah even walking the guest to the door like good little orphans. *Mr. Samuels seems okay. Hannah felt herself relax. And mom seems downright smitten. Okay, Samuels, you get the thumbs up from me.*

For now.

She was still going to change the audition song.

Hannah spent the rest of the week practicing "Home" from *The Wiz*. The song was higher and would suit her voice well. Every time Skylar asked about auditions Hannah dodged, skipping like Dorothy and friends down the yellow brick road.

Lions and tigers and Skylar, oh my!

Chapter Two
Gin and Fog

<Click to open your Evite>

While the cat's away...

 Party at Sky's

My dad is away this weekend, so Casa Clarke is open for business.

Friday March 6th
Anytime after 8 pm
House at the top of the hill
(you know the one)

Bring booze! Bring food! Don't bring losers.

By Thursday of that week, Skylar Clarke found a new problem to vex her. Will bought Zoe a small heart-shaped diamond pendant. A chip really, but Skylar wanted to possess that necklace the way she wanted to possess Will. The gift reopened all the rejection of the breakup. It wasn't pretty. It had been months since the Will-Skylar divorce. Countless rebound boyfriends. Even a rumor that Skylar let the Varsity basketball team have their way with her at Homecoming. And Derrick was around more and more.

But that stupid necklace made Skylar's whole world this festering crater of unrequited love. This void was surrounded by a pool of half-crystallized syrup—Skylar's overly saccharine interactions with Zoe. *If Will gave that necklace to Skylar, she would have laughed in his face.* The irony both bemused and incensed Hannah.

The only solution: house party. An impromptu get together, Skylar swore to Hannah. It was, after all, the night before auditions. But the Evite and fifty people would suggest otherwise.

Auditions were always the first Saturday in March at 9 a.m. sharp. The musical shared the campus with softball clinics, Speech and Debate, and Gaelic Society planning their St. Patrick's Day Bash. A motley crew they were.

Skylar's dad was away on business with his new wife Katrina Torres-Clarke. They went to Sun Valley to put the vacation home on the market. The home that Skylar's mom custom built. She adored that place like it was another child. Every detail handpicked. Skylar said that her dad wouldn't make back half of what he spent on it. But Katrina wanted a place somewhere warmer.

"Of course, she wants something else. Do you think Katrina Torres from the Boogie Down Bronx skis? You think she rides?" Skylar sniped. Hannah stood there irrelevant while Skylar whined to Derrick about Katrina's ridiculously long fake nails.

Wonder who she hates more…Zoe or her stepmom? Total toss-up. And look at Derrick. Skylar's just chatting away while he's conversing with her boobs. If there's one subject that could get the calculating Skylar Clarke chatting like a mom after a glass of Chardonnay, it was Katrina. *Derrick seems pleased with the attention though. Anyone would be.*

Zoe and Will were the only no shows for Skylar's party. Zoe doesn't drink. *Big surprise.* Will was with Zoe. *Another shocker.* Their absence was another bit of rage to fuel Skylar's reckless binge drinking. Straight tequila. Katrina's favorite bottle stolen from the liquor cabinet. No one was allowed to touch Mr. Clarke's scotch collection but everything else was fair game.

One of the sophomores stood staring at Mr. Clarke's bottle of MacCallan 1939, lit from beneath in a teak and cherry art deco curio cabinet. Skylar pounced, "Not that. That's Daddy's. If you want more parties like this, we don't touch it."

Mr. Clarke knew about Skylar's parties. He was permissive and largely inattentive after his wife died. A few things were off limits, like his car collection and scotch, but otherwise Skylar, a high school senior, had the largest, most luxurious property in Whispering Hills to use and abuse. High school party heaven.

Around half past twelve, Skylar launched into an unexpected tirade, kicking half the guests out. She just looked up from her phone and tore through the throng of guests around the enormous marble-topped kitchen island.

Greg Tate put his arm around Hannah with the love that comes three stiff drinks in, "She's been texting Will all night. This is not going to be good." *Bet you're excited to witness the carnage. I should get in the fray.* Like an experienced first responder, Hannah moved toward the action.

Glass broke. A few students rushed away. Skylar screamed at Cynthia. Hannah shepherded some party-goers to the exit. When she got back to the kitchen, Skylar was still laying into Cynthia who awkwardly attempted self-defense. *Save Cynthia. Then she'll tell Brody how awesome I am.* But the alcohol had really taken hold. *Forget it. Cynthia is a tool.*

Besides, Greg was getting Cynthia's coat. Greg would rescue her. Later, Greg texted that Skylar slapped a freshman for grinding up on one of her lacrosse groupies. *Like Skylar actually cared about some athletics douchebag.*

Hannah snuck outside to the back porch. Someone smoked a joint in the hot tub. The pot smelled good drifting over the chilly air. Earthy and mellow.

"Hey, come here," a baritone voice called from the hot tub.

Hannah squinted. *Who is that?* She looked closer but took baby steps. *If this is some random Speech and Debater, I'm going to barf. S&D think they're so cool because Dean Feldman is in love with them. Big deal. You're going to Princeton. Guess what? At Princeton, you're mediocre.*

Oh shoot, it's Brody Wolcott. Hannah's heart beat faster. She gulped down her drink and walked over, determined to play cool. *Brody is Cynthia's brother*, Hannah reminded herself in an effort to calm down. *Cynthia is horrible and annoying and should consider killing herself.*

Using that logic, Brody Wolcott was not worth Hannah's time. *Right?*

But Hannah Cross has had a crush on Brody since freshmen year. Almost four years of weird hormonal dreams and waking up sweaty. Brody invades Hannah's thoughts during the day too. When a teacher calls on Hannah and she fumbles an answer, it's Brody's fault. *You'd think I would daydream of the day I get to be on a real Broadway stage? But no, I fantasize about my cliché high school crush.*

She walked closer and pretended not to see exactly who it was. *I know, I'll lie and pretend like I think it's Greg in the hot tub.* Brody would be annoyed that his broad muscled shoulders were mistaken for Greg's skimpy silhouette.

"Hannah. Hey." Brody Wolcott smiled coyly and jiggled his beer. *Am I desperate enough to get him another beer?* She pretended not to notice the bottle hanging in the air.

He turned to face her. Brody's strong arms folded across the ledge. Steam rose off his shoulders. His hair wet and slicked back.

"Get in," he commanded.

Hannah laughed — but the sound was clumsily and stupid. She awkwardly brushed her hair back. *I'm so stupid. I'm screwing it up.*

"I don't have my bathing suit."

Hannah's feet wavered. She felt the tequila she'd been mainlining all night. *God, why did I take that last shot? And auditions are tomorrow too.*

But auditions were the furthest thing from Hannah's mind right now. Brody grinned again, wickedly this time. He had the swagger of a college kid. Had it since sophomore year.

"I don't have a bathing suit either," Brody's deep laugh danced through the air.

Hannah stepped a little closer.

"You look cold," he seemed genuinely concerned. It was disarming.

A few more seconds…

"Okay, fine. But don't look," Hannah conceded.

"Perfect gentleman. I promise," Brody turned his body back around and Hannah undressed slowly, keeping her bra and panties on. Her nipples were hard against the cold March air. Hannah folded her arms across her chest and looked down at her body. *Years of monthly moodiness and period cramps…and no curves to show for it. Nothing like Skylar's hourglass.* Hannah's hips might as well have belonged to a twelve-year-old boy. And breasts? Nonexistent. She sighed. She hopped in the water quickly and soaked down until only her collarbones were visible, "I'm in."

"Can I open my eyes now?"

"You never had to close them. Your back was turned," Hannah smiled flirtatiously.

Brody swam closer. The two were nose to nose. "I needed to take extra precautions. I don't trust myself around you."

She could play it cool no longer. It was as if teenage heaven opened up and little teen angels started singing the "Hallelujah Chorus." Brody never spoke to Hannah in school. It took Brody all of three minutes to break down all Hannah's artificial barriers.

Hannah beamed, "I didn't even think you knew who I was." *What a dork. I'm messing this up royally.*

"Hannah Cross. The girl I'm about to kiss." His right hand cupped her jawbone. Her mouth was immediately wet and ready to meet his. *This could go on for hours.* Brody's left hand slid around the small of Hannah's back and then she was on his lap. If all Brody just said was bullshit, the lower half of him couldn't lie. The bulge in his wet boxer shorts certainly knew who Hannah was. She felt empowered by it.

Hannah ran her fingers through Brody's hair and stuck her tongue in his mouth hard. They kissed and he got more confident, nibbling her ear and running his hands under her bra. Hannah's body responded—she let out a satisfied sound that was somewhere between a groan and an exhalation.

Then the crash of a sliding glass door shutting hard.

"Who's that sexing it up all over my hot tub?"

Skylar.

Shit.

Why did we have to be at her house? Why did Brody <u>finally</u> happen when Skylar Clarke could be around to ruin it?

"Oh, my word! Hannah? Who the hell are you with?"

She kept walking closer, the deep V-neck in her tight cashmere sweater revealing perfectly round cleavage. Hannah scrambled to cover her flat breasts and felt blood rush up through her neck and face.

Skylar threw her head back and laughed wildly, "Is that Brody? Oh, I'm *so* telling Cynthia."
She leaned against the Jacuzzi, "Do you have to biggest hard on right now? Hannah's hot, right?"

Brody lifted Hannah off him gently. Her whole body filled with rejection. Hannah knew he was just sparing her more embarrassment but still, she felt the rebuff strongly. Tears welled up in Hannah's eyes. *Thank God it's dark. That's all Skylar needs is to see me crying.*

Brody pushed his torso out of the hot tub, "Hand me that towel, Skylar."

"Nope, I want to see it."

Nothing from Brody—except a stare that even Hannah could feel.

"What's the matter? Equipment not working?" Skylar cocked her head to one side.

"Screw you." He hopped out quickly, splashing water all over her. Brody grabbed a towel from one of the lounge chairs, wrapped it around his waist and went inside.

Skylar squealed at the splash, "Hey! This is cashmere!"
She loves this. I hate her right now.

She turned back to Hannah, winking, "I'm telling Cynthia this. Obviously."

"I'm going home," Hannah lifted herself out of the water and Skylar pushed her down hard.

She laughed again, "You're so light! Tell you what, I won't tell Cynthia if you stay over."

"No." Hannah got out the other side and started walking towards the towels. Her underwear was white and sticking to every inch of her.

"Hannah," Skylar whined innocently, "Don't be like that. Look, I'm sorry I ruined your drunk make out sesh. And don't worry, I really won't tell bat shit crazy Cynthia. She probably has a crush on her brother. Wouldn't want to unearth any more of her Freudian bullshit."

Hannah wrapped a towel around her body and walked inside. Skylar grabbed her friend's elbow, "Hey, I'm serious. Stay over. No one is home and I'm afraid to be in this big house by myself."

Suddenly, Skylar looked harmless. It's cliché but maybe it was the moonlight. Maybe Hannah was actually just getting cold. Hannah was also abandoned by her father so maybe Hannah could relate.

Every time Skylar screwed up, even though Hannah had a right to be mad, she was afraid instead. *Shit will come crashing down at school if I actually stick up for herself.* It was a difficult pill to swallow.

But Hannah agreed. And Skylar bounced up and down with delight. And when they cuddled in her bed two hours later, Hannah told her best friend all about Brody.

Chapter Three
Auditions

Theatre is a series of insurmountable obstacles on the road to imminent disaster. – Tom Stoppard

»~-~»

Break a leg, Sky!

oxox

Bethany

Skylar's iPhone blared some obscene hip-hop song. The phone vibrated and fell off the bedside table, screen blinking frenetically. Get up, girls! You shouldn't have gotten inebriated last night, the phone seemed to say

Hannah rolled out of bed and laid face down on the floor for a moment. She grabbed the small card from under Sky's bedside table. *Must have fallen. Oh, it's from her sister.* Hannah read the quote and thought ruefully about how truthful it was. Theatre was indeed a bunch of obstacles on a journey towards a disaster. In other words, doing the play was a shit show. And every shit show began with auditions.

Hannah found Skylar already in her bathroom. *There is a solid possibility she's brushing her teeth with tequila.* Skylar's wavy hair was in a messy ponytail. She sat on the closed toilet.

"What the hell is wrong with us?" Skylar giggled softy.

Hannah rubbed her eyes, her voice hoarse, "Auditions are in 90 minutes. Hope Mr. Samuels runs some warmups."

Skylar shrugged, "Unlikely. Mr. Samuels seems like a tool." Then two second later, "Sorry, Hannah. I know your mom has the hots for him." She played with her ponytail and smiled fiendishly, "Aaron Samuels could be your stepdad one day. Too bad you'll be long gone from Whispering Hills. Won't be able to cash in. Hashtag nepotism."

Hannah searched the queen's face. *How does she know about Mr. Samuels and mom? It's too new. How many times did she drive by Thursday night? No, don't take the bait. Not this morning. Not before auditions.*

"I'm taking a shower," Hannah undressed completely knowing nakedness would silence Skylar.

"Save it for Brody!" Skylar shut the bathroom door behind her.

The housekeeper made breakfast, but the girls left it on the counter untouched. Instead, Skylar made Bloody Marys.

"I'm not drinking before we have to be at school," Hannah shook her head admonishingly. Still Skylar poured three shots of vodka into a travel coffee cup and topped it off with tomato juice and a dollop of horseradish. She was going in the fridge for Tabasco when Hannah's phone rang. They both jumped as if they were hiding a body and the police were at the front door.

"It's just my mom," Hannah exhaled.

Skylar finished making the breakfast of champions while Hannah checked in. She pressed the cup into Hannah's chest, "A little of the snake that bit ya!"

"Shh…Oh. Not you, mom," Hannah rushed her mother off the phone, jaw grinding involuntarily. *Wouldn't be the first time Skylar showed up to school plastered. I could never even be late to class, no less drunk at school. Not Gillian Cross's daughter.* Fac brats don't get to screw up. Wealthy kids, however, do whatever the hell they want.

Hannah looked at iPhone in her hand, one of many expensive gifts from her best friend. *Guess I'm on babysitting duty again.*

Skylar threw the keys to her Range Rover in Hannah's direction, "You're driving."

"No, I'm not."

Skylar stopped short, "I'm not wearing my contacts. I can't put them in until I sober up."

Hannah's whole body deflated. *How the hell am I supposed to drive down Lakeside Road?* All the winding and hairpin turns. The road was treacherous sober.

Skylar clicked her tongue, "We can have a drunk driver with bad eyes driving or just a drunk driver. Which one do you think can hit the most pedestrians? Come on, you know you love the Rover."

"Shot gun!" She climbed into the brand-new truck, one of many sorry-I'm-married-again presents from Daddy Clarke.

Hannah shuffled around in her bag looking for Advil, trying to balance both the keys and her morning cocktail. She popped two pills and chased them with Bloody Mary. *This is gonna be a long day.*

Skylar texted furiously, keypad clicking rapidly. The buttery soft leather of the Range Rover seats felt good. Worst part was Hannah really wanted to drive the Range Rover. Hannah wanted lots of stuff Skylar had. Once Hannah made a lame excuse about needing a Halloween costume to get an old blouse Skylar was giving to Goodwill. "Wait, you want this? Oh, for Halloween. Oh my God, it would make a good costume," Skylar had said as she tossed the shirt over to Hannah.

"Good luck today," Skylar's eyes were wide with expectation.

"Thanks."

Were those good wishes for the drive or the audition?

Skylar threw her phone in her bag, "Ugh, Cynthia. Wants a ride. Umm…NO. Stalker."

"I can swing by her house." *Maybe Cynthia would drive.* Plus, Cynthia lived in Lakeside Manor, a small, new subdivision of McMansions surrounding the lake. *It's sort of on the way.*

Skylar sneered, "Of course you don't mind. Brody might be there. Or maybe he's still sleeping, dreaming of…"

Hannah cut her off, "If he's fully clothed, I really don't care."

"Touché." Sky laughed and placed her elbow on the car door, gently sipping her drink.

The two started the long windy drive down the mountain. Hannah tried going slowly but Skylar egged her on. They'd be late for auditions if Hannah drove like a granny. Now, Hannah was going 50 mph—too fast even for residents who knew the lay of the land. The road was two single lanes. Narrow lanes at that. It was paved but tons of trees surrounded it. Morning sun barely broke through the canopy of branches. Even at this point in the morning, the road appeared dark.

"Floor it! We're going to be late, Hannah!" Skylar yelled at one point.

"I don't live up here. I don't drive this."

"You have eyes, just use them and go faster," Skylar returned. She was about to say something more when a Prius pulled out in front of the Rover from a secluded side street. Hannah barely had time to slow down.

Hannah slammed her hand on the steering wheel, "We are going to get in an accident if you don't calm down!"

"It's Will's car. Follow him," Skylar whispered, almost inaudible. The blinders were on. Will Bartlett drove his Prius at a responsible speed. The car was a gift from his father, a renowned environmental architect. If it's not evident yet why Will and Skylar were completely incompatible, the car choices should clearly define it. A Prius and a Range Rover. Will was quiet and sensible. Skylar was excessive, imposing, and luxurious.

"He's going to the same place we are, Sky. I'm already following him." Hannah rolled her eyes but spoke like she was placating a toddler.

Skylar leaned forward and squinted, "Zoe is with him. She slept at Will's house? What a slut. What a frigging hypocrite. Isn't she like the president of the youth ministry or some Christian club?"

The curves of the road were nauseating. Hannah moaned, "I don't know. Maybe youth group at her church?"

"She is! And she swore up and down that she wasn't having the S-E-X until she was married. Oh, my God! I hate her. She's such a whore! No wonder why he wants her. Perfect lady in the daylight and prostitute at night."

Thinking humor might diffuse the bomb in the passenger seat, Hannah offered, "Maybe Zoe and Will Bartlett got hitched last night?"

"Don't interrupt me! Follow them!" Skylar hollered and reached over to honk the horn. Absurdly Hannah was reminded of the red queen in Alice in Wonderland. Off with her head!

"Don't..." Hannah lost control of the SUV for a moment. The swerve was small but powerful. Her heart nearly jumped out of her ribs. "Shit! Skylar!"

Skylar honked over and over. Hannah pushed Skylar's arm away. Then came the slap. Warm tears rose in Hannah's eyes. *She just hit me. I can't believe she just hit me. Oh my God, she's insane.*

The cars approached a hairpin turn. More honking.

"Holy shit! Skylar—stop!!" Hannah's scream was loud and high-pitched.

The Rover made the turn with what seemed like angels surrounding the car. But when they were back on a straight stretch, Skylar started in again, unfazed by the near totaling of her brand-new car.

"Pass him! He's an asshole. And he's too much of a pussy to race you."

Wiping a salty trickle from her cheek, Hannah replied, "No!"

"Do it! Or I will climb over there."

She will too. Hannah checked the opposite lane. *No oncoming traffic.* The Range Rover accelerated and quickly caught up to the Prius. They were side-by-side in an instant. Hannah kept pressing the gas, but Will's car followed suit. *Why isn't he falling back? Just fall back.*

Skylar gave Zoe the finger. "Slut!" Her hands were on the wheel and Hannah swatted them away.

Hannah turned her eyes back to road and slowed down.

"What the fuck, Cross?" Skylar hollered, her voice screeched with rage. "I said PASS HIM!"

Hannah revved up and the cars were side-by-side again. But he wouldn't let up. Again, Skylar taunted the couple. Hannah floored it and started to pass Will's Prius when she saw the truck coming at her. An eighteen-wheeler headed straight for the dark navy Range Rover. The truck's horn was louder than anything Hannah ever heard.

"Shit!" Hannah screamed as she swerved back into her lane, hitting the front corner of Will's Prius. Or maybe Skylar reached over and grabbed the wheel. Hannah doesn't exactly remember. But somehow, they didn't hit the truck.

They did hit the Prius.

The SUV struggled to right itself. Hannah felt her entire body seize with anticipation.

And she could see the Prius in her rearview mirror. Well, a glimpse of it as the car ran off the side of the road. Down the tree-studded mountainside. The sound the car made as it careened down the hill was horrendous. It hurtled uncontrollably through trees and brush.

Hannah slowed down, panting wildly, "Oh my God! We hit them!"

"We didn't mean to. I swear," Skylar yelled back—her usually pink cheeks white with fear.

Sweat bubbled on Hannah's nose and forehead. Her mouth felt dry. "We have to go back. We have to help them." Hannah saw a place to pull over. It was dirt but looked level enough to stop safely. She turned to her best friend, "Shit! We hit them! We hit them!" She started to cry.

Skylar just stared straight ahead. Hannah shouted again and again. But Skylar was stone.

Finally, Hannah unbuckled her seatbelt.

Skylar grabbed her friend, "The truck probably pulled over already."

"So? We have to go back!...Get off me!...I'm calling 911!"

Skylar snatched Hannah's phone and threw It in the backseat, "Just give me a minute to think."

They could be dead. They could be dead.

"They could be dead, Skylar!"

Skylar replied almost involuntarily, "Good."

"What did you say?" Hannah answered.

"Nothing. Keep driving to school. We need to get to auditions."

"But we hit Will's car and it went sailing down a hill. They might be seriously injured. They could be dead. WE killed them!"

A beat. Then almost in slow motion...

"*You* killed them. *You* hit them. That is, if they are dead or injured. Who knows?" Skylar was calming down at an eerily fast rate. There was a meanness inside her that lived and breathed like another lung.

"What?! Are you kidding right now? You're blaming me?"

"You're driving. Think about Hannah. You're driving. Not me. You're drinking and driving. What are you going to say when we get back there? Are you ready for your life to be over?"

She continued. Hannah hated herself for listening.

"Your mother will hate you. The school will expel you and probably fire her. Not that Gillian Cross did anything wrong, but you know how Whispering Hills likes it reputation. Your future is gone the instant you go back there. And if you think that I'm going to down with you, you really don't know me."

But I do know you. Because I know what you did to that poor girl at camp. To Katie Greco.

But I also know that you're right. Hannah wept softly.

———

54

Skylar took out her phone and checked the time, "8:50. Ten minutes to auditions. Drive."

"I can't drive," Hannah sniveled.

Skylar put on her Prada tortoise shell glasses, something she never wears outside her home, "Get in the back. I'll drive."

When the two walked into auditions, Skylar was fine, a stoic queen overseeing an execution. Hannah, on the other hand, was a hot mess. She grabbed a number and ran to the restroom. Skylar told Ms. Panzini, the choreographer, that Hannah had personal troubles. Probably something about her father. He was never there for her. And Ms. Panzini probably said something about Skylar being a good friend.

In the bathroom, Hannah rushed to the last stall and muffled her sobs. Girls shuffled in and out. *Is that my name? Are they talking about me? No, it's okay. No one knows.* Not one person checked the last stall. It was the same stall Hannah hid in when she bombed auditions the first time. The time she picked the same song as Zoe.

It was an hour into auditions when Skylar came in.

Hannah opened the door and Skylar hugged her hard. "I'm sure they are fine," she purred.

They sat on the cold floor for a few minutes. If Hannah hadn't been so distraught, she be flattered that Skylar deigned to sit on the grimy tiles. It meant something.

The sound of Will's car swerving off the road and careening down that ridge still played in her head and made her sick. Every time Hannah told herself Will and Zoe were fine, that the truck stopped and called 911, that the ambulance probably got there in time, her head rang with the sound of the Prius. Like she lived inside a huge bell. Even her teeth rang with the scream of the tires. And Will and Zoe—jostled around inside like sneakers in a dryer after a rainy run.

Hannah swallowed hard, "We're terrible people. I'm a terrible person. I hit them."

Without blinking an eye, Skylar responded with logic and her usual get-over-it-attitude, "You didn't actually hit them. After I signed in, I told Ms. Panzini I left something in my car. I checked the whole right side. There's no like marks. Don't you think that if we hit Will, there would be a dent?"

Yeah, I guess. Surely there would be paint from the silver Prius visible on the dark blue Rover. She was right. Right? Hannah looked around the bathroom stall. *I need this story to hold up. Will lost control of his car. A terrible accident. But I didn't actually cause it.*

The restroom door swung open and Hannah jumped. Skylar put a gentle hand on her knee. The door to the stall jiggled, "Sky? Hannah?"

"What, Cynthia?" Skylar called back, her voice dripped with contempt.

"They are looking for you." Cynthia returned quietly.

Skylar rolled her hazel eyes, "Who is looking for us?"

"Can I come in? Mr. Samuels is looking for the next five singers. Hannah is number 32, right?" Cynthia jiggled the stall handle again.

Skylar pulled Hannah up and then faced the door but left it closed to Cynthia, "Okay, we'll be right out."

Cynthia moved toward the exit and muttered, "You're welcome," under her breath.

Baby steps to the bathroom sink. Skylar's arm around Hannah's waist. Hannah splashed water on her face. Skylar watched grimly in the mirror. Hannah half-expected a ghost to materialize behind them. Then the ghost would disappear immediately when the girls turned around. *Too much Macbeth essay writing this week.* Hannah shook off the thought of ghosts.

Skylar stayed to reapply lip-gloss, but Hannah had to get moving. On the way, her phone vibrated, and she looked at the number quizzically...

did you have
fun last night?
what about
this morning?
pretty rough,
huh?

Whose number is this? She started texting back and found herself face to face with a crew member, one of Sarah's lackeys.

"Turn off your phone. No more watching Idina Menzel crush it on YouTube," he sniped.

At the auditorium doors, Sarah Young, the head of crew who fancied herself a student director, stood up to usher Hannah inside, "Almost missed your vocals. You know how they feel about punctuality."

You nasty little hall monitor.

Sarah opened the door to deposit Hannah then turned back the rest of the kids lining the corridors. "Shhh!!!" They immediately stopped talking because Sarah was the gatekeeper on audition day. The head of the lesbian mafia arched an eyebrow smugly at the auditionees.

But Skylar shouted, "Get it, girl!"

The walk from the back of the theatre to the front row was excruciating. All the decision makers turned slightly and took her in. Hannah trembled as she scanned the teachers' faces. There was Jill Panzini, the choreographer. *I wonder what tale Skylar spun about my dad when we arrived.* Panzini's expression was all fake concern. Jill Panzini and Hannah's mom were good friends, so the dance teacher harbored a righteous hatred of Gillian's ex. But her worry about Hannah was artificial. *The only thing she really worries about is her freaking wedding binder.* "If I have to look at one more picture of a flower arrangement when we are supposed to be warming up," Hannah had complained many times this school year.

And then there was Mr. Samuels, a pen in his mouth, staring over his reading glasses. Unimpressed. *All business today.* As if 'Aaron' hadn't dined with the Cross family a few days before. *Do I look like the lead he's already cast in his head? Do I look like someone who could carry a show?*

Probably not.

Hannah handed sheet music to the accompanist and announced that she'd be singing "Home" from *The Wiz.* Ms. Panzini looked at Hannah like she was little baby who just did something adorable. Aaron Samuels cracked a smile. A sense of relief washed over Hannah. *He remembers talking about my audition song. He likes that I chose "Home."*

When she climbed up on stage, Hannah nodded meekly at the pianist to start. But when it was her turn to come in, she missed it completely. Nerves felt like they were growing all over Hannah's body, popping out like hives. The pianist offered closed-mouth smile and repeated the intro again. This time he gave big nod to count her in.

Nothing again. Little did Hannah know that the next ten minutes would be the most humiliating of her life. Mr. Samuels threw his hand up — a signal to the pianist.

"Something wrong?" He tried to say it as benignly as he could. The irritation was crystal clear. Hannah was a senior, a staple in all the Whispering Hills shows. No doubt he expected at least a solid audition. Maybe not lead material. But not this freshmen bullshit. He raised his eyebrows as he waited for a reply. Ms. Panzini said nothing, but her eyes were sympathetic.

Hannah pleaded to start again and got a nod from the director. Third time around and Hannah sang but messed up so badly that Mr. Samuels threw his hand up again. His neck red with agitation. *I even messed up the lyrics. What a newbie move!* You don't have a prayer of getting a lead if you mess up lyrics.

The adults put their heads together and whispered. Then Aaron Samuels spoke, "Hannah, you were Zoe Kellogg's understudy last year in *Guys & Dolls*, correct?"

"Yes, sir."

"Come down and stand next to the piano, Hannah."

"Let's sing 'If I were a Bell.' Pretend like you're at rehearsal." Aaron Samuels' fingers danced on the keys—he was a better than the rehearsal pianist. He played and hummed the song beautifully.

Hannah soaked up these moments—they were meant to calm her down. He wanted to get the best out of her. But she was reminded of Zoe and how much she wanted Zoe's role last year. And this particular morning that name made Hannah's stomach rise. *I can't even blame Skylar. I was driving that damn car.*

Mr. Samuels started playing and nodded empathically on Hannah's cue. Her throat was sandpaper. She showed everyone an uninspiring five-note range. As Hannah exited, she wiped the tears away. *Great. Senior year and I've just blown my last audition here. All they know now is that I'm shy, I can't remember lyrics, and my voice is about as good as my brother's.*

Skylar met Hannah at the doors to the auditorium and whisked her down the hallway. When Hannah sobbed about how poorly the audition went, Skylar petted Hannah's hair lovingly. But her expression gave her away. *So fake. She's using her "this is my sad for you" face.* Hannah knew it too well.

Sarah Young called Skylar's name like a drill sergeant and she flitted back to the theatre. The Clarke Theatre—one of the many spaces on campus that bore Skylar's last name. *Skylar doesn't care. Today I'm competition, not her best friend.* The betrayal was a gut stab.

She looked coyly over shoulder, "Wish me luck."

Like you'll need it. We put two classmates in the hospital this morning. And you're fine? Hannah grinded her teeth until her jaw hurt. *Sometimes...sometimes...I wish I'd never met Skylar.* Hannah wanted Zoe Kellogg to walk right through that door, on crutches, hobble down to the stage and sing her heart out. *On Zoe's worst day, Skylar still couldn't steal the lead.*

Cynthia and Greg were huddled close by. Both of them glued to their phones. "O...M...G," Cynthia scrolled the Whispering Hills Drama Club Facebook group.

"Is she really a no-show?" Greg's eyes were wide with the anticipation of juicy gossip.

"She never checked-in on the FB group," Cynthia answered. Everyone posts on that Facebook group. Good luck wishes. 'I'm-so-nervous' posts followed by a chorus of encouraging comments. Seniors posting about how it's their last show with hundreds of sad-faced emojis.

Greg leaned in close to Hannah, "Zoe Kellogg is nowhere to be found. All day. She blew off auditions." His mouth contorted until he looked like a clown. Hannah gulped hard. *Act giddy with excitement,* she told herself. *Remember this is big news. The operative word is "news."*

Then another gaggle of kids waddled over.

"She's not here!"

"Zoe Kellogg is missing auditions her senior year."

"Something must have happened. Something good."

"Maybe she got a role on real Broadway!"

Suddenly Hannah was surrounded with her sin. "What about Will?" Hannah blurted, immediately sorry she'd said it. Both Cynthia and Greg looked up, confused.

"What do you mean? Will said he wasn't doing the musical this year. He's been saying it for weeks," Greg's forehead crinkled. The grooves showed where his future wrinkles would appear.

Cynthia concurred, "Yeah, he's got an agent down in the city. Sending him to auditions like every weekend."

"Yeah," Greg continued, "Remember how he missed math the other day? Well, he got his schedule changed so that he can leave school by 1:45."

Shit, that was common knowledge. Hannah waited for Greg and Cynthia's rapid-fire interrogation. Hannah's locker was next to Will's. They'd assume Hannah had up-to-date info. The questions never came. A mercy. Facebook or twitter or snapchat caught everyone's attention again.

Hannah felt alone. She leaned against the wall next to Greg for a few minutes. *Don't say anything else. Don't say anything stupid.*

"How did it go, Hannah?" Cynthia tried to be sweet. Both Hannah and Cynthia were middle level performers in the past. Equals. Each year, they'd nabbed a feature or a small speaking role. But never a bona fide lead.

"I sucked," Hannah retorted somewhat rudely and walked away before Cynthia could see the tears.

Every huddle of students was abuzz with Zoe's absence. It meant a lot for everyone. When the top dog isn't in the mix, everyone moves up a rung on the talent ladder.

Hannah stood over Sarah Young's little desk. Sarah pretended not to notice for at least two minutes. *I hate the crew sometimes. Sure, act like I'm invisible.*

When Sarah finally looked up, she snarled, "Yes Hannah? You *can't* go back in and try out again."

Normally, Hannah would give Sarah Young a little lip. She didn't give a crap that Sarah had a big posse of bushy-eyebrowed crew members. Instead, Hannah shrank at the jab about her botched audition, "Umm, I was wondering if Zoe auditioned yet."

"It's none of your business who else auditioned or when," Sarah replied pertly, not even bothering to look Hannah in the face.

"There's just some rumors," Hannah tried to speak as sweetly as she could.

"Classified" was the response. Hannah wanted to reach over the table and strangle Sarah with her cheesy scarf. It had Shakespearean dialogue printed all over it, a souvenir from their class trip to London in sophomore year.

"Classified?! What is this? The CIA? You do realize that I'm asking about a person whose presence is way more important to the show than yours."

Sarah stood up, chair falling over behind her, "I'm the student *director.*"

"I believe last year the program read 'lesbian in a power struggle.' You don't direct shit," Hannah could feel other eyes on them, waiting to see this showdown.

And then tweet about it.

Sarah's baby lesbians gathered round. An absurd reenactment of a Jets and Sharks scene from *West Side Story.* Skylar came bounding out of the auditorium and the door nearly knocked over one of Sarah's crew. "Watch out, garcon!" She ran over to Hannah, ready to tell her about how wonderful the world was. Then Skylar realized Hannah was in a staredown with Sarah Young.

"Problem?" Skylar cocked her head at Sarah. Sarah tried to remain strong, but she fixed the chair behind her and sat down. Sarah was tough, but she was also smart. You didn't want to have a public fight with Skylar Clarke. It would be social suicide.

Sarah called for the next singer. Cynthia.

Skylar laced her arm through Hannah's and practically cavorted down the hall. Hannah told her what happened. A strong pinch at her elbow made Hannah wince. The friends walked so far down the hallway they could hear Speech and Debate practice. They were far away from *any* theatre kids.

Skylar whispered in a gnarly voice, "What the hell, Hannah? Why don't you just paint a bull's eye on your forehead? When the police come asking about Zoe, do you want to make it that easy? God, you're an idiot sometimes."

A lump rose in her throat. "I need to know if she's okay. Wait, did you say 'police'?"

Skylar pushed Hannah hard up against the lockers, "No. You. Don't. You don't need to know. The more you stalk this situation, the more you look like you know exactly what happened. So, stop being a retard about it."

She's right. The more I search for information the more people will suspect me. Hannah recalled Greg's expression just moments ago.

"Hannah!" Her mom called from downstairs. Hannah looked at her clock. 6:30 p.m. She had passed out after auditions. All the adrenaline from the accident, the aftermath, the auditions came crashing down.

"Hannah! I got some dinner from the deli. And it's almost time for Marvelous Mrs. Maisel. Season premiere tonight."

Hannah lay back down, eyes drifting right off. She still felt exhausted. The nightmares again. The incubus that drew her further into unconsciousness while preventing any true rest. It was the same dream that came every night since camp this past summer.

The lake at camp. Water deep and black. And the evil Skylar had woven there. In her dream she always saw the silver Tiffany & Co. necklace. A small aquamarine jewel set in the middle. The necklace pushed up from the sinewy mud that surrounded the lake. Hannah walks closer to it. And the mud swallows the necklace again. She knows that necklace. It's hers and Katie took it. So Skylar devised a plan to get it back. Usually it's Skylar's voice in the dream adapting lines from Macbeth and chanting them "Sleep no more. I have killed sleep."

But this afternoon, it was Will's voice.

"I'll be down in a few minutes, mom!" She hustled downstairs and kissed mom hello. *Try and act like nothing happened today*, Hannah repeated over and over. *Focus on the chicken cordon bleu from Jimmy's deli. My favorite.*

But Gillian looked anxious. She walked a plate over to Hannah. "You okay?" she asked with a love that made Hannah want to immediately confess her sins.

Hannah's mouthed wagged open. *She knows everything.* Word travels fast in Whispering Hills Country Day. "Uhh…umm…yeah."

Hannah's brother slipped behind her, "Whoa, put on a bra, Hannah."

"Ricky! Please." Mom snapped.

"Yeah, Ricky. Why are you looking at my boobs anyway?"

Ricky made his plate and left the kitchen, "What boobs?"

"Tease your sister again and you'll spend the rest of the night in your room. No X-Box."

He huffed as he plopped on the couch. Gillian called one more time, "Leave it on the news!"

Ricky growled. Hannah wondered why her mom was defending her with such fervor. Again, she dipped her chin down and looked tenderly at her daughter, "Hannah, wait. Aaron said auditions were—"

"Terrible? Awful? Disastrous? Yes, they were. No, I don't want to talk about it," Hannah reacted, not even realizing her tone. Her mom's expression changed—clearly hurt. *And what the hell was Aaron Samuels doing swapping stories with mom? What a dipstick.*

But as Hannah padded into the living room, she reminded herself that her reaction was completely normal. Her mom didn't suspect anything. Just a crappy audition. And Hannah's diva attitude. They sat around the TV. No conversation except an occasional "Oh my!" from Hannah's mom as the three watched the local evening news.

64

Hannah picked at her dinner, moving food around the plate enough so that her mom wouldn't raise an eyebrow. *How am I supposed to eat? Eating is for tomorrow. Tomorrow — when Zoe and Will would be back in school. Tomorrow — when Zoe had the lead because she showed up in the nick of time and blew them away.* Hannah indulged those thoughts for a few moments. The image of Zoe walking into school with Will on her arm. Will walking toward Hannah's locker after giving Zoe a modest kiss goodbye. Will's warm smile. He always liked Hannah. Will would ask how auditions went, trying to hide his interest in a show he'd decided to shun.

A loud gasp from her mother and Hannah came back to reality. Her mom was horrified. She pounced on the coffee table, scooped up the remote, and turned the volume up.

B-roll of the hospital. Then the too-chubby-for-network local news reporter began, "It was around 9 a.m. this morning when two Whispering Hills Country Day students were in a tragic car accident on Lakeside Road. The silver Prius was found mangled at the bottom of a hill and the students were rushed to Harrison Hospital in critical condition."

Then the b-roll of Lakeside Road and a voiceover retold the story in an even more gruesome tone.

Hannah's mother started pacing with her wine, "It's the school, Hannah. Who has a Prius?"

Hannah froze. *What do I say? Of course, I know the Prius. Is offering that information a confession? But I would know anyway — even if this morning hadn't happened. Will was my friend.* The word "friend" rung in her head, reverberating through every brain cell. *But of course, I know Will drives a Toyota. That car stuck out like a fat chorus girl in the senior lot among the Beamers and Lexuses.*

Wrapped up in her own dramatic digestion of this news, Gillian didn't even notice her daughter's distress. "I should call Aaron. Or Jill. Jill would know." Gillian paced with her phone.

Ricky piped up, youngest but manliest of the household calming down the womenfolk, "Wait till the news is over, Mom. They might have more."

And sure enough, after the commercial break, the news anchor came back with, "Looks like Lisa has new information on this tragic car accident that involved two kids from the local private school. Lisa?"

"Yes, Brian. I'm here with the truck driver who called 911. Thanks for taking the time to talk to us."

The truck driver. Hannah's heart sank down to her stomach where it was mixed around with acid and a few pieces of chicken cordon bleu.

"No problem," the driver grunted.

"Tell us what happened this morning."

He gulped hard, "Well, Lakeside is only a two-lane road. And I come around the corner and I see this black SUV, maybe navy. It was a dark SUV. And then I see the silver car. The black SUV is on my side of the road, so I nearly hit the side of the hill with my truck. There's not that much room for mistakes on Lakeside. That SUV should not have been passing in my lane at that point. I thought for sure I would hit the SUV. Or the side of the hill. But I didn't."

"What happened next?"

"I heard this awful crash. It was the car, the silver car, going down the hill. Caught a glimpse of it in my sideview. So, I pulled over and called for an ambulance. I made my way down the hill and saw the girl in—well, I guess it was her school uniform. She was breathing at least."

"And the boy?"

The driver took off his baseball cap, "Ma'am, I don't know. I just prayed that the EMT would get there soon. They both needed medical attention. And fast."

Lisa plied her witness some more, "Tell me about the dark SUV."

"I don't know. The SUV was trying to pass the Prius. It could've hit the Prius and forced it off the road. In fact, I believe that's what happened. But I was driving too, focusing on not crashing myself. So, I don't know for sure. That SUV didn't stick around though."

"Left the scene of the accident?"

The truck driver repeated himself, voice graver than before, "Yes, ma'am. That SUV didn't stick around."

"There you have it, Westchester County. Foul play on Lakeside Road and two students are in the hospital." She turned to the trucker, "Thanks for talking with us."

Hannah's mother shut off the TV in disgust. Ricky bused his plate and went upstairs, unfazed by the news. He didn't go to Whispering Hills until next year. Ricky went to public school. Often times, Hannah envied him. Ricky was popular. Plus, his background blended in with all the other painfully normal kids. In fact, Ricky's mom didn't work at the recycling plant so that meant he was considered pretty well-off.

In a frenzy, Gillian called Ms. Panzini who didn't even know about the accident. She'd been at the school all evening, fighting with Aaron. Jillian knew the Prius though. Will Bartlett. A moan came from the phone. That's why Zoe wasn't at auditions. Then Hannah's mom covered her mouth and tried to muffle a cry.

One of the football players made fun of Will's car once. Will overheard and made a snipe about the football player's enormous GMC Denali. "A car that big means you're compensating for something. You know, like the fact that our football team lost to the School for the Deaf. Or compensating for…well…what guys are always compensating for."

It didn't escalate much further than that. Will Bartlett was classy, respected, and scrappy when he had to be. A wave of guilt came over Hannah as she imagined Will's sweet face. He always asked how she was. What did she do over the weekend? Or did she finish that long AP Gov project?

———

"I'll break the news to Hannah. She's been downstairs with me," Gillian signed off with Mrs. Panzini and then sat next to Hannah on the couch. *This is how she looked when she told us about the divorce.* Hannah resented her mother's concern. *Zoe and Will are in the hospital and you're worried about me?* Then the fear set in. *Zoe and Will are in the hospital. That means they are going to tell their story.*

Before Gillian could even start, Hannah's phone blew up with five or six texts. She read the top one. Acid rose up her throat.

> GT: cast list
> Up! wtf? NO
> CALL BACKS.

From Greg. *He didn't see the news yet.* Then other texts from Cynthia and a freshman who followed Hannah like a puppy dog.

> CW: panzini
> must be
> pissssssed!
>
> GT: WHAT
> ABOUT THE
> DANCE
> AUDITIONS?
>
> AM: holy shit!
> cast list up
> already!

Hannah got up and walked toward the stairs. Her mother whined, "Hannah, talk to me. Are you okay?"

"Are you okay, mom? Jeez." Hannah replied sarcastically.

"Hannah!" her mom called, ready to scold then turn all guidance counselor again. "Hannah, come back here!"

The cast list was up. It was absurd, but Hannah's body instinctively moved to a computer and checked the musical Facebook page. Two students were in the hospital and Hannah was likely getting kicked out of school. *And yet all I can think about is the cast list. Am I this self-absorbed?*

It felt like forever before the browser loaded the webpage. Hannah knew exactly where to click. And there it was. Cast List for Spring Musical: Stagecraft.

Skylar got the lead. Hannah's hands balled up into fists. Her breathing slowed nearly to a halt. *The lead? Zoe was supposed to be the lead. And if not Zoe, then I should be the lead. I was Zoe's understudy. Skylar isn't half the singer I am!* The fury soaked into her skin, ribboning through her skeleton. *I hate Skylar Clarke!* Hannah searched for her name and didn't see it anywhere. She scoured again.

The phone rang. Skylar. She let it ring three times. Hannah was determined to let it go to voicemail. *Wait. Neither of us will even be in the show. Zoe will tell what happened and Skylar will be stripped of the role. The school has to.* How could they let a student behave like that and then reward her? The Clarke money wouldn't matter. Skylar and Hannah would be on the same playing field.

"Hey," Hannah answered, breathless.

"Jeez, girl. Phone on silent or something?"

Nothing from Hannah. Skylar didn't wait.

"Did you see? Can you believe it?" For a second, Hannah couldn't read her tone. *Was Skylar Clarke actually remorseful? Was she worried now that Will and Zoe were evening news material?*

Hannah remained silent but Skylar didn't notice, "I told you I rocked it today. I knew he'd give it to me."

"Not if Zoe had showed up. But we took care of that didn't we."

Skylar huffed at the pettiness, "Well, fuck you very much. Guess I should call Cynthia. I'm sure she'd know enough about Whispering Hills survival skills to congratulate me."

Hannah heard her mom lurking upstairs, probably folding laundry or tidying Ricky's pigsty. Dropping her volume a few notches, Hannah replied, "Skylar, how can you be happy right now? Did you watch the news?" *It's senseless to appeal to her moral compass though. That never pointed true north. Maybe appeal to her logic, her savvy.* "Skylar, we are both getting kicked out of school when Zoe and Will say what happened this morning. We ran them off the road, ruined Will's car, and put them in the hospital."

She laughed maniacally.

"What?" Hannah blurted, forgetting to keep her voice low. "What is *so* funny?"

"How is our school finding out? Hannah," then an awfully long pause, "Will is dead."

The tears came so fast they were rolling down her cheeks before Hannah even realized she was crying.

"Hannah, did we watch the same news program?"

Oh my God. Mom turned the TV off. The news wasn't over. Her mouth turned so dry it hurt. She wiped some tears away and did her best to keep the crying silent. "Dead? What…what…what about Zoe?"

And just like she was relaying chemistry notes, Skylar trotted right through the rest of the news, "Well, Zoe's dad is an ER doctor at Harrison Hospital. So, when the ambulance arrived, he identified them. She was pretty jacked up. Lots of broken bones and a messed-up jaw and oh, and she's in a coma."

Imagining Zoe's father, Hannah was nearly ruined. Dr. Kellogg loved his daughters, Zoe and Paige. They were his pride and joy. He even had this cheesy bumper sticker that read "Stage Dad." It looked so ridiculous next to the MD on his license plate. Hannah imagined Dr. Kellogg pouring himself over Zoe's half-dead body. Shaking his fists to the sky like he was auditioning for the Hudson River Greek Theatre festival. Why do the gods punish me?

Skylar continued, "They might transport her to Columbia Presbyterian in the city. Other than all that, I think she's okay."

"Okay? Skylar, she's in a coma! A coma! And Will..."

Skylar was all business. No time for feelings. Or a conscience apparently. "Need I remind you that the two people who would identify *you* as the driver are completely indisposed right now. They are two people who could ruin your life."

I interrupted, "Your life, too! You were there too!"

"But, Hannah, you were driving. And I'm me. You know, you're a terrible best friend. Even Derrick congratulated me. Granted, he wants in my pants...but still."

How everything would play out flashed before Hannah like a near death experience. *The school will blame me. The media will blame me. Skylar's name will come up but quickly dismissed. I was Zoe's understudy. Of course, I hated Zoe. Motive.*

The story was perfect in the sickest way: Poor kid in a rich school who never feels part of the group goes batshit crazy one morning. Hannah wiped more tears, "I gotta go."

"Fine. Try to get your head on straight." Skylar hung up and probably proceeded to call everyone on her favorites list.

Chapter Four
The First Rehearsal

MEMO

TO: All faculty & staff
FROM: Pat Feldman, Dean of Student Life
DATE: 9 March 2016
CC: Principal Hendrickson
RE: Services for William Bartlett

Whispering Hills has received communication from the Bartlett family about the services for their son William. Services will be held as follows...
Wake at Schumaker's Funeral Home March 9, 10, & 11
Wake hours will be 2:30-4:30 & 6:30-8:30 each day.
Funeral will be held on Saturday March 14 at 10 am @ St. Mark's Episcopal Church.
Please see me if you need a ride to the funeral. We have a few volunteers who will be at the school at 9:30 to take teachers to the church.

The memo laid flaccidly on the counter next to Gillian's work bag. Hastily written. Evidence of the administrative exhaustion a student's death unleashes on a school.

Police were spotted at school already. Detectives in civilian clothes. Hannah expected police would show up. But she thought they'd been in uniforms. Like when the police arrived at camp this summer to question everyone about Katie Greco's disappearance. Well, not exactly a disappearance. More a hiatus from camp. She came back a few days later. Hannah never blamed Katie for it. If Hannah had experienced the same thing Katie had, Hannah would have definitely gone AWOL. Skylar could be that scary.

Hannah slid the memo closer to her body but kept it on the counter, afraid to pick it up. Then she noticed her mother in the front hallway. Hannah strained to hear.

"Oh, dear. Jill, what is he thinking?"

A pause then...

"It doesn't matter if he's new. A student is dead."

Another pause to let whoever was on the other end agree with her.

"Exactly. The kids need time."

She's talking to Ms. Panzini. Is she talking about Mr. Samuels? Doesn't matter if he's new? Must be Samuels. Hannah heard keys drop on the oak floor. Her mother rummaged through a shopping bag.

"Dammit. No. Not you, Jillian. I dropped my keys....Well, you can't very well say anything with kids around. If you don't have a united front, the rest of the rehearsals won't go well. Remember *The Lion King*?...Aaron did what? What did Principal Hendrickson say to that?"

Her mother turned the corner and Hannah's heart stopped.

"Jill, I'll see you at work." She plopped the phone in her purse.

Hannah's mother gathered her bags, "Are you ready to go?"

What did Aaron Samuels do? I need to know. I can't believe he's causing drama already. She wanted to ask her mom, but the words just stuck in her throat—much like her abysmal audition song.

"Yes, I'm ready."

Will Bartlett's funeral took place a week after the accident. The beginnings of the investigation, a visitation that went on for three days, and an uncooperative local pastor prolonged his burial. The Bartlett family wanted it done and over with. The sooner the rituals of grief happened, the sooner they could deal with their actual grief.

For the first two nights of the visitation, Hannah couldn't go. "I'll go, mom. I will. I just have this project to finish" or "I don't want to fail this calc test." She did, however, drive past Schumaker's when she picked Ricky up from basketball practice. The air around the funeral home was thick with heartache. The line of mourners wrapped around the building. Cars parked everywhere they could fit. Even on the grass. People parked in the Stop & Shop lot across the street and walked over to keep vigil.

They went because it was the right thing to do. They went because they were sad. But mostly, they went because they were thankful they weren't the Bartletts.

It was the third evening of the visitation when Hannah finally mustered the strength to show her face. Hannah and Gillian Cross waited in that dreadful line. There they were — frozen by the March winds and the silent weight of a life cut short. Warm trickles fell down Hannah's cheeks. Her gloves felt scratchy when she wiped them away. Others took note of her sadness — and the more they sympathized, the more the guilt grew like a cancer inside her.

The Range Rover. She's here again? She went last night. And the night before. Sitting there in a handicapped spot was Skylar's truck. Hannah let out a wail then quickly muffled it. Gillian hugged her daughter hard. When they got closer to the car, Hannah spied the right side of it. No dents, no dings, no silver paint. *Just like Skylar said.* The relief just as strong as the remorse.

Inside the funeral home students paraded past, saying hello and some offering condolences. Skylar sat at the front with the Bartlett family. The two families were close for the year Skylar and Will dated. They would lean on Skylar.

In a tufted velvet armchair, Skylar Clarke dabbed her eyes with a tissue. In fact, the only two mourners sitting up front were Skylar and Will's elderly grandmother. The other Bartletts milled around and received guests. Every once in a while, Skylar would clasp the grandmother's hand.

Hannah excused herself from the line. She hurried to the bathroom. *Here I am in a bathroom stall again. Hiding from my hideous deeds. Hiding from Skylar. How did I get here?* She thought again of camp. *Maybe if I had down the right thing then, none of this would be happening. But the police were so careless. And Skylar was…well, she was and is Skylar. And Katie Greco was a dreadful human being.*

A human being.

She was still a human being. One I could have protected. Could have tried harder.

Hannah spent the rest of the night in the lobby, chatting idly or trying to look busy. Never approaching the casket. Lying to her mother about it. Later that night, a text from Skylar.

SC: saw u @
schumakers.

Hannah stared at the fluorescent screen for at least a minute.

SC: u don't
say hi?

Her stomach churned. After everything, the prospect of Skylar being mad could preempt any other concerns. Hannah hated herself for a moment then clicked the keys.

HC: just upset.
mom wanted
to leave.

Hannah closed her eyes. The phone vibrated once more. Greg this time.

GT: omg
check call
board.

Hannah sprung off the bed, sheets tangled and almost tripping her as she grabbed the laptop. Her phone continued to buzz with the same text from different people as she loaded the musical's Facebook page.

ANNOUNCEMENT:

REHEARSAL WILL BEGIN AT 2 PM on March 14 TO ALLOW STUDENTS TO ATTEND SERVICES FOR WILLIAM BARTLETT.

FULL CAST REPORT 2-6 FOR READ THROUGH.

What the hell? Samuels didn't cancel rehearsal? A student is dead. Another is in a coma. God forbid we should miss a rehearsal. Hannah, filled with righteous indigence, texted furiously for the better part of an hour, participating in the chorus of complaints. She forgot for a moment that she was the one responsible for the actual funeral.

"Hannah? Are you listening?" Aaron Samuels cocked his head. Hannah and Skylar stood at attention with the director. Skylar basked in his encouraging words. *Yes, I'm listening. I just want this lecture to be over.*

Hannah answered, "Yes, sir. Of course. Thank you for overlooking the audition. I'm happy to be part of the show."

Samuels sniffed. *He didn't want to cast me at all. Bet Ms. Panzini convinced him. Or worse, I only got a part because of my mom. Barf. I wish you were Mr. Jacobsen—our old director. He knows how hard-working and talented I am.*

"We're done here," Mr. Samuels glared at Hannah. Both girls started away when he called Skylar back.

"Hannah should take a page out of your book," he whispered to Skylar, but Hannah heard the remark. The rest of the cast were swarming around the front of the auditorium. Mr. Samuels was still complimenting Skylar's maturity and poise when Hannah reached her friends. She resolved to remain stoic. *I'll show him. Just relax. Do what you do. And then he'll see he was wrong.*

Greg Tate was first with a big hug. He didn't check Hannah off his list of hugs at Will's funeral.
"Oh my God, girl! I'm sorry. I know Will was like—your locker buddy."

"Thanks. It's—" Hannah was about to say something vapid about how hard it will be not to see Will every day. But Skylar pranced up and stole Greg away.

Greg immediately hugged her forcefully, "This must be *so* hard for you."

When Skylar pulled away, the most perfect tear fell from her right eye. She wiped it delicately, "I literally can't even be here right now."

No kidding. Another cast member — some nameless underclassman — walked up to pay respects to Skylar too. The tableau was a flawless illustration of the school's pecking order. Skylar suffered the pities of lower classmen gloriously, like the first lady of Whispering Hills. Quietly reverent and classy and all gravitas.

While Skylar continued her show, Greg and Hannah talked about the other drama of the day: the fact that rehearsal wasn't canceled. Cynthia walked up and rolled her big blue eyes at the director. His back was turned, of course. Ms. Panzini shuffled by — eyes still red from weeping at the services.

When she was a safe distance, Cynthia began kvetching, "I heard that Mr. Samuels didn't even want to start rehearsal late. We were supposed to be doing the read through this morning and then start learning the opening. We're doing a choreographed overture. Lame. And now he's all bent out of shape because Principal Hendrickson made him start late to let everyone go to Will's funeral."

Hannah interrupted, "The principal?"

Cynthia loved the attention, "Yeah, Ms. Panzini told the principal that Mr. Samuels didn't want to cancel morning session of the rehearsal. She tattled on him."

Cast members gathered around them — the magnetic pull of teacher drama. Greg looked around at the group and announced the obvious, "Will Bartlett was one of us. We need the closure."

Everyone nodded at Greg's sagacity. He used a fancy counselor term. Without even realizing, Hannah suppressed a vicious giggle that bubbled up in her throat. *I caused this. I can't believe I caused this.* The power one person could attain washed over her.

But Paige Kellogg, Zoe's sister, walked by and thoroughly murdered the Freudian slip Hannah was indulging. One of Paige's friends ran up and bear-hugged her. Tears rose to Hannah's eyes and she looked away from the group. Paige's small, frail torso heaved with grief. Ms. Panzini came to the rescue and ushered Paige out of the theatre.

A few minutes later, it was time to start. Mr. Samuels grabbed the mic and got the cast assembled on the stage. Everyone looked at each other with that collective expression of curiosity and confusion.

Aaron Samuels began, all the other adults in a row a few feet behind him, like drill sergeants at the first day of boot camp. Ms. Panzini even stood with her feet hip-width apart and her hands resting on the small of her back. It was comical. Still, Hannah sat up straighter, determined that she would make up for auditions.

"These next few months will ask much of you. I expect dedication to me, these fine people behind me, this show, and your fellow cast and crew. We are a family now…"

A dysfunctional family.

About halfway through the speech, Skylar leaned in close. Her breath smelled like hazelnut coffee and brown sugar, "That was brutal today."

Hannah's stomach clenched. *Why is she talking about Will's funeral?*

"I don't think we should talk about it here."

Skylar scoffed and continued pouring her warm breath on the left side of Hannah's neck, "After you left us, Samuels told me that I was the only 'adult' audition he saw. He totally didn't understand while Panzini likes you so much. I told him it's because of your mother."

"Why would you say that?"

"Hannah? Is there something you'd like to add?" Mr. Samuels barked from the front of the stage, "Or perhaps you think that you don't need to hear this? Above it all, are we?" His tone dripped with bile.

Screw you, Aaron Samuels. Hannah balled up her fists and dug her nails into her palms.

"Nothing, then? Okay. Let's…" The director told everyone to take five and report to the read through in room 104. He had a video from Stagecraft on Broadway.

When the group broke, Hannah found herself caught behind Sarah Young and her crew. Hannah swallowed hard to fight the tears.

Of course, they were discussing Will's death.

And Sarah Young is so damn loud.

"No, you're wrong Denise. That road is not a thoroughfare. It doesn't go anywhere. The other driver is from the neighborhood. Not some random person. It's someone who knew the roads. That's why the police are at school like every day."

Another chimed in woefully, "I can't believe someone from Whispering Hills would do that."

Sarah retorted, "Flee the scene of a horrific accident to save their own ass? I can believe it. People have a lot to lose here."

Denise offered, "The road leads to the park. It could be anyone."

Sarah lowered her voice, "The road also leads to Clarke mansion."

At that, Hannah ran past them, barreling through the group and knocking Denise into a row of seats. But Hannah needed a toilet and fast. Her hand clasped over her mouth.

"Hey! Watch it, Hannah!" Sarah called.

Hannah rushed to room 104 after heaving in that same last stall of the bathroom. *My second home. They should put my name on the door. Now I'll catch more attitude from Mr. Samuels. A chorus girl late for his precious read through.* She sloshed some water around in her mouth to kill the acidic sour taste. She inhaled sharply through her nose, forcing air through her nostrils. With her head down and deep in thought, Hannah rehearsed her explanation for Mr. Samuels and exited the girls room.

"Oh, Hannah. Hey." Brody Wolcott leaned effortlessly against the lockers.

"Brody?"

He stood up straight. Hannah looked down both sides of the hallway. *Just the two of us.*

"What are you doing at musical rehearsal?" Hannah smiled coyly, activating her inner-Skylar. He was a long way from the lacrosse field.

Brody took a few measured steps closer and Hannah felt the skin on her collarbones tingle. His expression contained all the weight and grief of the day, "I brought Cynthia to rehearsal and my mom wanted me to wait around. See if things were actually happening today. She'd rather have us home — you know, on a day like today. She's pretty messed up about Will. Dying young and all."

"Yeah, my mom was crying last night too. She hugged my little brother and lost it."

An awkward moment of quiet. Hannah's swagger vanished, "I — I don't think Cynthia is in the bathroom. She's probably in 104. Unless you just like hanging out outside the girls' room."

Gosh, I'm so bitchy. Why do girls always take every opportunity to ruin a moment with the guy they like?

Thankfully, Brody wasn't deterred by the immature snipe. He stepped closer again, "You never know if a pretty girl is in there. And she's sick. And you need to check on her."

"I wasn't sick. I — I just…"

———

81

Another step closer.

Brody dipped his head down and purred, "Good. You're okay, then?"

Hannah regretted moving away so quickly but a kiss? Right now? In the empty school hallway? *So cliché. And my breath would certainly make Brody regret waiting outside the bathroom.*

Hannah started to the classroom, "I have to get to the read through. Samuels already hates me."

Brody jogged a few seconds to catch up, "Hey, I just wanted to make sure you were okay."

"I am. Really."

He wasn't convinced. Before they made the corner, Brody touched Hannah's arm, "And Samuels doesn't hate you. He's just being hard on you because he's dating your mom."

"What? No, he's not…"

"Everybody knows. It's not a big deal. Nobody is talking about your mom in a bad way. I promise. Ms. Cross is like the best teacher here. And her letter of rec is why I'm getting into Hofstra."

"You're going there because Hofstra knows an excellent lacrosse player when it sees one."

Brody smiled — surprised at Hannah's interest lacrosse, the sport he lives for. "Yeah, but I still needed a teacher to vouch for me, you know, that I can read and write."

Hannah laughed, and Brody capitalized, "We should go out sometime. I know this isn't the time to ask. I'm sure you're…"

"Yes, we should. Text me. Okay?" Hannah felt giddy and somewhat scared at the same time. Like the feeling you get when the roller coaster makes its initial ascent. *Was it guilt or Brody nerves or abject fear of Mr. Samuels? Yep, all of the above.*

When Hannah neared the classroom, she heard voices arguing in the hallway. Hannah ducked behind a trophy display case. It was Ms. Panzini and Mr. Samuels.

"She needs to be with her family. Her sister is in a coma."

"No, she needs to be at rehearsal. I think distraction is a good thing right now."

Ms. Panzini sighed heavily, "Maybe next week. Maybe distraction will be good then. But not today. They all just buried their friend."

They were talking about Paige Kellogg. Hannah narrowed her eyes. The first of many teacher conflicts the cast would witness over the next few months. All too familiar. Usually, Hannah would just roll her eyes and wait for Mr. Samuels to proclaim the obvious "I'm the director of this show!"

But not today. Today, Hannah was the reason everyone was in upheaval. Not trusting her legs, Hannah held the display case for support. At any moment, her life could come crashing down. She couldn't shake the feeling that everyone, at all times, was talking about her and Skylar.

Another adult appeared. The rehearsal pianist. "Paige is a wreck. Let's call someone to take her home. And if you send her home, we can probably get a lot more done."

Smart. Appeal to Mr. Samuels' need to get something accomplished today.

But Samuels wasn't having it. "You too? Really? First, I have to cast Hannah Cross as understudy to the lead—when she shouldn't even be in the show. That was the worst audition I've ever seen. And now I'm sending the dance captain home the first day of rehearsal? And Jill. Weren't you planning on using Paige in the opening number?"

"Yes, but…"

"You coddle these kids, Jill. I heard it about you before I came. And now I see it. This is why I'm bringing in Zachary Cartwright to do a number."

Ms. Panzini stood aghast for a moment. Choking on the insult, she yelled, "I'm sending her home!"

"I'm the director!" he shouted.

And there it is. Time to get in that classroom. They are too annoyed with each other right now to yell at me. Hannah showed herself and the adults immediately hushed. Ms. Panzini turned and walked a few paces down the hallway, clearly crying.

Hannah was about to slip into the read-through unscathed. Mr. Samuels stared at the floor but then, as if the proverbial lightbulb had gone off over his head, "Hannah?"

"Yes, Mr. Samuels," and then before he could say anything, Hannah blurted out, "I think it's good that we're here right now. I'm sorry. I—I—overheard a little. I just wanted you to know that. It's a good distraction. For me, at least."

He stared blankly for a second and then uttered a surprisingly sincere "Thank you."

Once inside the classroom, Skylar flagged Hannah down and pointed to the open seat next to her. "I saved it for you, bestie," she smiled and basked in the green glow that was Cynthia Wolcott's jealousy. Skylar loved creating these little moments for Cynthia. They kept her obedient.

The students buzzed—apparently someone saw a police car circling in the parking lot. Mr. Samuels walked in and everyone quieted.

"Sorry about the wait, everyone. I had to get the DVD of Stagecraft from my office. Everyone has a script? Good."

Ms. Panzini came in and walked directly to Paige. She spoke softly and solemnly. *Maybe…if I'm lucky…just maybe Zoe died. Ms. Panzini is relaying the tragic news. No, probably not that lucky.*

Paige and the dance teacher left the room.

"Looks like Panzini just drew a line in the sand," Skylar leaned in and sneered.

Mr. Samuels cued up the video and the cast began the read through. It went on for three hours. So, Hannah had all that time to wonder about that police car.

84

Chapter Five
Fake it Till You Make It

The next week was spring break. Greg's parents usually go on vacation—they're both professors so they jaunt around Europe. Greg usually has a "kiki" on St. Patrick's Day with a few besties. "Just a little gathering," he told the Cynthia. "Gossip and some champs," Greg smiled as he turned to Skylar and Hannah.

CALL BOARD SCHEDULE FOR SPRING BREAK... March 16-20
Monday: No rehearsal
Tuesday: 11:00 am to 7:00pm
Wednesday: 11:00 am to 7:00pm
Thursday: 11:00am to 5:00pm
Friday: No Rehearsal

No kiki this year. Professor Tate and Professor Tate were too anxious about the recent tragedy and its effect on their newly out-of-the-closet son.

Hannah's mom tried several times to engage in a discussion about Will's death. It's the high school teacher in Gillian Cross, always part therapist.

"Yes, I'll be fine. I just feel bad for his family," Hannah repeated on autopilot. The high school senior avoided any fake "feels." The pretending might give way to a deluge of tears and confessions. *Mom needs to stay in the dark. I can't ruin her life too.*

Hannah treated these conversations the same way she treated the conversations after camp. "Yes, terrible what happened to Katie Greco. I'm sure she'll be fine though. It was just an accident. Skylar didn't know Katie didn't know how to swim." *This is so much bigger than pathetic Katie Greco though.*

And just as the theatre camp kids recovered quickly — even nailed their performance in the parent showcase — after Katie was found, the Whispering Hills students did the same. Necessary rituals of death were complete. The clique moved on. Eventually they even ceased caring about Zoe. Schoolwork and the play took over their collective unconscious.

Not really for Hannah though. She often imagined Zoe, a vegetable rotting away in a hospital bed while senior year came and went. Zoe missing her last hurrah on the school's stage. And no prom.

And then there were the nightmares of Zoe's waking up. In her dreams, Hannah keeps vigil beside Zoe who hugs her grateful family and then points an accusatory finger. In reality, Hannah hadn't visited Zoe yet. Other students had spent time at the hospital. Greg read the Stagecraft script to the sleeping beauty. Cynthia made a playlist of Zoe's favorite show tunes.

But at rehearsals, Samuels kept them so busy that no one had time to grieve. Would've been seen as self-indulgent anyway. And the upside? The play kids found their new place in the pecking order now that the star was gone.

"It's our duty to Zoe to put on an amazing performance of *Stagecraft*. We must press on…in this business we call show," Sarah Young had declared to her crew. Hannah rolled her eyes. *In this business we call show? I can't with this girl.*

Skylar found her new role effortlessly. She got what she wanted. She was the lead. After four years, Skylar finally had the lead. And she was good too. Samuels was impressed. Even Ms. Panzini was happy. One time, Skylar Clarke even deigned to talk to a freshman. The doe-eyed crew member walked away like an angel had descended from heaven.

The lunchroom smelled like chili on Tuesday. Disturbingly enough, no chili was being served. Willfully ignoring the noxious smell, Hannah choked down the sandwich her mom made. Rehearsal would run from 3:00 p.m. until 7:30 p.m. She'd need some sustenance.

A police officer walked in and chatted with Jill Panzini who straightened at his appearance. Everyone at Hannah's table fell silent—including Skylar who, for once, looked a tinge frightened. Greg craned his long neck to see who would be called in for questioning.

The police had been milling around since the accident. Hannah's circle was totally interested in being a part of this investigation. Greg didn't care about Will or Zoe. He was all about the drama. A real investigation? Yes, please.

"They're talking to Paige again," Greg slumped back down and sulked.

Hannah smiled knowingly at Skylar. Despite their recent tension, the two always inhabited the same wavelength. Greg probably binge-watched episodes of CSI to prepare for his big interrogation scene. *You got to auditions an hour early. Why bother questioning you?* Hannah scolded Greg in her head and kind of relished the idea that she should be the center of attention. Not Paige. Not Greg.

Cynthia rolled her eyes, "They need to lay off her. Paige is exhausted. And Samuels put her in like every number."

"The detectives questioned Will's friends last Friday. Brought them in one by one. Like suspects," Skylar added. "Hannah, have you been questioned yet?"

Hannah's head snapped around to face Skylar. *What the? What is wrong with her?* "No, uh, I mean, why would they want to talk to me?"

Skylar scoffed, "Cause you were friends with Will? Like everyone else was?"

Why is she putting me on the spot? She knows I can't play along like this.

———

88

Greg reflected, unaware of Hannah's impending nervous breakdown, "I think I'll get called soon."

Skylar agreed, "Probably sometime this week. They'll talk to everyone. The police are sure it was foul play. Right, Hannah?"

"Yeah, sure." Hannah practically buried her face.

Cynthia comforted Greg, "Don't be stressed about it. Just tell the truth."

Hannah wished she could laugh at their forced drama. Normally she would. In a moment though, she rallied, "Principal Hendrickson has been at odds with them. My mom said. He's just mad that they need to conduct the investigation at school and keep taking students out of class. Teachers are complaining that kids come back all distraught." Hannah swelled with pride at delivering her monologue. But deep inside, she wished the police would go away. And soon.

"The detectives are looking to cross-examine everyone. That's how they catch lies," Greg nodded.

Skylar looked around and considered the whole cafeteria, "Students are in a frenzy though. Teenagers are a fragile folk." She said it as if she wasn't a teenager herself.

Cynthia chimed in, always needing to be relevant, "If the police talk to you, they'll probably ask you the same stuff they asked me last week." Cynthia had enjoyed lording this experience over the rest of the clique. "Tell us about the morning of your auditions. What time did you leave the house? Do you remember how you got to school that day? Do you remember seeing Will Bartlett's car on the way down the hill…"?

God, she's incessant. It's like sitting across from a cartoon.

Later that day, Hannah nudged Skylar and whispered, "Did they talk to you yet?"

"No," she sneered. Then they sat in uncomfortable silence for another few minutes until the director called the cast to order.

It was a grueling rehearsal. And Hannah felt sick the whole time. *She's hiding something from me.* It was the same feeling Hannah got the day Skylar asked her to lie to the director at camp. "Just make up an excuse. I won't be there today. Neither will Katie. But you don't even have to mention her." So nonchalant. As if she and Katie were cutting rehearsal to smoke clove cigarettes. As if Skylar didn't loathe Katie Greco.

That day at camp, Hannah didn't really care what Skylar was up to. She was, after all, always up to something. But now, Skylar's avoidance of the conversation was vexing.

The two made their way to the dance studio. As deftly as possible, Hannah said, "You'd tell me right? If you got questioned, I mean."

Skylar took Hannah's hand and laced her long fingers between Hannah's, "Just not now, Hannah. Don't worry." She gave Hannah's hand a squeeze.

A text from the queen much later.

> SC: samuels says i get a tour of cartwright's new musical. going to bway this thursday night. BACKSTAGE!

Unbelievable. It's not enough that he fawns over Skylar in rehearsal. Like he's in love with her or something. Now she gets to go backstage at Girls & Diamonds.

Hannah stared at her phone. Typing…then deleting…then typing again. *If I got to meet Zachary Cartwright…I just know he'd like me. I just know I could stand out…impress him.*

HC: can i
come?

The response came swiftly. Like Skylar knew Hannah would ask. She just had to hit 'send.'

SC: leads
only.
#sorrynotsorry

Hannah rolled her shoulders back to release tension in her neck. Only one more flight up to the music room. The classroom was on the opposite side of the school from the theatre. And two floors up. But if you've ever heard eighth graders wailing on their violins, you'd understand why the school put the music room so far away from everyone.

A few giggles came from the room. *Weird. I'm at least ten minutes early.* Samuels blocked off time to teach the torch song "More Than This." As Skylar's understudy, Hannah was always at important rehearsals. But as a shadow. Sometimes the Call Board even had Hannah scheduled in two places at once.

However, if something were to happen to Skylar, Hannah would know every song and every line. Hannah smiled for a moment. *If only…*

The door was cracked open. Another laugh from the inside. *Mom? Is that my mom's laugh?* But Hannah couldn't tell. She stopped and noiselessly placed her backpack on the floor. *I'll just wait a few minutes. Skylar won't show until exactly the time she's due to be here. If Mom is in there...* She felt at once giddy for her mom's romance with the new director and totally grossed out.

Soft whispers came from the room now. Mr. Samuels let out this virile chuckle and Hannah almost gagged. *Just think about something else.* For a few seconds Hannah held her fingers in her ears like a toddler. *Skylar should be here soon. She'll break this up.*

Then Skylar laughed from inside the room. *Skylar? Wait, Mom is in there. At least I think it's Mom in there. Why does Mom sound like Skylar?*

A loud "Shh" from the director.

Hannah moved inaudibly to face the crack in the threshold. The muffled titters came again. *Definitely Skylar. Mom isn't there at all. Never was. Skylar is in there flirting with my mom's boyfriend.*

Filled with rage, Hannah threw the door open. They were completely taken unawares. Even Skylar had a startled look on her face when she turned. Across the room, Mr. Samuels, face half-hidden by the piano, sat at the bench with Skylar sitting on the closed piano facing him. Skylar had her elbows leaned up on the piano, her shirt stretched tight across her full breasts. Her long wavy hair fell down into the open piano. Hannah wished that the piano gears would come to life. They could coil around the strands of hair and yank her head back hard.

Shit, what the hell should I do now? Hannah's eyes danced between Skylar and Aaron. She looked for proof of foul play and hoped for evidence to the contrary. Samuels collected himself quickly, the only actual adult. Now he stared at Hannah like he always did.

"Am I interrupting something?" Hannah said pointedly at Skylar.

The director shuffled through sheet music aimlessly. Skylar met her friend's tone, "No. But you're late for rehearsal."

Hannah walked closer, slammed her bag on the floor by the piano, and replied in kind, "Call board said 5:45. Check the time."

Skylar turned slowly, her rear now facing the director. She leaned over the piano, looked at the clock on the wall behind Hannah, and chirped, "So it is."

Then Skylar's whole face turned bright and innocent, like she put on a mask, "Looks like — for once — I'm early! Crazy! Right, Mr. Samuels?"

He laughed uncomfortably then placed a few sheets atop the piano, "Here's another copy of 'More Than This.'"

Hannah shivered with anger, "I have the first copy you gave me."

"Oh, uhhh. Okay then." He played warm-up chords; eyes locked on the keys. Hannah felt triumphant imagining his thoughts:

Would she tell her mother?

Would she tell someone else?

What did she see exactly?

Hannah missed the first two steps on the scale as she relished letting Samuels feel her gaze. Skylar missed the first two steps as well. But she sang so clearly and angelically on the third that Hannah's thoughts were broken. Skylar glared at Hannah. Hannah found her voice. It was clear and strong too. Surprising even. Mr. Samuels couldn't help but press the keys a little harder. He looked up at the young women, horrified at the situation he'd created.

93

The rest of the rehearsal Hannah resolved to channel the anger into the song. For the warm-ups and the first twenty minutes of reviewing the song, her voice surpassed Skylar's. *Yes, I have the better voice. Skylar has always known it. And now you, Mr. Samuels, know it too. The bad audition was just that. A bad audition.*

And Skylar became frustrated. Four years of being together almost constantly and Hannah knew her tells. The skin under her right eye twitched ever so softly. She continually put her hair up then took it back down. And the biggest tell of all—Skylar echoed every compliment Hannah got from the director with a genuine sweetness that would fool a trained psychologist.

When Aaron Samuels stopped after the bridge to give notes, Skylar beamed with pride as she marinated in the constructive criticism and the praise. But he played again, the director looked directly at Hannah, "You sounded lovely just then, Hannah. Keep it up."

"Oh, uhh, thank you." Hannah was stunned.

"She just has to work on her game face for auditions now," Skylar interjected.

"Yes, if only that was the Hannah Cross I met at vocal auditions..."

The next time they sang Hannah didn't hit all the higher notes cleanly. Her throat tight from Skylar's spiteful remark. Mr. Samuels decided he would work with Skylar on the breathing for the last belt. So, Hannah sat and noticed her phone had two messages. Both from Brody. Hannah kept the phone inside her bag and read the texts, trying to deaden the smile that had unconsciously sprung to her face.

BW: sorry i
haven't been
in touch. mom
has me taking
SATs for the
third time on
saturday
morning.

Then a two minutes later, another.

BW: dinner
tmrw? want to
catch up. ☺

Without analyzing it, Hannah wrote back.

HC: sure.
olympus
diner? disco
fries <3

Hannah indulged some excellent thoughts about disco
fries covered in mozzarella and dipped in turkey gravy. Even
more indulgent thoughts about Brody braided themselves into
her mind too.

It wasn't until Skylar was standing over the desk that
Hannah realized rehearsal was over. Hannah walked out
without saying a word. The anger returned. Flirting with her
mother's love interest—even for gain in the show—was
treason. You don't mess with mothers.

On the way to dance rehearsal, Hannah kept a pace fast
enough where petite Skylar had to jog a little. *If I'm being
honest, I'm just buying some time. This is unusual. Skylar actually
doesn't know what my reaction will be, how much I saw. I'm going
to make her wait.*

Skylar stopped with Hannah at the restroom. She stopped with Hannah at her locker. She stopped with Hannah at Greg's locker where Hannah left the answers to the AP Gov homework. Skylar chatted the whole time. Trying different approaches. Taking the temperature of the room.

"That was nice of Samuels to give you a compliment. I totally knew that he'd notice you eventually." *The nice approach. Hmph.*

"I see someone was texting with Brody. Don't worry. I won't tell Cynthia." *The loyal approach.*

In the bathroom stall, she even tried this one: "Whoa. I *totes* need a bikini wax. The downtown is all 70s porn star." *The self-effacing approach. Never cute with Skylar. I think she's even a little nervous.*

By the time they arrived at the dance studio, Skylar was desperate. And Hannah had found the words to confront her friend. But Skylar took her arm, "The police questioned me the other day. I have a dark SUV and they are investigating everyone with that type of car."

"Why didn't you tell me?" Hannah turned white with fear. *Who knows what she told the police?* Immediately, Hannah's mind went back to the crash. *That sound. I still can't get it out of my head.* And Hannah saw Skylar's insidious expression right before they hit. The mania of an unchecked tantrum. *She wanted to hurt them. I could see it on her face.*

"I was waiting until we were alone. If you weren't being weird the past ten minutes, I could've told you earlier. God, I'm sorry I brought up the audition," Skylar rolled her eyes. "Listen, there's nothing on the car. I swear."

"How do you know there isn't anything on the car? We hit them. His car is silver. Yours is navy. There's bound to be a dent and paint on your car." Hannah remembered seeing the Range Rover at the wake. *There wasn't any damage. But it was dark too. And I was a few feet away.*

"I told you there's nothing on the car," Skylar huffed. "And I have more. We were supposed to be at auditions at 9, right?"

"Yeah."

"And we actually got here at 9:05."

Hannah put an indignant hand on her hip, "What's the point?"

"Cynthia was the last person to sign the attendance sheet. Cynthia signed at 8:35. So I signed both of us in at 8:38. Right after Cynthia."

The accident happened closer to 8:45. Hannah remembered that clearly. *If Skylar had signed us into auditions at 8:38, we have an alibi. A documented alibi.*

Skylar pranced into dance studio.

"Wait," Hannah blurted, "What about Ms. Panzini? She was at the sign-in table. She knows."

"She signed off on the sheet as accurate. Never noticed the time. Mostly because you walked in crying like a baby. See, your dramatic entrance actually worked in our favor. Panzini loves you and your mommy. When I told her that you were crying because of your deadbeat dad, she bought it."

Hannah stood frozen. *Skylar actually kept me safe. At least it feels that way. I think.*

"And I visited Zoe like two days ago. You should go too. I'll go with you if you want."

What did she just say? Like visiting Zoe was nothing. Like Zoe had mono.

Hannah felt the tears but suppressed them. *Will Bartlett is dead. Zoe rots in a hospital. And it's my fault.* She took a deep breath and pressed the guilt down as hard as she could. After all, she was safe from culpability. Her mother was safe from scandal. Even her silly brother was safe. *Just focus on that.*

Chapter Six
Blocking

To: Brody Wolcott
From: Coach Wilder

You're Invited to the
Annual Varsity Lacrosse
Dinner

Saturday March 28th
7:00 pm

Secret Location

Please RSVP by March 23rd.
(include the name of your
plus one).

See you there!
--Coach Wilder

Hannah stole a look at the paper in her backpack and nearly chuckled. *Is this an invite or a memo?* She thought of Coach Wilder playing with fonts and trying to make his invite to the Annual Varsity Lacrosse Dinner look exclusive. *Not exactly an invite to the Met Gala. But I'll take it. And I'm pretty sure the whole school knows the "secret location" is Applebees.* Still she couldn't believe she was going to be Brody Wolcott's date for the Lacrosse Dinner. Hannah looked forward to seeing him for their date that night too.

Even with Brody in her near future, dance rehearsal dragged. Learn a combo. Ms. Panzini changes something. Samuels and Panzini consult, and Panzini changes it again.

The dancers learned (and relearned) a small ensemble dance number in the first act. In Stagecraft, a small-town poor girl named Aurelia leaves her abusive father and horrible boyfriend to make it big in the city. Things don't go exactly as planned at first but in the end, she lives out her dream as a Broadway star. The Whispering Hills cast rehearsed "Make It," the upbeat song that Aurelia sings with her waitress friends in the cheerless diner where she works.

Mr. Samuels pulled Skylar up front, "Remember, Skylar, you're poor. You have nothing. No prospects. You depend on others. But now you have to depend on yourself." The motivation for the scene.

This is ludicrous. Skylar as a poor girl with no prospects? Her big decision lately was whether to play D1 softball (yes, Skylar was a wicked pitcher) at UConn or go to Daddy's alma mater—Swarthmore. Either way, she would meet some rich jock douchecanoe, get married, get her MBA, quit working as soon as her first baby came along, and live out the rest of her life terrorizing the other members of the Bronxville Junior League. But when the scene started, Skylar played the part effortlessly. Even Hannah pitied her for a few seconds.

Hannah, Greg, Cynthia, Skylar, Paige, and a few others were there to learn the dance. For once, Hannah was actually in the number. Just a patron in the diner but still…

———

Cynthia played the salty old crow who warns the beautiful ingénue about staying in "this no-good town." Greg played the cook at the greasy spoon. He got to bust through the swinging kitchen door at one point and yell at the waitresses to get back to work. "Blue plate specials aren't going to serve themselves, ladies!"

Close to the end of rehearsal, Ms. Panzini and Mr. Samuels got into an argument. No one dared leave the dance floor. No one dared sit down. No one dared to check a cell phone. Both adults were hyper-aware that the room was watching. *This is intense. But maybe, if they get pissed enough, they will let us out early. Then I'll have more time to get ready for my date with Brody.*

Suddenly, Ms. Panzini turned to the group, face red with stress and physical exertion. She called to the student director, "Sarah, run the dance from the bridge. Keep running it until the timing of the turns are right."

Crap. Sarah is definitely going to make us work until the end. No chance of getting an extra twenty minutes to prep. Sarah Young popped up from the floor, a misty area left on the mirror where she'd been leaning. Skylar turned to Hannah and made a face. Hannah raised an eyebrow back. No one can stomach Sarah—especially when Sarah has been given permission to yell at the cast.

Sarah drilled the same three counts of eight over and over again. Everyone was sweaty and exhausted. Hannah rubbed the stitch in her side. Greg went to grab a drink of water.

"I didn't say you could get any water yet," Sarah put her hands on her hips.

Greg stood his ground. He didn't answer but took a swig of water, licked his lips and let out an "ahh" like he was trying out for a Pepsi commercial. Sarah cocked her head and gritted her teeth. Mr. Samuels and Ms. Panzini were still squabbling. Panzini motioned with her arms. Samuels pointed at his chest and then at the floor.

Greg walked over to Paige who was panting for air. "Make It" featured Paige heavily. Even though the song was short, Paige just did the choreography several times. She needed a break. Greg handed her the bottle of water and leered at Sarah, "When you can get up here and do this dance fifty times full out, then you can decide when we get water breaks."

Sarah looked over at the teachers for back up but neither adult noticed. She put her hair up in a tight ponytail, the bottom half of her head shaved, her neck tattooed with a Chinese symbol.

Is she going to fight, Greg? For a moment, all the grief and anxiety faded as Hannah waited for what would be the greatest confrontation in Whispering Hill's history. Hannah stared at the back of Sarah's head, spying Sarah's ridiculous tattoo placed beneath her half-shaven bob. She remembered when Sarah explained the tattoo to everyone in Study Hall. "It's the Japanese symbol for honor," she had said pedantically. "It's a samurai thing. Do you even know…"

"What a samurai is?" Skylar interrupted. "Yes, we know. Doesn't change the fact that you just inked the Mitsubishi logo on yourself…permanently."

Hannah smirked at the tattoo now. She wondered if tough Sarah Young would escalate this exchange with Greg even further. The whole cast held their collective breath.

"Run it back," Sarah called to the crew geek at the sound system. Then she stared at Greg with a force that could've turned him straight again, "Line up."

Paige took a dainty sip, "I'm okay. Thanks Greg. I'm okay, really."

Panzini and Samuels erupted. Horrific and glorious at the same time.

"Then I'll just get someone else to do it!" Mr. Samuels threatened. Beastly veins popped out of his neck.

Ms. Panzini grabbed her bag. It almost hit Mr. Samuels in the chest. She shouted back, "You're going to fire *me*, Aaron? Go ahead and try. I've been here for over ten years!" She turned to the cast, tears rising to her eyes, "Rehearsal is over. Go home!" She stormed out, slamming the door and shaking the speakers attached to the wall around it.

Mr. Samuels brushed his shirt downward and ran his tongue between his cheek and his teeth. "Everyone except Skylar is dismissed. Get your things quickly and go," he announced. Then, as an afterthought, "Good job today everyone. Especially you, Paige. Good job."

Mr. Samuels took Skylar to the center of the room by the elbow. She looked up at him demurely, her face barely glistening with perspiration. Hannah saw herself in the mirror. Her face was cherry red, and her hair line soaked. *I look like I just ran the marathon and Skylar looks like she just had a romp in the bedroom. No wonder everyone is attracted to her.*

When Hannah arrived home from rehearsal, she only had about thirty minutes to shower and get ready before Brody would be at her door. *Do I do my hair or my make-up? Only one of these is getting done well. At least I don't smell like feet and dance studio and drama.* Hannah stepped out of the shower and started toweling off. However, she paused when she noticed herself in the mirror. Dripping wet and naked, Hannah couldn't help but take notice of how her body responded to the longer, more challenging rehearsals. Her thighs looked slender but powerful. Her abdominals were tight, defined even. She noticed the small shelf on each side of her oblique muscles, just above her hips. And her damp hair trickled down on straighter, stronger shoulders.

She pulled on her underwear, grabbed her phone, and took a mirror selfie. Then another. Then another. *Crap, I don't have time to get this pose right. Oh well.* Hannah put her phone down and decided she'd find the right filter later.

Dashing back to the bathroom vanity, she painted her face full of make-up. She stared for way too long at her open closet. *What says I don't care and makes me look hot at the same time?*

When the doorbell rang, Hannah was still standing in her panties. "Shoot!" *Why did Brody Wolcott have to be so damn punctual? And so damn polite?*

Hannah overheard Brody talking to her mother. Just the diner. Yes, they wouldn't be out too late. Then he delved into the end of Death of a Salesman. Hannah could only imagine the dorky look on her mother's face. She fought with her leggings as she wondered how perfect Brody could be related to insipid Cynthia Wolcott. *They actually shared a womb?* Hannah coiled a scarf around her neck and put her damp hair in a loose ponytail. Out of the dirty clothes pile, she grabbed her Citizens of Humanity denim jacket—a birthday gift from Skylar—and gave it a sniff.

"Hannah, your date is here," Gillian Cross almost sang the words.

Date? Seriously?

"Be right down!" Hannah pulled on her Uggs.

Hannah trotted downstairs to meet Brody's bright eyes and even brighter smile.

A denim jacket doesn't cut it on a cold March night. She wished she'd put on her school fleece instead. Brody was right behind her by the time they reached the car. *Is he going to open the car door for me? Wow, chivalry isn't dead.*

But it was even better.

"Here," he whispered as he slipped off his varsity jacket and put it around her shoulders, "it's pretty cold." Brody rubbed Hannah's shoulders and chuckled a little.

And then he opened the car door. This impromptu date was turning into a cinematic romance starring Hannah Cross.

They discussed school and the play and sports on the way to the diner. It was polite and small. Play conversations were too often weighted with history and emotional turmoil when Hannah talked with the clique. So, it was a nice respite.

Brody found a parking spot under a broken streetlamp. No one around. He leaned in and kissed Hannah. Just like that. Soft and tender. Goose bumps rose up all over Hannah's neck when his cold fingertips explored the bottom of her hairline. "Sorry, just couldn't wait until after we ate, I guess," Brody grinned mischievously.

All of a sudden Hannah felt hot in her scarf and Brody's huge jacket. She yanked the scarf away from her neck and pulled Brody in awkwardly. Now his whole torso was on the passenger side of the car and the two were kissing again. Faster, harder this time. Hannah opened her mouth readily and let his tongue in.

After several glorious minutes, Brody pulled away, "Wow. We need to go inside because…" He looked at his crotch and laughed, "We need to go inside while I can still walk inside." Hannah giggled knowing that if she pulled him in again it would drive Brody crazy in the best of ways.

"Let's go inside then," Hannah started getting out. *If I pull him in again, I might be getting more than I bargained for on a first date.*

They sat down and ordered drinks—Coke for Brody and hot water with lemon for Hannah.

"Such a performer," Brody smiled.

"What?"

"My sister lives on hot water with lemon and honey. You know, during play season," Brody used air quotes when he said, "play season." Typical for someone who played three varsity sports. But Hannah just tilted her head and gave him a flirtatious grin. *Okay, you can make fun of the play kids a little bit.*

She was about to ask what Brody was ordering when he continued, "Yeah, Cynthia drinks that all day. And she practically lives on salads with no dressing and Cliff bars. It's ridiculous."

Do we have to talk about Cynthia? Like ever?

"We all do," Hannah replied then pretended to read the menu. Then she had a brilliant idea. *I should say something nice about Cynthia. Evidently, Brody doesn't realize how colossally annoying she is.*

"Well, all the lemons and honey are working out well for Cynthia. She sounded amazing today in rehearsal," Hannah beamed and waited for the compliment to register. Brody looked up and searched Hannah's face for a moment.

He asked, "What are you going to have?"

"Greek salad." After seeing her drum tight body in the bathroom mirror, Hannah was determined to keep it that way. *No disco fries for me.*

"Well, I'm getting a burger with fries and onion rings." And when the food came, he placed the basket of fries and rings between them and asked, "Is ketchup on the side okay?"

She was halfway down the wedding aisle when Brody did his impression of Ms. Panzini teaching intro to jazz dance—a class all freshmen, even the jocks, had to take.

Freshmen year was the year Ms. Panzini got engaged. She's been planning her wedding ever since. And as each year passed, it seemed everyone but Ms. Panzini realized that no matter how big her wedding binder got, this guy wasn't committing.

"And that binder she has. So many sheet protectors and spreadsheets and seating arrangements," Brody laughed. Hannah almost snorted her drink.

Things were going well. Maybe too well. Because Skylar walked in. *The universe clearly hates me.* And then Cynthia and Greg walked in too. *Great.* Brody had his back to the door. *Pretend not to notice them. He doesn't see them.* Hannah looked down at her food and then back at Brody. *The diner is huge. Maybe the hostess will sit them far away.*

She rapid-fired a bunch of tedious questions about Lacrosse. Brody answered, more emphatically with each question, probably warmed by Hannah's increasingly detailed thoughts about his favorite sport. The distraction worked for a few minutes. Hannah didn't catch where the hostess sat Skylar and company. *Maybe they didn't see us either.*

But that feeling was short-lived.

"Cyn!" Brody waved at his sister. Hannah turned around too. Skylar gave a pageant wave, Greg nodded, and Cynthia just stared blankly. Brody couldn't detect it yet, but Hannah could see it right away — Cynthia was shocked and furious that Hannah was out with her precious twin brother.

"Sorry. Probably should've gone to Valbrook over in Pemberton, right?" Brody took a big bite of his burger and continued eating. His apology was a shoulder shrug at best. *He's so blissfully unaware. Bet the lacrosse guys don't deal with this level of tension. I envy him.*

It wasn't Brody's fault he had Cynthia for a sister. It also wasn't Brody's fault that Cynthia hated Hannah. Cynthia hated Hannah because of one person: Skylar Clarke. And it wasn't long before Cynthia stormed out, crying of course. Hannah rolled her eyes and Brody saw.

"What was that?" He turned his whole torso to see his sister barrel through the doors of the diner. "Do you think Skylar said something to her?"

Hannah's infatuation with Brody gave in to her extreme dislike of Cynthia. "You know Cynthia," she answered flippantly and went back to her salad.

Cynthia was pacing outside, waiting for big brother to come and ask her what's wrong.

Brody's face flushed, "What's that supposed to mean?"

Hannah lifted her shoulders dramatically, fully committing to the position. *I just can't with Cynthia. I can't be diplomatic. I can't pretend to like her. Even if she is genetically connected to the hottest guy in school.* It was a decision Hannah would rue for weeks. Nevertheless, she persisted, "I don't know. They were probably talking about the play. Or maybe Skylar asked Cynthia to pass the salt."

"Asked her to pass the salt?" he scoffed. "And that stupid play. You guys act like you're on Broadway." Brody huffed again, this time louder. "And Skylar Clarke is a real—"

Okay — that's it. No one calls the play stupid! Hannah interrupted, "Whispering Hills puts on the best shows in Westchester. More than I can say for the lacrosse team. Good job spending all your time playing a sport no one gives a shit about."

As soon as the words were out, Hannah wished she would take them back. *Holy shit! No, no, no. Why did I say that?* Why? Because the play is everything. No one talks shit about the play. Her friends were the hardest working kids at Whispering Hills.

"I'm out," Brody reached across the table and grabbed his jacket that was lying next to Hannah. The weight of it upended Hannah's bag. All her make-up, tampons, cell phone...her everything fell out onto the sticky floor.

"You know, Skylar has been a colossal bitch since middle school," Brody simmered. "She's been terrorizing Cynthia for years. But you, I liked you. I asked you out despite your association with self-proclaimed queen of Whispering Hills. Guess I was wrong." And just like that he was gone. He stopped briefly at the hostess station, pointed at their table, and handed over some cash.

What did I just do? Hannah pushed the salad away and grabbed the basket of onion rings. Hannah always knew that Skylar was broken. *But she's always been good to me. The past four years would have been hellish without Sky.* She vouched for Hannah in the rich kid school. Skylar gave Hannah cache. Then the past few weeks welled up inside Hannah. *Brody is totally right – Skylar is an awful human being. Can she be saved?* As tears came to her eyes, Hannah realized something important. Skylar was reason Cynthia and Hannah hated each other. Sure, Cynthia was childish and annoying but Skylar pit them against each other. She did it for power…or maybe for sport.

    Speak of the devil… and she'll appear.

"Trouble in paradise already?" Skylar Clarke plopped down where Brody had been just minutes before. Hannah boiled. *She knew we'd come here. I shouldn't have told her about the date.*

Skylar dipped a fry in ketchup. "It's not your fault that Cynthia has awkward taboo feelings for her brother."

"Shut up, Skylar. For once, just shut up."

"Hey, screw you. I was going to invite you to sit with me and Greg. The Wolcotts are douchebags. Have been since forever. Their daddy owns that Lexus dealership on Pembroke Road. They think their shit doesn't stink. Don't take it out on me."

Hannah leaned over the table, "Maybe if you weren't so horrible to Cynthia, she wouldn't freak out when she saw me and Brody together."

"I don't have to take this crap, Hannah. You are terrible to Cynthia too. I seem to remember you're apologizing to her last year after she overheard you saying that there are some people in this world who should just kill themselves." Skylar raised her eyebrows. She grabbed Hannah's arm and dug her nails in hard, "So pot meet kettle. Cynthia hates you because of you. And now Brody hates you because of you. You never had a chance with him."

108

She trotted away triumphantly.

Hannah walked out—unsure of what else to do. She hoped her friends didn't see the tears.

It would be a cold, long walk home. But Hannah needed the time to cry and let the crisp air clean out her sinuses.

Later, four texts.

BW: cynthia
has been
crying for
hours

BW: u used
me to make
her miserable

BW: don't talk
to me anymore
and lose the
invitation to
the lax dinner

BW: u can tell
that bitch
skylar the
same

Hannah sat up in bed. She grabbed her pillow, pressed it onto her face, and screamed as loud as she could. She wept bitter tears. And screamed into the pillow again for good measure.

Her brother knocked on the wall separating their bedrooms and yelled, "Go to sleep, weirdo."

Hannah looked at the clock. 11:45 pm. *I'm never getting to sleep now.* She opened her laptop with good intentions. *I'll get some work done.*

But instead, Hannah scoured the Internet for news about the accident. She'd already watched the News 12 Westchester clip about a thousand times. That article had a follow up about Will's services and a message from the Bartlett family. But that was all. The local news story got cross-posted on the Daily News and the New York Post. But again, same information. *This is going to blow over. If the police had something, the news would spill it.* She tried to relax. *I would know if the investigation was getting somewhere.* At least everyone at the lunch table agreed.

12:30 am. Still no sleep. Reading the news made Hannah feel restless. Almost involuntarily Hannah pulled on a jacket and shoes. She took the keys to her mother's minivan and went for a drive. Her mother was none the wiser, fast asleep and likely dreaming of Aaron Samuels. And Ricky, if he was awake, didn't care enough to stop her.

She got to Skylar's about twenty minutes later, not even really knowing what brought her there. Hannah had no plan. But deep inside, she wanted to see Skylar, like an invisible thread connected the two of them forever. And Skylar could wind the string up and Hannah would be pulled back, never able to get too far.

Hannah pulled up to the front of the house. She bundled herself tight and walked around to the service entrance. Skylar never set the alarms or locked the doors. Clarke mansion was just an extension of Skylar's own personality. This enormous expensive house and no security. That's the kind of wealth the Clarkes had. It was as if the house said, "Go ahead. Come inside. Steal something. I dare you."

When Hannah got to the back of the house, she saw a gray pick-up truck. Skylar's Range Rover parked behind it. *That's not the groundskeeper's car. Why do I recognize it?* The truck had a busted taillight and its fender hung askew off the back.

A light came on in the house. The second floor. *Skylar's room.* Two figures moved. Hannah looked back at the truck again. *Derrick Sullivan's car. Ugh, really? You had Will Bartlett and now you're screwing Derrick Sullivan. His greasy hair. His even greasier eyes.*

Peering into the flatbed of Derrick's truck, Hannah saw a bunch of wrenches and screwdrivers, a car jack, something that looked like a hair dryer, and a small plunger-looking tool. Then Hannah spied the spray bottles. *How nice of you to take a break from graffiti to have a tryst with Skylar. What a loser.* Hannah leaned closer. *It's not graffiti.* She let out a moan. *Auto paint. Navy blue. Dammit Skylar.*

Hannah watched the windows again. Just light now. No figures. She leaned against the truck and waited. A light suddenly streamed from the kitchen windows. *Shoot!* Hannah tried to get behind the truck. But a piece of her hair that had cascaded down into the flatbed caught on something. She worked the tangle free quickly and hustled behind the pick-up. *If Skylar sees me here, I'm so over. She'll lose her shit.*

Hannah sat in the minivan, not daring to start the engine yet. The rumble of her mother's minivan—dubbed "Lunchbox Lightning" by Ricky—would demand the attention of those inside the house.

Is that a Whispering Hills bumper sticker on Derrick's truck? I did not see that coming. Did he actually like Whispering Hills? Derrick may have smelled like an odd mix of pizza and car engine, but he never smelled of school pride.

Derrick Sullivan was a scholarship kid. One of about twenty who went to Whispering Hills on the Clarke Fellowship. Yes, that Clarke. This endowment was part of an initiative started about four years ago. Bring students from underprivileged communities, namely Pembroke, to Whispering Hills. Even the wording of the initiative on the school website was awful. "We at Whispering Hills want to offer our challenging academic curriculum to a broader base of students. We want our current students to be exposed to racial and socioeconomic diversity for the benefit of the whole learning community."

Gillian Cross had reeled after the faculty meeting, claiming she would talk the principal and demand a revision. She never did though. And from then on, the Clarke Fellowship brought twenty "diverse" students to Whispering Hills. The privileged student body benefited from a small dose of life outside the bubble. And students like Derrick? Who knows? The Admissions Office always teemed with applicants for the Clarke Fellowship though.

The two figures appeared in the upstairs window again. This time, the figures melded into one. The shadows mingled together in a clandestine dance. *I might throw up.* She thought of Derrick's mouth and Skylar's mouth. It made her queasy.

But Hannah's disgust gave way to hurt. She hated herself for it. After all that happened today, Hannah was most hurt that Skylar wasn't available right now. Like before. Like she always was. *I want to go back to before.*

Skylar ruined Hannah's chances with Brody. Skylar flirted shamelessly with Aaron Samuels. Skylar never missed an opportunity to tear Hannah down in front of…just about anyone. And yet, here Hannah was, outside the service entrance to Clarke mansion, completely devastated that her best friend was with Derrick. *God, I hate myself right now.* Hannah's chest heaved, and she thought again of Katie Greco, of summer camp. Hannah so readily covered for Skylar when she wanted to take Katie out on that little canoeing trip. The trip that ended in Katie Greco almost drowning. And then Katie running away from camp, away from Skylar.

How Skylar ever got Katie to come along was a wonder. Go out to the middle of the lake? No life vests? And Katie was a pathetic swimmer. *At least Skylar got the necklace off her. It was my necklace.* Hannah thought of the little aquamarine pendant.

I covered for her. Because, that day, Skylar chose Hannah. And it felt good to be chosen.

Chapter Seven
The Scorpion

March 27
Attention ALL CREW

Please put body mics back properly by winding the wire around the mic.

The silver glitter in the prop closet is for the <u>SHOW!</u> We are using gold glitter for rehearsals.

After "All I Need is a Stage" it's all hands on deck to clear the glitter. **<u>This is a trip hazard and a major safety issue for the dancers.</u>**

--Sarah Young,
Student Director

The note was hastily scrawled on a piece of yellow legal paper. Likely torn from Sarah's clipboard.

Hannah listening through the backstage door. Sarah Young lectured her cronies. Hannah relished interrupting the castigation. After all, Hannah's errand was a priority. Mr. Samuels needed the top hats. And he needed them five minutes ago.

The cast was rehearsing the second act of Stagecraft already. If nothing else, Aaron Samuels moved through rehearsals at a faster clip than the previous director. Everyone sang his praises.

"He's just a hard ass. But we needed someone like him," a junior commented.

And another, "He's so passionate."

Still another replied, "Passionate people misfire sometimes. It's because he wants the show to be great."

The cast even forgave Mr. Samuels for never bringing in that Broadway choreographer he promised in the first rehearsal. "Zach Cartwright is a dear friend of mine. And, despite his demanding schedule, he's agreed to choreograph one number," Mr. Samuels had beamed at the group, his eyes locking for a moment with Ms. Panzini's.

But Zachary Cartwright didn't matter anymore. Samuels had proven himself a formidable leader. Every minute of rehearsal time was utilized. The cast and crew felt empowered by it.

Whispering Hills had long been known for its stellar theatre program. "A Broadway farm team," a local review once said. But this year would be spectacular. Hannah felt a difference in her body, now taut from pirouettes, hitch kicks, and endless 5678s.

Outside the door, Hannah listened closer. Now Sarah talked about the accident. Again. *Ugh, I wish I wasn't the reason for all the speculating. Then I could barge in and make a snide comment about how Sarah watches too much Criminal Minds.*

"I'm telling you. It's someone who lives around here," Sarah said. *Please someone debunk this theory. It's someone else. Someone passing through. Just a tragic accident.*

"We shouldn't be talking about the accident so much. For Paige's sake. She needs the distraction of the play," another voice interjected.

Sarah cut her off, "No, the body mics don't go there. And make sure you wind the cord around them neatly. It's a nightmare if you don't." She huffed loudly then continued, "Seriously though, it wasn't an accident. It was a crime. the police are close to figuring this out. Between the time and location, it has to be someone from Whispering Hills. Someone who lives on that street. If the police thought it was just an accident, the investigation would be over by now."

Another voice added, "They need Zoe to wake up out of that coma."

And another voice — male this time — answered, "There's like three people who live on that street. The Wolcotts, the Stewarts, and Skylar Clarke."

And that's my cue! Hannah threw the door open.

"Hey Hannah," the male voice was Tim Reilly, a senior and stagehand for the past four years. His dad built the bigger parts of the set.

"Hey, Tim. I need..."

"What are you doing back here? Panzini is rehearsing in the dance studio," one of Sarah's eyes opened larger than the other.

"Well, Sarah, since you know the Call Board so well, you'd know that we're doing 'All I Need Is a Stage' today," Hannah marched over to the stack of satin hats, "So...top hats."

Sarah rolled her eyes. *Okay, where's my backtalk? You've got your posse.* When Sarah didn't respond, Hannah snarked, "Please don't let me interrupt your in-depth discussion about the storage of body mics."

A few crew members muffled a laugh. Sarah glared at them. "Screw you, Hannah," she whined.

On the way back to the dance room, Hannah's phone vibrated with a new text.

116

She hoped it was Brody. Just like she hoped it was Brody every time her phone made a noise. But he hadn't even looked at Hannah for a week. And he unfriended her, unfollowed her, un-whatevered her on all social media. Hannah was coming unglued.

The text was from Greg, Hannah's new best friend since the diner incident. Skylar had been a little distant. Too busy being amazing at everything to care. She was even awarded Most Compassionate Leader at the recent Student Council Assembly for her work on the softball team. *I literally can't even.*

Oddly enough, Cynthia and Hannah were becoming closer. Now that Hannah wasn't a threat to Cynthia's borderline incest fantasy, the two could be friends.

Balanced the top hats in one hand, Hannah checked her phone. *This is the twentieth text from Greg today.*

GT: where r u?
we need hats

GT:
SAMUELS =
FLIPPING
OUT.

Hannah hustled but when she arrived the director had completely forgotten about the top hats. He was at it again with Ms. Panzini. Furious whispers and gestures and students watching. *Hmmph. Glad I rushed back to watch mom and dad fight again.*

In the center of the floor, Paige showed a scorpion. She stood on one leg with the other arched behind her. One hand holding the foot as it grazed the crown of her head. Paige's weak smile spoke her trained ability to acquiesce, but her sunken eyes spoke her exhaustion. Her sister rotted in a hospital bed and she was here, a pawn for two grown-ups to use in their silly war.

I can do that move too.

Ms. Panzini interrupted a fuming Mr. Samuels, "Hannah! Show Mr. Samuels your scorpion."

Hannah walked to center, feigning confidence. She swung her right leg around in an effort to loosen her hips.

"Well?" Mr. Samuels huffed impatiently.

A beat.

Then Hannah nailed it. In the mirror, Hannah could see that she was just as graceful and impressive as Paige.

"Fine," the director conceded, "but can Hannah do the turns into the that pose? It's the final pose of the song."

Oh, God. Turns into a scorpion? With a top hat on? And on my left leg?

Sarah Young walked in. Pressure was on. The dancers all stood against the ballet barre. The music started, and Hannah waited impatiently for Ms. Panzini to count her in. *You can do this. It's just you and the music.* As she turned, Hannah concentrated hard on spotting, so she didn't notice anyone else. But she could feel them. And many of them hoped for a fall.

Just as Hannah finished the last rotation and threw her leg back to catch it, Skylar shouted, "Get it, girl!"

Doesn't she sound supportive? The star of the show who was both lead and leader. I know her too well. There are no friendships in theatre. She wants me to miss. Hannah gripped the muscles of standing leg even harder. And she hit the pose perfectly. Some people clapped.

Ms. Panzini turned to Mr. Samuels, "See? Hannah can do this stuff."

The director's lip curled upward. Now he had to give Hannah the feature. "Okay, but Paige does the rest of the solo bits in this number. I can't leave it to chance with an unknown quantity."

An unknown quantity? Hannah let out an audible sigh. *Fuck my life if this guy is my future stepdad.*

"Well, Aaron, perhaps if you held dance auditions like we've always done, you'd have *known* quantities."

Samuels didn't even react. "Let's run it again from the top," was all he said.

The cast found their places. This time Hannah wasn't so lucky hitting the turns. Everyone danced, mugging fake smiles to the damp mirrors. Paige did her parts perfectly. The last beats of the song played, Skylar singing her heart out and Hannah turning. But her ankle buckled, and she fell out of the last turn.

"Thank you, Hannah," Mr. Samuels uttered with a cruel sincerity. "Paige will do the scorpion. I believe your rehearsal time is over, Jill. I'll speak to my cast alone now."

"You won't be happy until Paige is injured! That's where this is going. I promise you." Ms. Panzini slammed the door before he could answer.

Mr. Samuels muttered something to Sarah and then followed Ms. Panzini. Hannah shook her head and almost laughed. *Teacher fights are the best.* The assembled cast collected their belongings, but Sarah ordered, "Mr. Samuels said that I should talk to you before you're dismissed."

Why? Just Why? Why did Aaron Samuels endow such an ass with this much power?

Skylar looked pointedly at the clock, "You only have four minutes. People's parents are outside already."

But Sarah Young was ripe with interim power. She began solemnly, "This is super important, guys. There will be glitter EVERYWHERE after 'All I Need is a Stage.' So…some of you will need a second set of shoes. One for the glitter and one for all the other dances. My crew can get the floor clean but if your shoes track more glitter out on the stage, that's not my problem." Her hands propped on ample hips, Sarah went on, "And I'll need three of the boys to help with moving props while the rest of my crew gets the glitter swept up."

Cue eye roll from Greg. There it is!

"Greg. Thanks for volunteering," Sarah winked at him.

"I have to change for—"

Skylar chimed in, "I can do it. Greg should change. I don't have a costume change."

Did Skylar Clarke just offer to help the crew? Where were the police when you needed them? We've got a guilty conscience on display.

As she left, Hannah overheard Sarah threatening her crew about the glitter again. *Will we ever hear the end of the glitter situation?* "If we don't get all of it up, Paige could seriously injure herself. Do you want that on us?"

In the hallway, Paige broke down. A few sophomores ran over to her.

"It's nothing."

It's never "nothing." The information reverberated through the throng of students leaving rehearsal. Mrs. Kellogg had texted. Paige's aunt would be picking her up from rehearsal. Zoe got worse.

What does worse mean? I'm relieved. Is that horrible? But if Zoe is gone, then I can put this behind me. Just like I did with Katie Greco. It will be just like Skylar said. Hannah mind bounced around though. Zoe. Katie. Skylar. And then *I can't believe I just lost that feature. I had it. And then I screwed it up.* Hannah wished everyone knew how good she really was. *When will they see it?*

Hannah found herself at her locker. A voice came from down the hallway but when Hannah looked up, the place was empty. She put her hand on the locker next to hers—the one that belonged to Will. She wished he was there now. Making small talk and not dead.

Then another ghost laced its arm around Hannah. Skylar started in about how much she hated her dad's girlfriend Trina. "You know she's from the Bronx, right? From the Bronx to Whispering Hills, that's some social mobility for you. That's America," she smirked and fixed her bra. "I mean, really. I'm waiting for Trina to come in with gold hoop earrings on."

"You have hoop earrings. I do too. Really Skylar. Maybe your dad is happy. Doesn't he deserve someone? I mean, with your mom gone."

Skylar recoiled at the last sentence. Hannah regretted it. Hannah looked at Skylar's eyes and paused. She saw the years they'd spent together, bodies entangled during sleepovers, secret plans, and inside jokes. Hannah was Skylar's right hand since freshmen orientation at Whispering Hills.

"My hoop earrings don't say 'Skylar' on the side in ghetto script. But I'm sure lots of your friends from Pembroke Middle School had earrings like that. Sorry if I hit a nerve."

Hannah threw her bag over her shoulder, "My mom is waiting outside."

"Okay, friend. Talk to you later," Skylar yelled sarcastically as Hannah rounded the corner.

Screw this! Hannah turned right back around and marched toward the queen, "Speaking of people from Pembroke, what the hell was Derrick Sullivan doing at your place after midnight?"

"Well, look at you. Someone stole mommy's van went stalking. Jealous? Do you want to be our third now that Brody ghosted on you?"

Skylar's voice pronouncing Brody's name stung like hell. *I'm not going there with her.* "I'm not jealous. I'm disappointed. Can't you do any better than Derrick?"

"You should be thanking me for Derrick."

"You lied to me," Hannah's voice trembled, "You told me there was nothing on your car. I saw it at the funeral home." *Of course, Skylar lied to me. She's a pathological liar.* Maybe Hannah was angrier with herself than her friend?

"And when you saw the Rover at the funeral home, there was indeed nothing there. Derrick fixed it. You're welcome. I've been selling my body to save your ass."

Hannah scoffed, "Thanks Mother Teresa. And you think Derrick's graffiti spray paint will cover up the dent in your car? The one that likely matches the dent on Will's car?"

121

"He used auto paint, Hannah. They sell that shit at Home Depot," Skylar looked at her friend incredulously.

Like you've ever been to a Home Depot. Hannah shook her head, "We have to go to the pol—"

"Shhh!!"

Hannah turned to see a freshman walking toward them.

Skylar moved right in the freshmen's path, "Are you lost, froshy?"

"I was just cutting through to get the gym. I have practice," she waffled and looked at Hannah for support. But Hannah just sucked her teeth and effortlessly fell into place behind Skylar.

Skylar lifted her chin ever so slightly, "This is the senior hallway. Only seniors. Go back the way you came and take the long way."

"But it's after school hours. I'll be late for practice."

"But, but, but," Skylar mimicked, "Vanish, frosh. Have fun running those suicides."

The freshman left. When she was a safe distance, Skylar turned to Hannah, "Were you about to suggest that we go to the police? Are you insane?"

"Zoe got worse. I want to be done with this. Even if it means coming clean. It was an accident."

"If you want to be done with this, you shut the hell up about it. Katie Greco never squealed. She messed with you. I handled it. And we never heard from her again."

Well, everything did turn out okay with Katie. Hannah looked at the floor for a pregnant moment. She hoped the tiles would rearrange themselves and show the answer to the problem at hand. Then a wave fear came over her body and she shook, "Was Derrick in school today?"

Skylar shrugged, "I don't know, Hannah."

"What about yesterday?"

She sighed, "I don't know. Who cares? He's probably home crushing up opioids and putting them in his addict mom's yogurt."

He does disappear every now and then. Still, Hannah couldn't shake the feeling that the dots were connecting in front of her. If she could just think on it. If these damn rehearsals weren't so long and exhausting. If the show wasn't so important. *I'll deal with this after the show is done,* Hannah told herself.

Hannah finally made it out to the parking lot. The cold, damp March wind hit her hard. The sky was a dark gray. It defied the sun to come out after this winter that never seemed to end. *Please don't let mom ask about the rehearsal.*

Aaron Samuels was sitting shotgun when her mother pulled the beat-up minivan around to the theatre entrance of the school. *Good God. Give me a break.*

"Hi sweetie. How was rehearsal?" Without waiting for an answer, Gillian Cross bubbled, "Aaron says you're doing great. We're dropping him at the train station."

Neither of them noticed Hannah the whole ride.

Police stopped by rehearsal the next day. Mr. Samuels was in the middle of changing the opening number according to his new cuts. Harmonies drilled over and over. Samuels played Cynthia's part on the piano harder and harder until she finally got it through her tone-deaf ears.

The blue uniforms were a welcome distraction from the dreariness of relearning music. At least they were for Greg, Cynthia, Sarah, and even Skylar who made eyes at the younger cop.

"Sorry to interrupt," the officer said unapologetically. His large belly hung over his utility belt.

"Not a problem. How can we assist you, officers?"

The younger one said nothing. He stood erect with feet hip-width apart, eyes like a Marine. His head was cylindrical, shaped like battery.

The fat one made his way to the piano. "You've probably seen some detectives around the school. Detectives John Barry and Terrell Jones are leading the investigation about the accident that killed, er, I mean, the accident in which one of your students died. They asked us to come around. They want everyone to know that <u>anyone</u> with <u>any</u> information — <u>anything</u> whatsoever — should give the precinct a call." He handed Mr. Samuels two cards, "There's a number for the precinct on there. And a direct number to Detective Barry. One for Jones too. Would you share it with your students, sir?"

"Of course. Are the detectives at school now?"

The younger one piped up, voice much lower that Hannah expected, "No, sir. They're at the station questioning a suspect."

The fleshy officer shot him a look.

Cynthia blurted, "A suspect? So, you'll find out who did it? Who murdered Will Bartlett?"

Murder. Really? Great choice of words. It wasn't a murder. It was an accident.

The fat uniform coughed, "We're all working on it. Everyone wants to get to the bottom of this."

Greg, emboldened by Cynthia's outburst, responded for the whole group. "You clearly don't think it was just an accident though. You've ruled that out." He looked around the group, "Someone murdered Will."

Jeez, Greg I didn't murder anyone. Hannah gritted her teeth.

The policemen looked at each other. The younger one sighed audibly, "If you have any information that can help, please call the number on those cards. We won't take up anymore of your time."

They left as unceremoniously as they walked in. Samuels handed the cards to Sarah. She wrote the phone numbers on the board. She bubbled the text and then wrote in red Expo marker DO NOT ERASE.

Without saying a word, Samuels played the song again.

On her way out, Hannah slipped one of the detective's business cards into her pocket. She had no idea what she was going to do with it. But she realized Derrick hadn't been in school the last two days.

Chapter Eight
Cue the Alibi

Inbox

From: Pat Feldman <pfeldman@whisperinghills.edu>
To: Gillian Cross <gcross@whisperinghills.edu>
Subject: AP English & Ongoing Investigations
Date:

Gillian,

I'm sorry to report that the detectives will be calling some students tomorrow during AP English class. I've tried to keep them from removing students from advanced classes. They will need to see the following students this week:

Sarah Young
Skylar Clarke
Hannah Cross
Greg Tate
Cynthia Wolcott

They will be meeting the students in English Resource room.

Thanks for your cooperation. I have assurance that the investigation at the school will be over soon.

Best,
Pat

Pat Feldman, Dean of Student Life
Whispering Hills Country Day School
914-555-1060 ext. 110

Gillian read the email and sighed deeply. The dean promised the students wouldn't miss AP English. They were in the middle of A Raisin in the Sun. What would they miss? Could she help Ms. Brewster make up the lost class time? But those concerns were rendered ridiculous when Gillian's mind went to Will Bartlett. So much potential.

The front door opened.

"Knock. Knock! Just had to stop by before rehearsals tonight." Aaron called from the front hall.

"In the kitchen," Gillian sang.

He strode into the kitchen and his hands gripped Gillian's waist. The kiss was almost cinematic — long and deep.

"Aaron!" Gillian pulled away, mock scandal on her face, "My kids are home."

"I don't see them in the kitchen," Aaron kissed her neck and she laughed.

A thud on the dining room table. Hannah intentionally slammed her textbook down.

"Hannah!" Her mother exclaimed, smoothing her shirt down.

Mr. Samuels smiled devilishly and started to the cabinets for a glass. "Would you like a glass of water, Gill? Hannah?"

Hannah scoffed, "No. But best put some ice in yours."

"Hannah! Your tone. What are you thinking?" Gillian chastised.

Hannah took two powerful steps closer, placed her hands on the kitchen island, and stared unflinchingly. *Don't back down now.* She thought of that rehearsal — the one where she caught Skylar and Samuels. She thought of Skylar's hair falling into the piano gears. She thought of Mr. Samuels' face — the same coy smile he wore right now.

How could mom be this stupid? And why — of ALL people — did her crush have to be Aaron Samuels?

"I think the real question is 'What are you thinking?'" Hannah growled, "You're practically going to second base in the kitchen."

"That's it! Apologize to Mr. Samuels. And me!"

"It's okay, Gill." Mr. Samuels took a drink of water before continuing, utterly unperturbed by the outburst. "Hannah, I'm sorry. I should've been more respectful. I know this situation is a challenging one. And I promise to navigate it more delicately in the future."

Challenging? Great word choice. My English nerd mom definitely won't notice that one.

Gillian just stood there, paralyzed by her daughter's denigration and her boyfriend's reaction. Hannah thought of Samuels and Skylar at the piano again. That giggle of Skylar's echoed through Hannah's head. *It's as if Skylar is in the kitchen right now.* Hannah mentally returned to that afternoon, to the sensual humidity. The air hung heavy with wanting.

"Hannah, you see," Aaron smiled at Gillian, "your mother in an amazing woman. And I just love being around her."

"Really? I would have thought you were into younger women," Hannah sneered then left the kitchen.

"Hannah! Oh, I'm sorry, Aaron. I'll talk to her." But Gillian's embarrassment was half-lived. Her focus was caught up in his use of the word "love."

Rehearsals carried on as usual that night. The detective's card burned a hole in Hannah's garishly printed Vera Bradley gym bag. Samuels argued with Panzini. Kids gossiped about the show, the accident. And Hannah's scorn for Skylar grew ever stronger. Hannah now knew all of Skylar's songs, even out singing her a few times in the past few days. Skylar boiled when Hannah held a note longer. Mr. Samuels would nod approval but every time he complimented Hannah, he followed up with a compliment for Skylar.

"Great. Strong finish. But we don't want to go overboard," he said after Hannah finished a perfect trill and Skylar didn't keep rhythm.

Hannah poured over YouTube every night and hummed harmonies in the shower. Skylar had the part already. With success came complacency. But Hannah still had that smoldering need to achieve. And every once in a while, she'd get a glimmer of being the lead. No longer a shadow.

Once Mr. Samuels patted Skylar's hand after her voice cracked on a high note. With no context, the gesture would have been romantic. Hannah couldn't ignore the longing pout on Skylar's pretty mouth.

At night Hannah lay in bed and tried to suppress the thoughts of their illicit relationship…and the anger that accompanied those thoughts. But her body would give in to the exhaustion and she'd fall fast asleep. Dreams of Katie Greco and camp returned.

Katie was from New Canaan, a place which, according to Skylar, was even snobbier and wealthier than Whispering Hills. "You should see her house. She thinks she's the shit. Everyone from Connecticut thinks that though," Skylar had said while the two were cuddled in her bed binge-watching Riverdale.

Katie and Skylar were camp besties since sixth grade. Despite living about a 45-minute drive from each other, they never hung out during the school year. But at camp they were inseparable. For three weeks of upstate New York bliss, the two rehearsed scenes, took hikes, ate s'mores, and played pranks. All the while Hannah toiled the summers away hanging clothes at the local dry cleaners and busing tables at the local dinner theatre.

But this past summer Hannah won a scholarship and got to join Skylar at drama camp for one week. Hannah excitement quickly fizzled when she walked into Bunk 14 though.

"Oh! Look gals, fresh meat is here!" Katie called from the porch.

Hannah trudged up the path to her assigned bunk. She couldn't wait to see Skylar. In fact, most of her friends would be there. Camp In the Round was the premiere acting camp on the East Coast. Therefore, all Hannah's rich friends needed to be there.

Skylar walked out onto the porch and squealed. "Hannah!" she ran to her friend. Skylar even grabbed one hulking bag off Hannah's shoulder. Katie's face darkened as she drew closer.

"Where's your trunk?" Katie looked at the bags. "You don't have one?"

"She's only here for a week," Skylar retorted, and Hannah felt grateful. *Why do I need a trunk? Do all campers have one?* When she got inside, she saw the bedazzled trunks at the edge of each bed. Then she looked at her bags, one was her Whispering Hills gym bag and the other borrowed from her brother — a Mamaroneck Hockey Club bag. It was the only thing big enough to fit everything on the camp's 'must bring' list. Her bags looked woefully out of place among all the monogrammed trunks.

"You're sleeping here," Skylar motioned to the empty bunk atop her own. "I never let anyone have it but you're an exception!"

Katie glared at them both then sat on her own bed, the one adjacent to Skylar's. *Wow, someone is marking her territory.*

A few legs dangled from top bunks topped with girls twirling hair or weaving hamsa bracelets. One girl laid in bed with her arms behind her head. Another was reading by the windowsill.

The scene was idyllic and dangerous at the same time and Hannah was excited by it. That is, until Katie broke in. "So…you're Hannah?"

"Umm, yes."

"You need a camp name." Katie played with the end of her perfect French braid.

Hannah face twisted, "A what?"

"Hannah Banana," Katie announced and peered around the room. Everyone stood up a little straighter.

Skylar interjected, "She's only here for a week."

"I know. On scholarship. But all first-year campers get a nickname," Katie checked, and the room agreed with her. It is known. All first-years get a nickname. "Since you're on scholarship, would you prefer 'Affirmative Action'?" Katie snickered. All the other bunkmates followed suit. So easy to dislike this new girl who would only be 'one of us' for a week.

Skylar shoved Katie, "Stop it, bitch!"

No one was supposed to know about the scholarship. Skylar must have let it slip. Hannah felt her stomach twist.

"Okay, okay!" Katie laughed harder. "Hannah Banana it is then." Katie clapped her hand on Hannah's shoulder. "We have vocal lessons in five. I see you eyeing my braid though. I can do one for you when I get back, okay?"

"Sure, thanks." Hannah just looked at the floor.

"Welcome to Camp in the Round, Banana!"

Police lurked around campus. The two detectives invaded the English lounge with their coffee cups and their leather jackets and their man smell. The school was aroused. Whispering Hills was on the map. Kids from other schools were talking.

Hannah's AP English class was reading A Raisin in the Sun when the office secretary knocked on the door. Cynthia was playing Beneatha and one of Brody's lacrosse bros was playing Beneatha's boyfriend Asagai. In the scene Asagai confronted Beneatha about her straightened her hair and denying her African heritage.

Thank God someone is saving us from ourselves. A bunch of privileged white kids discussing dreams of an African-American family on Chicago's Southside. What a charade.

"Excuse me, Miss Brewster. Sorry to interrupt. Mr. Barry and Mr. Jones, I mean, Detective Barry and Detective Jones would like to see two of your students."

Miss Brewster's eyes widened, and the secretary continued, "He needs to ask Greg Tate and Cynthia Wolcott a few questions. It's nothing to be nervous about, kids."

"Sure!" Miss Brewster replied obsequiously then nodded to Greg and Cynthia. "Will they be returning to class this period?"

"I don't know," the secretary shrugged, somewhat put out by the follow up question. Hannah smirked. *All she cares about is the Greek yogurt getting warm on her desk.*

Greg's body swirled around with all the drama of an accused innocent, "I should take all my books then?" His eyes darted around, "Do you think they'll have many questions? I mean, of course, I want to help…"

Wait for it. Here comes a swoon. He's gotten taller this year. I might have to duck out of the way if Greg faints.

"Hey, don't worry. It's going to be okay," Hannah whispered as Greg passed.

"Oh my God, Hannah. I'm totes nervous. I'll text you."

"Be strong. You'll be okay. Just tell the truth."

Eager for Scarlett O'Hara to depart, Miss Brewster motioned to Greg, "Just go. Take your things."

Cynthia's departure was quiet but just as shocking. Eyes big as dinner plates and golden complexion turned stark white. Cynthia blinked rapidly and looked at the floor. It was the I-just-blew-the-audition look. *Wow, if I didn't know for sure that Zoe's coma was my fault, I would think Cynthia was the guilty party. Maybe the police will pin it on her.*

Classes went by at a painfully slow rate. Every time someone walked by the classroom door, Hannah held her breath.

Then her phone blinked. So many emojis. *This could only be one person.*

> GT: that was
> awful. they
> think it was
> one of us. i
> could tell. no
> skid marks on
> the road—at
> least where
> skid marks
> should be.
> shows it
> wasn't just an
> accident.
>
> GT: it was a
> murder.

Then a slew of crying faces, gritted teeth, drama masks, daggers, and googly eyes.

> GT: you know i
> have a gut
> feeling about
> these things.
>
> GT: i'm never
> wrong.

What the hell do I text back? This is same way he reacted when Robert Meyer stole Jessica Trambull's cell phone in ninth grade. Dean Feldman told the students that no one — NO ONE — would be dismissed until the someone fessed up. Greg worked himself into such a tizzy that he almost confessed to a crime he didn't commit.

It was classic hyperbolic Greg Tate. But still, the phone beckoned for an answer. *How does an innocent person react to these texts? And the skid marks? Shit, why didn't I think of that?* She typed but didn't send it.

> HC: oh god.
> one of us? as
> in…one of the
> musical cast?
> AWFUL

No, that won't work. I have to text something. He knows I'm in Econ right now. The economics teacher was out sick. He would expect an answer. Hannah eyed the substitute. Mr. Pollix just stewing up at the desk. He hated covering classes. He was engrossed in his own work, so Hannah's fingers flew across the keys.

> HC: it can't be
> one of us. it
> was just
> someone
> passing
> through.
> maybe
> someone
> looking to
> burglarize one
> of the houses.
> nice places up
> that road.

Yep, that's it. Send Greg spinning with a new possibility. Still Hannah's heart raced. It didn't matter if Greg thought someone from outside the neighborhood did it. It mattered what the police thought.

Now I need to talk to Skylar. It was only a matter of time until the police questioned them. Hannah doubted a "friendly conversation" with a detective was a place where she could text a friend quickly. *Detective, before I answer that question, do you mind if I text my psychotic friend? I want to make sure we are on the same page about the horrific crime we're trying to cover up.*

The bell rang. Skylar in the hallway chatting up those same jocks, Thing One and Thing Two. One pushed his hands into his letter jacket pockets. Two spit his gum into the trashcan four feet away.

"Impressive," Hannah snarked, "Three pointer?"

"Surprised you know that term, Hannah. Now that's impressive," Thing One retorted.

"I need to talk to you," Hannah directed her body towards Skylar. No time for passive-aggressive flirting with these sportsball guys.

Skylar smiled disarmingly, "Sure, friend. Talk."

"Privately."

"I don't have any tampons if that's what you need," she laughed, and the guys giggled too. Hannah colored involuntarily. *She's such a bitch.* So many possible replies.

Of course, you don't have any tampons, Sky. Dragon Witches don't menstruate.

Or…

Of course, you don't have tampons. You don't need those when you're pregnant with the director's baby, you slut.

Hannah felt sweat bead under her breasts. "Greg and Cynthia got called by the detectives today. Looks like the police are talking to everyone in the play. I just wanted to tell you because they both seem upset."

Now I've got your attention. The look on Skylar's face revealed that neither Greg nor Cynthia told Skylar about being questioned. *Hmm. Interesting. Normally, they would have both run to mama for consolation.* Hannah began to see cracks in the overlord's veneer.

The queen entwined her arm through Hannah's and guided her into the girls room. For a few seconds, Hannah stupidly basked in the attention. This was the Skylar she fell for. She could make you feel like you were the only person in the world. Voice mellifluous and body warm.

"It's okay, Hannah. Don't freak out," Skylar checked under a few stalls. Her hair glistened in the early afternoon sun that broke through the frosted bathroom windows. Hannah breathed and remembered the plan. *All we have to do was stick to the story. We were already signed in at auditions when the accident happened. We had the party the night before. Sure, we were drinking but…*

Hannah's head and chest pounded with anxiety. She tried refocusing on formulas for the chemistry quiz. She paced and breathed heavily.

"I need to go. This was a mistake," Hannah rushed for the door.

"Hannah!" Skylar took hold her upper arms, "Hannah, please stop freaking out. Your eyes are all glazed over. We were together that morning. That means that except for maybe some small details, our story is the same. Remember, you don't need to know exact times other than when we were supposed to be at auditions. Don't be all 'We left at precisely 9:33 and it took 7 minutes to get to school.' That will sound weird."

"Yeah, you're right," Hannah nodded furiously. *No reason for more lives to be ruined from this.* Hannah's mantra. *I have to protect my mom. She could be fired.*

Skylar put on nude lip gloss. Through puckered lips, she relaxed and whispered, "This is probably the one and only time we'll talk to the police."

They left for class. Hannah (sort of) felt better. Back in the bathroom, in that last stall, Sarah Young and her girlfriend popped down off the toilet they had been crouching on.

"Well, I'll be damned," Sarah said.

Chapter Nine
Improv

CALL BOARD April 3rd

Special Friday afternoon rehearsal...

3:30-4:30: All leads report to the music room.

4:30-5:30: Aurelia—female lead, private lesson on More Than This and other solos
*no understudy necessary

Hannah double checked her phone. *Yep, I don't have to be there today. Awesome.* She thought of the long nap she would take when she got home from school. Her duvet and pillows beckoned. *I could sleep on this gross cafeteria floor. I'm so exhausted. But I got lucky. For once, I don't have to be in that music room or the dance studio for hours after dismissal.* Hannah closed her eyes for a moment.

"Hannah! Look!" Greg tapped her and pointed to the cafeteria doors.

Another grand entrance. If Skylar Clarke was upset, people were interested. Cynthia wrapped her arms around the most powerful girl in school. People in the lunch line stared. This was quickly turning into a scene. *I guess someone has met with the detectives. Time to amp up the grief.*

"I know, Skylar. It's so hard." Cynthia cooed, still shaken by her own interaction with the detectives. Later on, Skylar divulged that the police asked a lot about classmates, about the theatre kids.

"They seemed hot to know if Zoe had enemies. Girls jealous of her talent," Cynthia agreed.

"They know people were envious. I mean, Zoe could sing like an angel," Greg's eyes misted over.

Starting to weep, Cynthia's tiny back heaved with grief and fear. *I'll just wait patiently while she finishes.* Hannah tried to think of something encouraging to say. Cynthia continued, reveling in the concern of her friends. *Okay, this is getting old. I need this intel but giving Cynthia Wolcott the spotlight for any amount of time is feat of strength. And just look at Skylar.* Skylar's face turned from feigned grief to feigned concern to barely hidden impatience.

Hannah made her way to the vending machines.

"Is Cynthia okay?"

Startled, Hannah pushed the wrong keys and got potato chips instead of a protein bar. She turned in a huff to see Brody. "No, she's not. The police talked to her during English yesterday. She's pretty messed up."

Hannah took a deep breath. *You've been giving me the silent treatment for days. She's your twin. Ask her yourself!* She wanted to scream. Brody's big brown eyes softened despite Hannah's attitude.

"Here," Hannah handed him the chips, "I pressed the wrong button and got these."

Brody smiled, put money in the machine, and chose the protein bar. When it dropped the bottom, he reached for it but stared at Hannah the whole time, "Almost every day you get this bar. You need some serious protein to get through Connors' class, right?"

Hannah giggled girlishly despite herself. *Brody knows about my protein bar.* She started back to her table.

"Thanks," he called.

"For what?"

"For being there, you know, for my sister. She's real torn up about this stuff."

Hannah's gut churned. She put the protein bar in her bag and never touched it.

"Are we boring you, Hannah?" Ms. Connors looked over her glasses. Skylar, of course, was sitting with perfect posture and taking notes dutifully. But Hannah had the afternoon yawns.

"No, Ms. Connors. Just tired," Hannah replied, steadying herself as the quiet panic that only Ms. Connors could produce filled her body again. The chem teacher muttered something to herself. Something about musical season. Something about students caring more about afterschool activities than academics.

The lecture went on. Skylar moved her notebook so that Hannah could copy what she missed.

I wish we could go back. Hannah pretended for a few moments that chemistry was still the biggest stressor in her life and that she and Sky were the truest, best friends. But the luxurious moment of fiction was interrupted when the office secretary appeared at the classroom door.

"Ahem, sorry to interrupt, Ms. Connors. Hannah Cross is needed," Ms. Murray announced.

Hannah blinked. *It's my turn. Of course, it's my turn. I was the last of my friends to be questioned. It has to be my turn.* As she gathered her books, a folder with all her chemistry work dropped to the floor. Lab reports, notes, quizzes, Scantrons spread out under the surrounding tables. Skylar bent down to help. Hannah caught her eye — her face unperturbed. *I envy you. You really think you aren't culpable.*

As Hannah and Ms. Murray walked down the corridor, Ms. Murray was silent and conscientious. The office secretary was likely instructed *not* to talk to the ~~suspects~~ students. Hannah lagged a few paces behind, still zippering her bag, hands shaking. Foot falls and muffled discussions from behind classroom doors were the only sounds that attended them. Soon they would reach the English-lounge-turned-interrogation-room. *I have about four minutes to convince myself that I didn't do it…that I'm shocked and saddened and angry about what someone else did to my friends. All the auditions I've done, and this is the biggest one. I guess we're about to find out how good my acting really is.*

Just before the secretary opened the door, she nodded lovingly at Hannah, "It's alright, sweetie. They just want to ask a few questions. Most kids have been in there…only…fifteen minutes."

Hannah forced a smile. *Annamarie Murray broke protocol by talking to me. Another uninvited "perk" of mom working at Whispering Hills.*

The room smelled stale. Burnt coffee and inexpensive cologne and clothes steeped in cigarette smoke. *It's just the English lounge. It's just the English lounge. Where mom works.* Unconvinced, all Hannah could see was an interrogation room. The two detectives stood across from her. Their arms folded. With eyes that have seen too much.

The good-looking detective stood at the other end of the room. Hannah guessed thirties. He wore a nondescript gray suit, but his tie betrayed a wealthy upbringing. It was a butter yellow Hermes. Same one Brooks Clarke wore to the school's centennial. *This guy probably grew up in Whispering Hills. Maybe even went to this school. This is a steppingstone job for him…just another stair to climb on his way to US Attorney or something.* His cheeks pulled in as he swallowed. He rubbed his jaw and examined the small video camera perched on a tripod. He wouldn't say much the whole time.

The other detective sat right across from Hannah. He was older. Maybe early fifties. His large shoulders pulled the material on his shirt taut. His immaculately white smile shone brilliantly against his dark skin. He had a little gray hair, just on the sides. A gold band on his left ring finger and a college ring on his right. Hannah stared at the onyx inlaid with gold on his college ring. *John Jay. The College of Criminal Justice.*

"Hi Hannah. I'm Detective Terrell Jones and this is Detective John Barry," Detective Jones gestured to the camera and Detective Barry turned it on. "We'll be recording this conversation. We've done the same with your classmates," his baritone voice had no emotion. Hannah knew it immediately—this guy was economic with his words, but when he spoke, people listened.

It's okay to be nervous. Everyone was nervous. Cynthia was a mess. Greg probably treated it like an audition for a crime procedural on network TV. The only person who isn't nervous is Skylar. But she's a sociopath.

Hannah nodded meekly and tried to ignore the scallop of sweat under her arms. She noticed dampness on Detective Barry's shirt too. Beads of sweat formed on Detective Jones' head. It was hot in the room. All of a sudden, everything was heat. *The questions didn't even start yet and I feel like I'm being boiled alive.* The red light from the camera seared her face. *Get a grip. Get. A. Grip.*

"Please state your name for the record," Detective Jones began.

"Hannah Cross."

"And your grade?"

Hannah coughed involuntarily, "Sorry. I'm a senior. Twelfth grade." *They think I'm lying already.*

"Thank you." Detective Jones looked at this partner. *He knows,* Hannah thought. Detective Jones turned to his partner again, "Can we crack that window?"

"Yeah, it's hot in here." Detective Barry worked on the ancient window lock. He fiddled with the blinds first. It took him a minute to get them gliding right.

"Are you warm, Hannah?"

"It's always hot in certain rooms here. The heat in the building doesn't distribute right. So, some rooms are freezing, and some are really hot," Hannah continued because he seemed interested, "Sometimes this room is freezing. This is my mom's office. That's her space heater."

Stop talking! What am I doing!

"Your mother works here?"

"Yes, she's the English chairperson." *Actually, maybe the faculty connection will make me look less guilty. I'm not a person who could be involved in a fatal car crash. Right?*

They conversed for a few minutes...

What's it like to have mom at school?

Did you ever have her for English class?

Does your mom oversee the musical production too?

It was somewhat pleasant. The room remained sweltering hot. There was no March wind swirling through the trees and through the cracked windows. Besides, any air that came through was immediately thawed by the beastly radiator that sat directly beneath the opening.

Then Detective Jones started talking about the musical…

What parts has Hannah played in the past?

When did she start performing?

Did she want to study theatre in college?

Detective Barry interjected rudely, "Do you think you're any good? I mean, do you enjoy it? That's what matters right?"

Hannah pondered the first question but only answered the latter, "Yeah, I love it. That's the only thing that matters."

Then she had a brief moment of clarity. She interrupted Detective Jones before he could start his next question. *Answer like Skylar. Look directly at Detective Barry. Action!* "And yes, I'm pretty good. Not nearly as good as Zoe. She had a beautiful voice. We all miss her during rehearsals this year."

It was sincere. Hannah felt her heart calm with the honesty. *Yes, I am really good. A good singer, an excellent dancer, and a better actress than most. And yes, Zoe was better. And yes, most of the cast missed Zoe anchoring the production this year.*

Instead, her performance gave the detectives the perfect segue into discussion of Zoe.

And her coma.

And dead Will Bartlett.

"Speaking of Zoe Kellogg—did you know her well?" Detective Jones' voice was smooth and effortless.

God, it's hot in here. Hannah felt her chest tighten. She was too busy running through the symptoms of a heart attack to come up with an answer.

"Hannah? You okay? Did you hear my question?" Detective Jones asked almost sweetly.

The other one moved to the corner behind her.

"Sorry," Hannah began, "yes, I knew Zoe but not very well."

"Really? I would think you were friends. Same year at school. Both in the theatre program. I have your schedule here and it looks like you had several classes together too."

He has my schedule?

"Umm, I guess. Yes, we were friends," she stuttered.

Detective Barry had enough. He moved in and forcefully put both hands on the table, "Were you friends or not? Like if she wakes up tomorrow, would Zoe Kellogg say you two are friends? It's not a hard question."

Hannah's ribs closed in on her frantic heart. Detective Jones gave Detective Barry a look. "Sorry, Hannah. We have a lot of interviews to get through. We are just getting the lay of the land. You know, ruling out kids who had nothing to do with the accident."

Hannah felt her face redden. "Of course, I had nothing to do with it."

Barry continued, "Just to clarify, are you friends with Zoe?"

"Yes."

"Good friends? Best friends?"

"Just friends."

Jones moved on, "Okay then. And were you friends with Will Bartlett? I see your locker was next to his."

They know so much. How do they know so much? How the hell did I not realize the police would know so much? The room was boiling now. And dry. Her throat was dry. Hannah thought she answered but apparently nothing came out.

He tried again, "Hannah, the truck driver we talked to said that the suspect's car was a dark SUV. The SUV fled scene. Do you know anyone with a dark SUV?"

"Yeah, y-y-yeah, I guess."

Detective Jones prodded, "The truck driver said the SUV was probably a BMW X5 or a--"

"Lots of people have SUVs here," Hannah interrupted. She didn't even realize words were exiting her mouth.

"Yes, I would imagine," Detective Jones replied stoically.

"There are a lot of rich kids here. Lots of people have their own car. Lots of them are SUVs."

Both hands still on the table, Detective Barry leaned in, "Rich kids like Zoe Kellogg and Will Bartlett?"

"Uhh, that's not what I meant."

"I mean, you don't have your own car. Do you, Hannah?" Barry's eyes looked small and black, like marbles.

Jones cut in, "Hannah, do you know the difference between involuntary vehicular manslaughter and assault with a deadly weapon?"

The room started spinning. *Assault with a deadly weapon? What were they talking about? Are those tears on my cheeks? Oh God. No, don't cry. Don't cry!*

"Are feeling alright?" Detective Barry's voice the other corner now.

He's all over the place. How can he be in two places at once? Hannah stared at the table, focusing on the grooves of the wood. "Yes, I'm okay. It's just hot in here," she managed.

Detective Jones responded, "We're almost done. Just a few more questions. We know you have to get back to class."

"Okay."

"It seems a lot of your friends go to theatre camp during the summers. Do you go to…" he flipped through a notepad, "Camp in the Round? It's upstate. Looks like a Greg Tate, a Cynthia Wolcott, a Sarah Young, and a Skylar Clarke also have attended."

Why were they asking about camp? Hannah's head pounded. *What did camp have to do with the accident?* "Umm, yeah. I went this summer. Just for a week. Most of my friends go for the month of July though."

Detective Barry made his point again, "Why only a week? Why not the whole month like your friends?"

"I usually work during the summer. It's an expensive camp. I got a scholarship to go this past summer. My mom can't afford to send me for a whole month," Hannah explained. Each sentence dug deeper into the narrative Detective Barry was writing. *He thinks I did this out of spite. He thinks I did this because everyone is rich and I'm jealous of them. He thinks I'm the poor kid at the rich school who snapped.* Forgetting that she actually did commit the crime, Hannah burned with anger. *That's not who I am. Screw him.*

Then the words came out before Hannah could measure their value. "I know what you're trying to say — that I'm guilty because I'm poor. You're trying to make it sound like I'm jealous, so I did something awful. Well, that's not true," Hannah cried violently now.

A few awkward moments passed before Detective Jones pushed a box of tissues across the table. He sighed, "Try to calm down. Detective Barry didn't say that. We are just trying to get all the details straight. Just doing our jobs."

The door swung open and slammed into the bookcase. All three turned to see who was interrupting.

"Oh! So sorry. I'm so sorry. Please continue. The sheet said you were done by 2:15 today," Gillian Cross squeaked and held up a memo.

Detective Barry rolled his eyes and sighed. Detective Jones half-stood up, "Yes, ma'am. We are almost done. If you could just…"

"I just need to grab my laptop. So sorry," Gillian made no moves to leave. This was her office. She needed her laptop. Investigation be damned. Hannah almost laughed out loud at her mother's oblivion.

Detective Barry raised his voice, "Ma'am. Please leave. This is official police work. We will let you know when we are done."

Gillian bristled at the scolding. "Yes, I'm leaving now. Please do let me know when you're done with your official police work as this is officially my office." Without waiting for a reply, she shut the door hard.

Hannah looked from one detective to the other. She crinkled her nose, "Sorry. That's my mom."

Detective Jones stacked his notes and folders. "Turn off the camera. We're done. You can go."

"This is already a harrowing experience for our students. Can you be sure you're not making it worse?" A stern male voice echoed from inside the dean's office. Hannah waited outside the closed door. Her mother told her to wait down the hall, but Hannah had inched closer to the office, dying to hear the adults argue without the burden of student presence. Inside Dean Feldman's little hobbit hole were Mr. Samuels, Gillian Cross, both detectives, and the dean himself who played referee.

"I'm sorry, Sir. I didn't catch your name." *That was Detective Barry. Such a douche.*

"My name is Aaron Samuels. I'm the director." *Well, douche meet double douche.*

"Of what?" Detective Barry's tone dripped with sarcasm. . *Touché douché.*

"The musical!" Mr. Samuels met his tone. If Hannah wasn't the cause of all conflict, she be lapping up this epic pissing contest. These detectives had a job to do. But many adults at school figured the accident was just that—a horrible accident. Mr. Samuels considered the "investigation" a word to put air quotes around almost every time he mentioned it.

Gillian's tone was an attempt at reconciliation, "Your work is very important, detectives. But I must say, it was ridiculously warm in that room. A student could have fainted."

"Perhaps the police could continue their work at the station? Ask parents to bring the students?" Dean Feldman offered. It was no secret that the faculty's patience with the detectives was wearing thin. The constant interruptions, The students coming back to class a mess. And no clear answers. No arrests. Everyone just wanted to move on. A police presence was a reminder of the tragedy and the school was beginning to resent them.

Then Mr. Samuels broke in. Angry, dramatic, and never going to hide it. "And are we getting anywhere? Is this investigative work yielding any results beyond disruption of learning? These kids are fragile right now. They need counseling not questioning. They are not the enemies," he was yelling by the end of his monologue. His voice came closer to the door, so Hannah backed up considerably.

Samuels opened the door with a flourish. *And scene.*

Detective Jones wasn't having it and followed him out, "Sir, this is investigation is bigger than your music class. A student is dead. Another lies in a hospital bed. Help us. Don't hinder us."

Both men spied Hannah waiting in the hallway and stopped the confrontation right then and there.

Later that evening, Mr. Samuels came over to play "house." Gillian picked up some Panera Bread and the four gathered around the small butcher block island in the kitchen. Aaron attempted some small talk with Ricky — a pathetic show for Gillian.

Well Mr. Samuels, you can't even fake interest in sports. Hannah shook her head as she listened to Aaron try to relate theatre to Ricky's hockey team. Ricky moved to the dining room table to deal with loathsome algebra homework. Gillian flitted back and forth to check him. After finishing half her sandwich, Hannah formulated a reason to get away. *They are talking about money. Can I just leave? Or do I need to give an excuse? I could always claim more homework.*

"I heard they are freezing the pay scale this coming year," Aaron groaned. He continued through slurps of his tomato basil bisque, "I know the economy is tough, but can't they find the money to give us a cost-of-living raise?"

Gillian sighed, "It won't change for another few years. I heard from the financial director…or Joan's assistant rather — and you didn't hear this from me — that 22% of the students are in arrears by months. Months!" She looked over Ricky's shoulder and nodded her head. *Like my English teacher mom actually knows if my brother is doing the equation correctly. The paper might as well be written in Chinese.*

Despite herself, Hannah chimed in, "I know Sabine's dad lost his job. He worked for AIG. She was crying at lunch the other day and Skylar said so. Sabine might leave the school."

"Hannah, are you going to eat more of that?" Mom gestured at her sandwich.

"I'm not hungry."

"You should eat some more, Hannah. After the stressful day you had…"

The doorbell.

"I'll get it," Ricky shot up. Anything to get away from word problems.

Hannah started the kettle for tea and noticed Aaron still eyeing her sandwich, "You can have it. Really, I'm just not in the mood." *Why did you just get soup? It's not like you have to wear the lycra and sequins and tights you chose for costumes.*

Aaron nodded gratefully and quickly grabbed the untouched half. But then his face went blank.

"Hi Hannah," Skylar stood at the opening of the kitchen. "Hi, Ms. Cross. Hey Mr. Samuels," she grinned kittenishly.

Unable to rally, Hannah blurted out, "What are you doing here?"

Gillian's mouth hung open, as far as she knew Skylar and Hannah were great pals. Why the hostility?

Skylar didn't flinch, "How are you? I heard you got questioned today. I came over because, well, I figured you wouldn't remember to do our chemistry lab. I thought I'd come help."

Gillian handed Hannah a cup of tea then started assembling one for Skylar who continued to chat effortlessly with both adults. Like the tea kettle next to her, Hannah simmered. *Look how Mr. Samuels looks at her. Peeling off clothes with each furtive glance.* All the Call Boards with Skylar's name listed for a private lesson with Mr. Samuels flashed before her memory too. *They are sleeping together. This asshole is sleeping with Skylar AND my mother.*

"Honey, are you okay?" Gillian asked gingerly.

Hannah snapped out of the bad dream, "Yeah, it's that...that darn chem lab."

"Colleen is tough. But she gets great results. You'll ace the exam in June," Gillian smiled at everyone at once.

In their tight kitchen it was hard for four people to get around. Hannah watched Skylar get to her tea. Her chest brushed up against Mr. Samuels' back as she squeezed between him and the fridge. He shuddered.

When the two got into Hannah's bedroom, Skylar wondered, "So when do you think Samuels will propose to your mom?"

"What?"

All the muscles in Skylar's face worked in unison to give the sweetest expression. "You heard me," she repeated. "Your mom looks so happy. I think they will totally get married."

She rifled through her backpack for the chem notes. *What if I accused her of sleeping with Samuels? I could watch her contort and squirm at the revelation. The part when she knows I know.* An anger like spoiled meat bubbled up in Hannah's gut. *I have the words. Just speak them.*

A white fear struck Hannah. *What about my mom? The humiliation. If I don't say it aloud, it is still just speculation,* Hannah breathed slowly. She knew the truth. But until you speak the truth, what you know can remain imaginary.

"Here's the chem notes. Nancy let me use the copy machine. Little snot nose gave me shit but I told her it was for you and that you were questioned by the police today."

"I'm surprised Nancy let you…even so," Hannah tried to make nice. *Put it from your mind.* But the truth was they'd been distant from each other since the accident. Hannah was hurt that Skylar moved on without her. The lead in the play. Probably even a new boyfriend Hannah didn't know about.

For those first few awkward minutes, Nancy Altman provided common ground. She was a hopeless nerd, the stereotypical hall monitor. She was the "Sarah Young" of the Student Council. Whispering Hills had the most ridiculous Student Council too. Every year the school would let ten seniors run for student body president. The nine who didn't win would all be vice presidents. But each got a different role, usually something that parent volunteers or office staff didn't want to do. In fact, Greg's crush was VP of the Balloon Store. That's right. He was the vice president of selling balloons. Nancy Altman was the VP of Photocopies. She had her own code for the office Xerox machine. They didn't want students wasting paper. Crazy how a school with a helipad had to worry about copier paper and toner. Nancy took her job very seriously.

In fact, Nancy was a catalyst in Hannah's friendship with Skylar. Being the teacher's kid at her new school meant Hannah was a ball of anxiety those first few days of freshman year. Nancy took the liberty of explaining that if Hannah didn't return some forms to my homeroom teacher, she would get an automatic detention. Hannah could still smell the starch on Nancy's crisp uniform shirt.

Skylar leaned in, freshman but fully a woman, "Nancy, stop making everyone as neurotic as you." Then she picked up a pencil off the floor, "I think it's yours. A wonder how it fell out of your clenched ass."

Nancy muttered something about detentions. Skylar turned her body to Hannah, "Hi, I'm Skylar Clarke. You're Hannah Cross, right? You're Mrs. Cross's daughter."

And that's how the friendship started. And Skylar's introduction, while poised and warm, might as well have said, "Hi, I run this school because I have more money than God. You're a peon whose mom's salary is about the same as the cost of my watch, right?"

But what would you have done? Attach yourself to the diligent nobody Nancy? Or become friends with Skylar Clarke? The choice was simple. High School is disturbingly similar to prison. You associate with strength and you're strong. Associate with weakness and it's going to be a long four years.

Hannah looked through the chemistry notes. *Wow, Skylar actually took good notes.* Hannah felt relieved and oddly thankful. Skylar cracked the bedroom door open and listened to the downstairs noises for a few seconds. "Good, Ricky is still down there with them. We would hear him coming up, right?"

"Yeah," Hannah replied, "Ricky isn't exactly soft-footed."

"Okay, good," Skylar closed the door and ran her hands along the seam. As she turned, Skylar looked like an actress in a noir film — half gravity, half glamour.

"My dad is lawyering up."

"What? Why?" Hannah exclaimed, too loud. She stupidly looked around the room for confirmation that no one downstairs heard.

"The police have a warrant to search the Rover," her mouth turned down in a pout. She looked more like a girl whose favorite Uggs had a stain than a girl whose just been involved in vehicular manslaughter.

Hannah panicked, "You said that there's no dent. You said that the car looks fine. I saw the Rover."

Skylar threw her hand up, "I've already sat through one lecture about this tonight. My dad didn't even have the decency to tell me himself. He stood there silently as Trina relayed the whole thing. Apparently, the police paid her a visit this morning—interrupted her private yoga lesson. Gag me."

She went on. If there was anyone Skylar hated more than Zoe Kellogg, it was her father's new wife. "And do you know she was wearing my grandmother's pearls? Those are supposed to go to me or Bethany," Skylar fumed, totally derailed from her purpose.

Hannah smirked as she thought of Katrina Torres-Clarke twirling pearls and drinking some Sauvignon Blanc as she explained the morning's happenings to Skylar.

"So, I had to stand there, getting lectured, by Trina of all people. But I guess my dad let her take the lead on this one. Seeing as she probably has some experience with law enforcement," Skylar cocked an eyebrow.

"You didn't say that to her, did you?"

"Not exactly like that," Skylar replied, a little meekly this time. "My dad would have flipped out if I said that."

Well, now at least I know why Skylar is here. It's not the chem notes. And it's not to talk about the investigation. Hannah sat on the bed, her vitriol for Skylar tempered briefly by pity. Skylar came over because she mouthed off to her stepmother and her dad took Trina's side. Besides musical theatre, this was all they really had in common—shitty dads. Hannah's dad never showed up and when he did he was only half there. So, she half-loved him. Skylar watched her dad wait for his wife to die. But all the while Brooks Clarke courted some young upstart at his company, licking the wounds of his loveless marriage. His devotion to the first Mrs. Clarke—the real Mrs. Clarke—was a lie.

Skylar plopped down next to Hannah and rehashed the story. When she was finally exorcised, she cooed, "I know this Zoe stuff is hard for you, Hannah, but think of how shit will affect your mom if it gets out." She looked pointedly at business card on Hannah's desk. Hannah gasped. *The detective's card. The one I took from rehearsal.*

"What will get out? I swear I didn't tell the police anything." *Could Skylar see into my heart? Did she know that I took that card a few weeks back? Does she know why I took the card?* They had been distant. Hannah wondered if this was her friend sitting next to her or an abuser grooming prey. Or both. It's probably always been both.

"I know you would never say anything. It just hit me about your mom though. She would lose her job."

Surrounded by the glow of Skylar's expert gaslighting, Hannah thought of her mom too. *I need to be better the next time I talk to the police. If there is a next time…*

I need to protect my mom. Hannah saw it clearly now: protecting Skylar was protecting her mom. A sense of purpose set in as Skylar continued.

The police will search the Range Rover tomorrow. The only information they had from the truck driver who witnessed the accident was "dark SUV." Skylar began weaving the silky latticework of manipulation. The same threads she braided around Hannah since ninth grade.

But it will be all right, Skylar affirmed. And Hannah believed her.

There was no dent on the SUV. And Hannah believed her.

Derrick fixed it. Why did Hannah think Skylar was hanging around with him in the first place? Skylar gave a rhetorical giggle. And Hannah giggled too. How silly she felt now. That late night she stalked Skylar. *Of course, she isn't close to Derrick. Not the way Skylar is close to me.*

"When they come tomorrow, I'll nail the interview. Just like I did this morning," Skylar laughed. And Hannah laughed too.

"I think I'll be just fine," Skylar sighed smugly.

And the whole time Hannah heard "we" in Skylar's sultry low voice. And the whole time Skylar said "I" with a confidence that comes from being raised with money and opportunity and power.

Too bad Hannah didn't notice. Too charmed by the most powerful girl at school. Too relieved that her best friend was back. *We just need to get through this.*

Skylar left soon after that. She offered a ride to Mr. Samuels. "I can take you," she purred.

Gillian immediately took off her coat, grateful for the favor. She had papers to grade. Skylar could bring Aaron to the train station.

Chapter Ten
The Cameo

Please Respond by

March 20th

_____Aaron Samuels_____

_✓_accepts with pleasure
___declines with regret

The RSVP card sat at the top of the stack. *Wow. He's coming? Has a director ever come to this before? We'll see if he shows after the last few days of rehearsal. He's not exactly Skylar's favorite person right now.*

"Very strong, Hannah," Mr. Samuels had looked up from his sheet music. Skylar just stewed and drummed her manicured fingernails on the piano.

"Thanks," Hannah smiled and stood up a little straighter, ready to run it again.

They sang the song two more times, the bridge four more times, the same three chords resolving the bridge at least ten more times. And every time Skylar just couldn't hit the end note.

"Listen to Hannah do it," Mr. Samuels nodded. "You can hit this note. It's tough for you because you're almost an alto. And this is a mezzo role. But you can hit it. Right, Hannah?"

Hannah looked around the room for the right words. *What the hell am I supposed to say here? What response will keep me in good graces with Samuels and simultaneously keep me from Skylar's wrath?* Hannah nodded silently but basked in the praise. Rehearsals had been steadily improving for her. *He's finally seeing how hard I work. Maybe whatever flirtation Skylar has with Mr. Samuels is over. Or maybe it was all in my head.*

She ignored the snide remark from Greg earlier in the day. "Well, of course he's paying attention to you. He's totally sleeping with your mom," he'd laughed. *Unlike Greg to be so cutting. Skylar probably fed him that one.*

Skylar had enough of sitting through tedious runs of her songs and listening to the director compliment her understudy. "Too bad you didn't hit the note at auditions," she'd sighed. Her tone sounded genuine.

What a sociopath.

Mr. Samuels didn't even catch it. "That's right. This song is much harder than 'Maybe This Time.'"

Skylar sneered, "Maybe next time indeed." *Why is she such a bitch? Does she have to possess everything?*

"Let's not be unkind," Samuels turned to Skylar, "I know you're frustrated with this song but there's no need to take it out on Hannah. That's not what leaders do."

Skylar sucked her teeth. There was a pause that seemed to last ages.

Mr. Samuels faced Hannah again, "You know, I've got a few tickets to Cabaret tonight. The director is a dear friend. Why don't you and your mother come with? I'd love to introduce you to Stella McKay. She's just joined the cast as Sally. I think you'd enjoy it."

Skylar looked at her phone again, "Mr. Samuels, it's 4:45. Hannah has dance practice."

Hannah gathered her things quickly, "Thank you for the invite. I'll ask my mom."

Mr. Samuels smiled and penciled a few more notes on his sheet music. When Hannah left the room, she heard whispering between them. She shook it off. *It's over. Whatever it was.*

And it was probably nothing to begin with. Hannah chided herself — maybe she just read into all those exchanges and looks. He was dating her mother. Mr. Samuels was an adult and a teacher. And Skylar was a girl and student. Nothing was happening.

Tickets to Cabaret! Tonight. And Stella freakin' McKay! Hannah nearly floated to Ms. Panzini's dance studio downstairs.

Hannah brushed her fingers on the pile of RSVP cards. She wanted so badly to know if the Kelloggs and the Bartletts would come to the annual Easter Luncheon at the Clarke Mansion. It was an event started by Skylar's mother. The property had the most exquisite view of the lake and by Easter, Westchester County had thawed enough to show the initial signs of spring. Small chartreuse buds adorned the large trees—trees that, once fully leaved, would block the view of the lake from the house. The grass was peppered with purple crocuses and the beginnings of daffodils. The forsythia was in its yellow majesty. Naked brown branches now filled with bright yellow petals. And the Clarkes had tons of forsythia. Skylar's home showed such voracious signs of natural life that it almost made you forget the hard New York winter.

And you could see the property best from the grand dining room with its floor to ceiling windows. Skylar's mother had an Easter luncheon to showcase the family's "blessings." Yes, they had the best property on the lake. Every year as Hannah sat through the luncheon—her whole family invited to witness the Clarke largesse (and celebrate the Resurrection, of course)—she imagined the other family events she'd have to endure. She was sure Mrs. Clarke planned this entire wing of the home—the enormous chef's kitchen and breakfast room, the hotel-sized dining room, the adjoining butler's pantry and wine storage, the large stone patio emitting from the back of the house—this part of their home would be the locale of engagement announcements, bridal showers, weddings, and baby showers for both daughters.

Skylar sat down at her desk, putting her body between Hannah and the cards.

"The usual suspects are coming," she said flippantly and fastened her strappy heels.

"Mr. Samuels isn't a usual suspect. I'm surprised you invited him," Hannah remarked.

"Why? We always invite the director of the play. Besides, Mr. Samuels would be your mom's plus one anyway. Since they are totally doing it," she laughed. Hannah cringed. Not at the thought of her mother having sex. Well, yes at that too. But she cringed because once again Skylar inferred correctly about Hannah's life, something that was usually right under Hannah's pert nose.

Hannah didn't recall the previous director ever being at the Easter luncheon. *Boosters, yes. But Mr. Jacobsen? I'm not going to argue with her though.* She stole once last look at Mr. Samuels' RSVP card. *Yes, he is really coming today.*

"Still," Hannah tried to come off indifferent, "he never leaves the city on the weekends. I'll be surprised if he actually shows."

"He texted me last night and said he wouldn't miss it," Skylar applied some lip gloss and smacked her lips loudly.

Hannah moved away from the mirror. *He texts you? No, she's lying. She made it up. Call her buff.* Hannah steeled herself. *What was Mr. Samuels doing texting a student?*

As if on cue, Skylar baited her friend, "Do you want to see my phone?" She unlocked her iPhone and began to pull up her messages. "You don't believe me, do you?"

Hannah stayed quiet.

"Well, don't worry about it. I know what you think. And it's not what you think."

"What do I think?" Hannah stammered, and her façade cracked.

"That Mr. Samuels and I have a relationship that borders on inappropriate," Skylar took off her robe revealing her curvy body. She walked into her closet and continued, "We have a connection, yes. But, Hannah, it's a professional connection. It's artistic."

"He's a teacher. You're a student" *I want to say so much more. Why can I never find the words when I need them?* Hannah fiddled with her phone, a weak attempt at disinterest.

Suddenly, Greg burst in the room. Hands raised, head back, and hips jutted forward, he took a deep breath. "O.M.G.!"

Cynthia followed and shut the bedroom door.

"Greg! I'm changing!" Skylar scolded.

Greg wrinkled his face, "Oh, get over it, Skylar. Like I care about your huge boobs." He sat down next to Hannah and put his long arm around her. *Thank God Greg is here. I have no idea where that was going.*

"So, bitches, I have gossip. Three golden nuggets of gossip. First is this: the word on the street is that Mr. Samuels is doing the nasty with drumroll please…a student!"

Hannah the lump rise in her throat immediately. *Greg was such an ass sometimes. Did he actually forget that my mom and Samuels are an item? Or is he just borrowing a recipe from Skylar's wicked spell book?*

Cynthia noticed Hannah's change in demeanor. But before she could comment, Greg squealed again, "And second piece of gossip is, drumroll, please…" This time he actually played the "drums" on his thighs, "The police think someone in the cast is responsible for Will's death."

"And Zoe's coma," Cynthia added.

"Yes, and Zoe," Greg dismissed her.

Skylar stuck her head out of the closet, "What?!"

Does Skylar know this info? Is she hearing it for the first time?

"Well, Greg has deduced that the police think someone in the cast did it. He doesn't know that for sure," Cynthia rolled her eyes.

Skylar zipped her dress and walked purposefully to Greg, "Explain your theory. I talked to the police too. They don't think shit about the cast. I could tell."

Greg got up and Skylar sat next to Hannah.

"Yes, I deduced. But it's watertight, people. The car had to be from someone in the neighborhood. And the police have started reexamining all the members of the cast. Ipso facto — someone in the cast did it." Then with a flourish, "Was it you, Hannah?"

Hannah nearly jumped out of her seat. Her face turned white.

"Omg! Kidding!" Greg guffawed. But Cynthia noticed Hannah's face. *Come on. Pull it together,* Hannah repeated to herself.

Skylar to the rescue, "It was probz Cynthia."

Greg cracked up again. Cynthia turned bright red, "Don't joke about this, guys. Someone is dead."

Her face darkening, Skylar replied, "I know Will is dead. I was the one who dated him for almost two years. We talked about getting married."

Greg glared at Cynthia, "Yeah, it was their 22-month anniversary when they broke up. I remember because it was my birthday too."

Cynthia slouched into a chair. Hannah stepped in, "I think all Cynthia means is that what happened was awful and we shouldn't be here laughing about it. Zoe is still in a coma."

Cynthia smiled at Hannah, "And it's just Greg's theory."

There was an awkward silence. Skylar stared at her phone. She played the part so well. Reminded of the love of her young life, Skylar would now hold everyone in quiet contempt while she grieved and looked at pictures of him on Instagram. The light from the screen caught her glittery eye shadow in such a beautiful way. *It's almost as if she had nothing to do with his death,* Hannah thought. Then a scarier thought set in. *Maybe she's convinced herself that she didn't kill Will. Maybe she's convinced herself it's all my fault.* And if that's the case, well then, Hannah had no chance with the police. If Skylar could persuade herself of her own innocence, she could surely prevail upon the police.

Now they all stared at their phones awkwardly.

Greg gasped, "Hold on people. Katie Greco is dead."

A collective "What?!" rippled through the group.

Greg showed his screen. It was a Facebook page in memorial for Katie. "Well, either she's dead or someone is playing a sick joke." He scrolled and mumbled the posts aloud.

"Services were last week."

"RIP Katie. You were the best actress."

"So sad! I miss her so much."

Greg looked up, "This is nuts. We just saw her camp."

Now Cynthia had the page pulled up. One hand over her mouth, brow knitted, her thumb lightly passed over the screen. She wept softly, "Will and Zoe. And now Katie. They're so young."

"How did she die?" Skylar asked. Despite this shocking reveal, she continued flat ironing her hair.

Hannah had pulled up a news story on her phone. "It says here that Katie killed herself after she was bullied at school." *Skylar, I hope you didn't have anything to do with this.* A sense of comfort passed over Hannah. *The news says the bullying happened at school. Katie went to school in New Canaan. That's in Connecticut. So, Skylar wasn't involved.* Hannah remembered that afternoon at camp when Skylar asked for Hannah's help. It made so much sense back then. Would still make sense to her now?

"Okay, so all you have to do is hang out in the bunk for a little while," Skylar cooed.

"But what if one of the counselors comes by? What do I say?" Hannah fretted. *Why was Skylar always putting me in these situations? I'm always covering for her.*

Skylar huffed. Did she really have to explain this to Hannah again? The plan was a simple one. Skylar would get that necklace back from Katie Greco. Katie had been sour and acting out since Hannah got to camp. Katie owed Hannah an apology.

"One of the counselors will probably come by. Katie and I will be missing from rehearsal. But it's not the first time, I've skipped out on rehearsal. I mean, it's still summer camp, right? Just say you haven't seen us. Besides, I'll just be on the lake. When we're alone, Katie will be more comfortable."

Hannah nodded. She couldn't actually vocalize a disagreement with Skylar. She never could. "Okay, but don't be too long. And don't make a big deal about the necklace. She just needs to give it back. It's all good."

I do want that necklace back. I want it back badly. That little silver thread was a Christmas present. Skylar had bought it from Tiffany's. Aquamarine. Hannah's birthstone. Not quite as cheesy as a "Friends Forever" heart, but sentimental enough. And truth be told, Hannah was elated that Skylar was standing up for her.

"She stole from you. Even just for a prank. She needs to return the necklace. I'm going to make sure she does. But don't worry, Hannah. It will all be fine."

And then she just walked away. Didn't even wait for a response. When Skylar Clarke made her mind up to do something, it was getting done. Hannah just dreaded Skylar's methods.

Soon after, a counselor came to fetch Skylar and Katie for rehearsal. He was the new counselor. A Yale drama student. And he was gorgeous. His name was Josh but there was already another counselor named Josh at Camp in the Round. So, Greg dubbed new Josh "Hot Josh."

Hot Josh took a look around the porch, "Oh, hey! Hannah, right? I'm looking for Katie and Skylar. They are supposed to be running lines for *Antigone* right now. And they're like fifteen minutes late."

Before he could finish, Hannah responded, "I haven't seen them."

The counselor was taken aback by Hannah's tone. She waited anxiously for him to leave. But Hot Josh just stood there. Then he knocked on the door to the bunk, "Anyone in here? Katie? Skylar?" He opened the door, "I hope everyone is dressed."

"There's no one in there."

Hot Josh looked at Hannah curiously then walked into the cabin.

Skylar shouldn't be messing with Katie Greco. Even if it's on my behalf. And I probably shouldn't have made such a big deal about Hot Josh liking Katie. I mean, I thought he was looking at her and flirting with her a lot. But maybe he wasn't. Maybe I didn't see what I think I saw.

"Josh, I think I saw them walking to the lake. Maybe they went canoeing," Hannah felt proud of herself. She'd obeyed the instincts that told her Skylar was about to do something awful. And she played it off perfectly. She didn't rat on Skylar, but this will send Josh straight to the lake to save Katie from whatever Skylar was about to do.

"What? The lake? Nah, they wouldn't be going there."

Hannah replied curtly, "Why not?"

Hot Josh smiled, "I know you're only here for a week. But there's no way Katie Greco is going to the lake. I mean, maybe you saw Skylar going that way."

Now Hannah was thoroughly confused. *How can he be so sure? Maybe I was right. Maybe Hot Josh and Katie are hooking up.*

"Katie would never go canoeing. She's afraid of water. Can't swim," his tone was playful but patronizing.

A panic set in. *That's not what Skylar said.* Hannah ran through the conversation from earlier that day in her head.

"I just want to talk to Katie alone."

"She loves the lake."

"It's so peaceful out there."

"I can smooth things over and get your necklace back at the same time."

Hot Josh started trotting away, "Don't worry about it, Hannah. They probably just skipped out on rehearsal. I'll find them though."

God, I hope you do

Greg was still glued to his phone. "Aww, look. Hot Josh wrote the sweetest message," he passed the device around. "Should I write something?" Then Greg looked at Skylar, "Are you okay? You haven't said anything. You and Katie were tight. She was like "Hannah" before Hannah came along."

Oh God. Shut up, Greg.

Cynthia assented, "Yeah, Sky. It's okay to be upset."

"I'm fine!" Skylar snapped then took a deep breath and laughed a little, "Jeez, you guys are worse than my therapist. You need to stop watching so much Dr. Phil, Cynthia."

A knock at the door. Everyone collectively swiveled their heads toward the would-be intruder. Hannah waited for the "Miss Skylar" from behind the oak.

"What is it?" Skylar called.

The door cracked open. *It's not the maid. It's Trina.*

"Your father wants you to come downstairs."

Skylar curled her lip, "I'll be down when I'm done with my hair."

"He said he'd like you down there as soon as possible. So…finish up, okay?"

A big sigh and then Skylar popped off the bed. She threw her phone down on the satin comforter. "If he wants to talk to me, he can come up here. I said I will be down when my hair is done, Trina."

"Fine. Make sure you put a cardigan over that dress. You know what your father will say."

And…fireworks. Greg, who was melting into Skylar's couch cushions, sat up quickly. Hannah glanced at Cynthia. *This is a relief. Thank God for Trina. And no more talk about Katie Greco or Will Bartlett or Zoe Kellogg.*

Hannah braced herself. *Ooh, will Trina get the full Skylar treatment?* She held her breath. About halfway through the initial standoff, Hannah grabbed a pillow to her chest. The same way she would sit on countless nights when she and Skylar stayed up late watching episodes of American Horror Story. Terror and pleasure equally mixed.

"What did you just say to me?" Skylar began.

Trina stood straighter and walked a few steps into the queen's quarters, "I said that dress is too revealing for the Easter luncheon. You know what your father will think. You know he will…"

"Think I look a lot like you? You're right," Skylar interrupted, "This house doesn't need two women who dress inappropriately and prey on old rich men." Her voice dripped with sarcasm, "The Easter luncheon certainly doesn't need two women who, even with an American Express Black Card, can't seem to pick out a classy outfit. What was I thinking? You're right. You've got the trash thing down. I'll change. Then we can both pretend like it's completely fucking fine that my father married Diet J-Lo."

Trina's complexion reddened.

Almost forgetting himself, Greg whispered, "This is epic." Cynthia shot him a look.

But all Trina said was "That's completely uncalled for. I'm getting your father." Then she marched to the door.

Just then, Hannah noticed a light and felt a vibration from Skylar's phone. Only a few inches in front of her, she couldn't ignore it. It was a text. From Aaron Samuels.

> AS: Can't
> make today.
> We need

The screen went dark. Across the room, Skylar's face went dark too. This fight was far from over. Little did Hannah know how bad it would get.

"Go ahead, run to my dad. He's already rescued you from your shit existence in the lesser boroughs. He will…"

Trina exploded. She closed the gap between her and Skylar, "That's enough. I've tried so hard with you. But you're a spoiled brat!"

Skylar fired back, "AT LEAST I ACTUALLY BELONG HERE! Have you looked in the mirror lately? You don't fit in here. This is Whispering fucking Hills! Did you even know what the word 'luncheon' meant before my dad?"

And then came the slap. Trina's right hand made contact with the side of Skylar's contoured cheek. The world literally stopped. Skylar clutched her face in horror. Trina cowered backwards. Her expression terrified. Her new life was now in jeopardy. Cynthia ran to Skylar who melted crumbled into her arms. Greg, for once, was completely silent.

The phone vibrated again.

> AS: Can't
> make today.
> We need to
> stop this

Dark again. *This what?* Hannah didn't even know where to look.

Brooks Clarke walked in the room. "Enough!" he bellowed as walked toward Skylar. She lifted her face to present the red hand mark on her cheek. Brooks turned to Trina and scowled.

"Everyone get out! Greg, Cynthia, Hannah — take Skylar downstairs. Get her some ice."

Then to Trina, "Pack your things and go to your mother's."

The friends heard Trina stammer a response as they left. But Brooks was stone. Too many important people were coming to Clarke Mansion today. Traditions started by his first wife were never altered or abandoned. A slap wasn't going to change all that.

Hannah sat next to her mother at the luncheon. Gillian was more distracted than usual. Hannah was accustomed to her mother dazzling at these events. Her charm and ease in conversation is why she was promoted to English Chairperson. But it seems like all Gillian could do this afternoon was steal looks at her phone.

But her daughter already knew why she was upset. Aaron Samuels wasn't there. *I know that he is a no-show. But does mom?*

Across the table, Skylar glowed. Her older sister had finally arrived. Trina was gone for the day (guests were told she fell ill and was resting upstairs). Skylar could be engaging and sweet…when she was winning.

Gillian glanced at her phone once more and sighed.

"What's wrong?" Hannah whispered.

"Oh nothing," Gillian smiled widely. "Don't worry."

"Mom, you keep looking at your phone. Is everything okay?"

Gillian stuttered, "I—I just thought he'd be here by now. I hope everything was okay getting out of the city."

"Did you text him?"

Gillian feigned disinterest, "No, I wouldn't bother him like that."

"Bother him?" Hannah checked the volume in her voice. A sudden rush of fury came over her. *Those texts to Skylar. What a piece of shit.* "Mom, you're dating him. He said he'd be here. You have every right to ask where the hell he is."

"Hannah!" her mother retorted then checked to see if anyone else noticed their side conversation.

"Just text him," Hannah cajoled, momentarily reversing roles with her mother.

"Fine."

Well, thank God. Maybe this will all come to a head. Maybe mom will realize Aaron Samuels is a dog and dump him. Unreliable just like dad. Except dad wasn't sleeping with teenagers. Hannah found herself deep in thought.

"How's the soup, Hannah? You look like you hate it," Greg snickered.

Shaking out of the daydream, Hannah laughed it off, "It's good. Sorry. Was I making a face?"

Cynthia smiled, "You looked like you just tasted something rotten."

"No, it's great. Hey, did you start studying for Ms. Connors' test on Ideal Gases?"

Ricky, who'd barely said anything, interrupted, "This soup is going to give me some ideal gas."

"Ricky! Enough!" Gillian chastised and he sulked. *The Clarke Mansion is the last place my brother wants to on a bright spring day.*

Hannah leaned in toward her mother, "Well? What did he say?"

"He's on Long Island. It's his nephew's bris this weekend. He says he totally goofed and mixed up the dates. He said his brother David would kill him if he missed it."

Before she could stop herself, Hannah answered back, "Sounds like a lie."

Her mother was silent. Gillian tightened her jaw. *She knows something is up. I have to figure out a way to get mom to dump him. He doesn't deserve her.*

Hannah tried again, softer this time, "Mom, you should call him out. I mean he's —"

"I'm not talking about it right now, Hannah."

The hospital lights were assaulting. Hannah tried to focus on the tile floor instead. *Why did I let her talk me into this? Why can she not be alone for even one night?* Hannah thought of the pile of homework on her desk. *I was just at her house for hours because of the luncheon.*

Around 6 p.m., Skylar had called in hysterics. Her dad left abruptly after the luncheon, flying to Sun Valley for a few days.

"He said he needed to think in the quietude of the mountains. He said that even though Trina was wrong, I'm awful to her and I need to be held accountable," she screamed into the receiver. "As if he can't be around me for even a day! We were supposed to go see Wicked tomorrow and then pick up my Easter present in the Diamond District."

Hannah rolled her eyes on the other end. *How many times is Skylar going to see Wicked on Broadway?* Still Hannah's heart ached as Skylar recounted the afternoon. Skylar had that effect on everyone.

Trina had called her dad. "So many tears when your billionaire lifestyle hangs in the balance? What a gold digger!"

Brooks Clarke called for his private jet. "It's just so typical of him. This is exactly what he did when my mom was mad. He just up and left. Went to Sun Valley or West Palm or London."

And so, Skylar had a bright idea. "We should visit Zoe tonight. You've never been, and you need to go. It looks weird."

What if I go to the hospital and see Zoe and can't control my reaction? What if I'm overcome with grief? Won't that look suspicious? But Hannah didn't say that. She hung up the phone started to get ready. She'd barely said a word the entire conversation. When you deal with Hurricane Skylar, you just listen and obey. It's the best policy. *On the flip side, I got myself a front row ticket to Wicked and probably free lunch.*

And that was how Hannah Cross came to visit Zoe Kellogg in the hospital.

The first time at least.

It was about 9 p.m. as they walked under the bright lights of the hospital. Lights that stayed bright no matter if it was 11 a.m. or 11 p.m. Lights so bright that Hannah felt naked, all her sins written on her body. Her eyes darted around—night nurses, carts that beeped and pumped, paintings with inspirational quotes.

"Hi Skylar," a nurse said warmly.

"Hi Amy! Just popping in for a minute. I can't let a holiday go without seeing her," Skylar's voice honeyed and warm.

How many times has this psycho been here? I thought she'd only come to the hospital once. Her ability to lie is terrifying. Yet Hannah felt impressed by it. She steeled herself and flashed Amy a smile too.

"Who's your friend, Skylar? I don't think I've seen you here before," Amy asked.

Before Hannah could muster a response, Skylar broke in, "This is Hannah. Hannah and Will were really close. His locker was next to hers. I thought it would be good for Hannah to visit Zoe."

Hannah piped up, "I just adored Zoe too."

"Adore not adored," Skylar admonished with a high pitch voice like she was addressing to a toddler. "We love Zoe. She's going to wake up soon. We just know it."

"Well, with friends like you, Zoe has a lot to live for."

With that hefty dose of irony, the two made their way into Zoe's room. The space looked more bedroom than hospital. So many artifacts from home and school. Hannah pictured Mrs. Kellogg pouring over message boards and websites for advice on how to get your comatose child to wake up and start living again.

Then she looked at Zoe. But no pang of guilt coursed through her heart. Hannah wondered a moment if she was truly the villain. *Why don't I feel like shit right now?* She recalled the reading scenes from Macbeth last year in English class. She thought of Macbeth's friend — the one he has assassinated. She thought of how Macbeth's friend returns as a ghost. *Here she is. Looking just like Banquo. A life-size reminder of my mistake.*

Yet, Hannah's reaction was nothing like the tragic hero. Upon closer inspection, Hannah began to realize why. This patient lying in the bed wasn't Zoe at all. Her face and neck melded with the hospital bed. Her chest rose and fell with such subtlety you had to really pay attention to make sure she was breathing. This was half-dead Zoe. All at once, Hannah felt sadness for the young girl in the bed, disgust at the semi-grotesque scene, and relief that Zoe probably would never wake up.

And rehearsals are going so well. And Mr. Samuels had called her mom after the luncheon. He apologized profusely for having his dates mixed up. He wanted to make it up to Gillian. Could he take her and Hannah to see Cabaret this week? He knows Stella McKay. He'd love to introduce Hannah. He invited Hannah the other day but rehearsal ending up running late. He was sorry about that too.

Hannah thought of meeting Stella McKay. *It's going to be magical.* Hannah's number one Broadway woman crush since sixth grade. *If Zoe were awake right now, she would have been invited to the show. And Zoe would have met Stella McKay.*

Skylar stepped beside Hannah, placed a cold hand on her shoulder and whispered, "See? She's never coming back."

This moment is the closest we've ever been. Skylar and Hannah were connected, the most connected they'd ever been. Two conspirators breathing with one body that deep sigh of liberation from their sins.

Hannah gazed at her laptop later that night. An attempt at her Raisin in the Sun analysis essay. But sleep visited her too fast. The blinking cursor like a hypnotist's pocket watch. Soon she was hunched over the desk and snoring.

It wasn't Zoe that visited Hannah's dreams but Katie. Visions of Katie Greco mixed with scenes from *Macbeth*. A psychedelic pixelated tableau: Macbeth and Lady Macbeth stood there with Katie and Hannah on the Clarke Theatre stage. Of course, Skylar was conspicuously absent. Excused from the scene. Macbeth's neck was bloodied, his decapitated head reattached for the benefit of Hannah's dream. He mostly stood there staring at the three other women.

Katie's voice sounded distant, "She said she'd leave me out there. Out in the water if I didn't give it back." Katie's hair was wet, her skin swampy, almost green.

Hannah looked at the necklace around her own neck—the one Katie had stolen—then she fixated on Lady Macbeth's hands. The blood on them.

Katie spoke again, "But I asked her. I asked Skylar. 'Why did you give me the necklace then?' If it was such a big deal, why would Skylar give it to me?" She was crying now and looking at Hannah for answers. And Hannah felt the visceral choke that comes with dreams and silence.

"There's some blood on your hands now, Hannah." Lady Macbeth pointed slowly and stared with deep, starless eyes.

Startled awake, Hannah breathed fast and hard. *It's just a dream.* She checked her hands. *What am I doing? It's just a dream. It's only a dream. Skylar would never threaten to drown someone. She's crazy but not stupid.* Hannah shook her head lightly and gripped her desk. *Wake up, Hannah.*

The light from her laptop hurt her eyes. Her fingers found the keys and she searched for Katie's memorial page on Facebook. She scrolled through dates and times for services, countless compliments and wails of grief. *Do I write something?* The guilt of Zoe and Will oozed into Hannah's feelings about what to do for Katie. *I had nothing to do with Katie.*

She started to type.

> I know I was only
> at camp for a
> week, but Katie
> was the sweetest
> girl. So welcoming
> and so talented.
> oxox
> #ripKatieGreco
> #missyou
> #tooyoung

Wow, that's a complete lie. I mean, I didn't want her to die but Katie was awful to me. Stole my necklace as a prank. Hannah thought of how Katie convinced other campers to call her 'Hannah Banana.' She thought for a moment on what she truly wanted to write. How she wanted to call everyone out for how fake they were being. But then she just deleted her words and kept scrolling.

A post with over fifty comments. Whoa, none of the other posts have any comments. This post talked about bullying at New Canaan High School.

> It's a real problem
> at NCHS. I hope
> now they will
> address it.

The comments were fiercely defensive of the high school. Hannah was surprised. *There needs to be villain. Why not make it something big with no face? Like the high school? Seems like a big enough thing to blame for a student's death.* That's what people do in these situations. They heap all the collective anger on the high school to alleviate the heartbreak of a life ended too soon.

Hannah leaned in and read some of the comments.

> She was
> cyberbullied. It
> wasn't kids from
> the high school.

Hmph. Cyberbullying can still be from your own school, genius.

> everyone loved
> katie

I doubt it.

> i'm not naming
> names but it
> wasn't kids from
> NCHS. it was def
> those theatre kids
> she hung out with
> in the summer.

Skylar. I need to talk to her. What if she… No, she wouldn't… Hannah wanted — no — she needed this to be false.

Yeah, not the
school's problem.
Sure it's a tragedy
but maybe Katie
just hid how sad
she was. Maybe
we didn't know to
help her.

After shutting her laptop, Hannah grabbed her cell and dialed Skylar. *Please be awake. I need to hear that you had nothing to do with this.*

Voicemail. *Shit. Of course.*

"Hey, it's Hannah. We need to talk. Can we meet tomorrow somewhere? We need to talk privately, Sky. I don't know if you've read some of these comments on Katie's page but…"

An automatic female voice cut her off. "If you're satisfied with your message…"

Hannah threw the phone on the bed.

Chapter Eleven
All That Glitters

To: Hannah Cross <hannah.cross@whcds.edu>
From: Gillian Cross <gillian.cross@whcds.edu>

You got an audition! Do you know how to get there on the subway? Let's chat when you get back from rehearsal.

Mom

To: Gillian Cross <gillian.cross@whcds.edu>
From: Aaron Samuels <aaron.samuels@whcds.edu>

See below. Hannah is going to be so happy!
Love,
Aaron

---------Forwarded message-------
From: Stella McKay <smckay@yahoo.com>
Date: Thu, Apr 16, 2018 at 12:02pm
Subject: Hannah audition
To: aaron.samuels@whcds.edu

Aaron!

So lovely to see you again! And Gillian is a doll. And Hannah is a such a sweetie. Yes, I got her an audition. Tell her to be at the Farkas Auditorium at 10 a.m. on Monday. She needs to be ready with at least 16 bars. And be ready to sight read for us. Dennis is a stickler for the theory stuff.
Oxox
SMc

It's actually happening. Hannah sneaked another peek at her phone. *Yep, it's real. Still there. I didn't hallucinate that. I actually have a shot at one of the best performing art colleges in the country.*

"Hashtag movin' on up!" Greg sang in his lowest, raspiest, sassiest voice. *Someone's been watching Nick at Nite again,* Hannah mused. He used a moist toilette to rub his hands.

"Glitter?" Hannah asked.

"Oh my God! It's so annoying. Mr. Samuels makes us run the scene changeover more than the actual scene. Like, okay, we get it. The stage needs to be clear of glitter. But whatevs! Don't want to take away from your big moment, Hannah!"

Cynthia put her lunch tray down and joined in the celebration, "And a Tisch audition this late in the year! I blew my Tisch audition. Oh my God, it was awful. But you'll be great." *She sounds genuine. Wait, am I starting to like Cynthia? Maybe there's something I never saw before. I think she likes me too. Could be why Brody texted me the other night. Just a question about AP Gov homework but then a few smiley face emojis too.*

"I doubt I'll make it. Besides mom wants me to do Westchester Community for two years to be sure about where I want to go," Hannah replied.

Greg scoffed, "WCC? When did that happen? I thought we were doing a gap year together. Remember dance classes at STEPS. Auditions. Non-equity at first. But then we get our first jobs and boom! Equity Actors!" He picked a few more glinting squares from his nails.

Cynthia interrupted, "Mrs. Cross was never going to let Hannah do a gap year."

Hannah sighed, "Yeah, Greg. She would flip out if I didn't enroll somewhere. But if I'm at Westchester Community, I'll be around."

Cynthia beamed, "No, you won't be at 13th grade because you're going to be at NYU!"

Hannah tried to appear humble, but she enjoyed the attention. She was indeed movin' on up. The dinner, the Broadway show, the trip backstage—everything about that evening at Cabaret had been magical.

Apparently, Mr. Samuels had been raving to his classes about Hannah's impromptu sing along with Stella McKay. The one that got her an invite to audition for NYU's Tisch School. Ms. McKay was a resident artist. "Who cares? I'll get you looked at. They will be blown away. When you're this good and this beautiful, they ignore all that red tape," Stella had smiled brightly as she took off her stage make-up.

Hannah could almost ignore her lingering suspicions about Mr. Samuels. He was a perfect gentleman to her mother the whole night. The dinner was scrumptious. Gillian was a little tipsy by the time they got to the theatre and dozed off in the middle of Act One. But Mr. Samuels didn't seem to mind.

During intermission, he took an opportunity to talk alone with Hannah while her mother used the restroom. "I know I was hard on you the first few rehearsals. I feel like I owe you an explanation," he began.

"Oh, no, you don't owe me anything. I know my audition was bad. Like really bad," Hannah answered meekly and pretended to leaf through her Playbill.

"No, I do. I owe you an apology actually. See, Hannah, your mom was the first person I met at Whispering Hills and well, you know, she's pretty great. I knew right away that I wanted to see if something was…something was there with her. But Ms. Panzini pointed out that you were Gillian's daughter and that I should be careful," he paused and looked around the theatre. "People talk in Whispering Hills. I didn't want to be seen as giving you any preferential treatment because of my relationship with your mother."

Aaron sat back, content with himself. By bringing Hannah to the show, he'd done a good thing. He'd smoothed things over with her like Gillian asked. Confident in Hannah's seemingly complicit silence, Aaron continued, "I mean, teachers talk. I had heard that you were a fantastic singer and dancer and I really wanted you to nail the audition. But I don't know, maybe it's because you came in late. Maybe you were frazzled. I heard that party was a doozy," he chuckled.

Late? Did he just say I came in late to auditions? Skylar and Hannah's entire alibi was predicated on their being on time to the audition. *He's mistaken.* She debated excusing herself to go to the restroom. But the house lights flashed on and off, signaling to the crowd to find their respective seats. *At least the second act will make this awkward convo stop.*

"Oh, yeah. Skylar's parties are always a little crazy. But I don't think we were late for auditions. I think it's just that you were a new director, so I choked. But I'm totally over it now," she lied and smiled broadly.

"Hmm, I'm pretty sure you and Skylar came late. I remember thinking I was going to set the tone by pulling you both aside. But then I decided against it because the cast was so nervous to begin with. But it's not a big deal," Mr. Samuels patted Hannah's leg. "I'm glad to hear that you're over it. You are shining in rehearsals. Sometimes I even wish that Skylar drop so you could play Aurelia," he whispered that last part.

"Aaron!" Gillian sat down and laughed conspiratorially, "You shouldn't say that." She mock scolded him. Gillian was happy to see her daughter finally getting the recognition she deserves and stepping out of Skylar's shadow.

181

The conductor walked out, and Hannah never loved a stranger so much in her life. For the entire second act she sat in wild imagination, emotions tossed around in her gut like a docked sailboat in a storm. Her mind raced but she was unable to keep up with her thoughts. She felt tethered to her seat and the show and etiquette. Finally, her mind focused solely on Mr. Samuels last words about replacing Skylar. From that point on, Hannah ignored his assertion that yes, indeed, both girls were late to auditions.

Back in the lunchroom, Sarah Young and Paige Kellogg plopped down at the table next to the Hannah, Cynthia, Greg. *Why are they sitting there? Sarah and Paige have been spending way too much time together. This is getting creepy.* Hannah searched their faces for answers. Sarah's crew friends had glanced over to check on the new seating arrangement too.

"I'm not staying. You can close your mouths," Sarah looked at Greg.

Cynthia responded first, "Oh, Sarah, you can sit wherever you want." *Whoa, Cynthia's sweetness extends to everyone today. A Christmas goose for everyone!* Hannah smirked, and Sarah caught it.

Sarah looked directly at Hannah, "No, I'll eat with my actual friends. But Paige and I thought you guys should know that the there's been some developments in the case. I know everyone is still really broken up about Zoe being in a coma and missing her last show as a Whispering Hills student. The show she should have had the lead in," Sarah puffed up her chest.

Okay, we get it. You're Team Zoe forever and ever. Hannah stopped her eye roll halfway when Paige glanced over.

Interest piqued by mention of the accident, Greg put down his fork. "What did you find out? Did the detectives finish questioning everyone from the cast again? Because I was never called in for the second interview," he rambled to everyone. Then just to Paige, "I feel like I could be helpful."

Paige nodded, "Thanks Greg. I'm sure the detectives will let you know if they need to talk to you again."

Sarah called them to order, "So, the truck driver remembered some more details. Apparently, the SUV was either a Range Rover or a BMW X5. But it definitely high-end."

Hannah tried to stop herself, but it was no use. Anxiety took over. "How did you even get this information?" she said a little too forcefully. "And how does the truck driver just suddenly remember details? Wouldn't he know more when the accident actually happened?"

Everyone looked at Hannah, but she didn't notice. Her cheeks reddened, and her heart raced.

Sarah began to stand up from the table, "Just thought you might want to know. I'm not here to get interrogated. I wasn't involved in vehicular manslaughter." She swaggered to her usual table but turned back, "Oh, and my dad is the Whispering Hills fire chief. So yeah, he's got some friends in the PD. Come on, Paige."

"Sorry to upset you, Hannah," Paige stuttered.

Hannah finally found her proverbial footing, "Oh no, I just get sad about Will. And I hate for you to get your hopes up about a break in the case."

"Well, it's not so unusual for witnesses to remember more details as time goes on. I gotta go."

"She's drunk again," Cynthia sighed deeply and all three looked at Skylar walking into lunch late. No boys on her arm. Cell phone out. Brazenly texting. Paige looked over her shoulder too. Noticing Skylar's impaired state, Sarah found a new level of confidence. All of them braced for Hurricane Skylar. But Sarah was the insane local news meteorologist who was going to stand in the rain. She was ready to defy the destructive winds. She was ready to throw down.

Hannah imagined a movie camera was in her face waiting for the extreme close-up reaction.

Skylar had a Range Rover.

Skylar lived on that street.

And Sarah Young has hated Skylar Clarke since freshman year when Skylar outed her as a lesbian in art class. "Drawing another vagina," she had said. "You've been drawing those since elementary school. Why don't you just buy a pair of Doc Martens and get it over with, lezzie?"

This confrontation was a long time coming. And Skylar had been coming to school drunk all week. Still hurt about her father's departure, she was in a free fall. No one, not even Hannah, could get through. As for Sarah, who put her lunch tray back down and sat next to Hannah. This was the perfect time to pounce.

Skylar arrived and immediately knew the game, "I think the island of Lesbos is missing their Wonder Woman."

Sarah laughed, "Funny. Offensive as usual and a poor mixing of narratives. You can do better. Try again when you're sober." She began eating her lunch.

Hannah tried to diffuse the situation, "Sky, did you have anything to eat today? I have some unopened…"

Skylar ignored her best friend and glared at Sarah, "Get out of my fucking seat." She slammed her backpack down on the table. The bounce caused Sarah's lunch tray to rattle. Tacos spilled all over her plate.

"You know. You're right. I was just leaving. I just thought that you'd want the information I came to bestow."

Skylar cocked her head and folded her arms, "Well, what is it?"

"Only that the police have a better description of the car that hit Will Bartlett and Zoe. Dark Range Rover. Maybe black. Maybe navy blue." Sarah began to rise.

Skylar just stared ahead — her legs swayed a bit beneath her. Paige attempted to get around the table with a meek "Excuse me."

Skylar snarled, "And when did you two become besties?"

Now a safe distance away, Sarah called, "Don't you drive a navy-blue Rover, Skylar?"

Skylar bolted toward Sarah whose face went from sanguine red to ghost white in a millisecond. Greg jumped out of his seat and wrapped his spaghetti arms around Skylar's drum tight torso. It was one of the few instances where 5'3" Skylar appeared short in stature.

"Skylar, no!" Greg yelled. Teachers began taking notice. A few of the lunch monitors swooped in. Fighting was a no-go at Whispering Hills. Automatic expulsion. If you wanted to fight, you could go to public school.

Skylar screamed at Sarah, "Do not fuck with me!" Then she wriggled out of Greg's arms, but he reattached himself with mind-blowing speed and agility.

"Get off me, Greg! Dammit!"

Sarah walked closer. Hannah shook her head and sighed. *Calm down, Skylar. She wants you to hit her. She wants you to do it.*

As the teachers approached, Skylar's eyes glistened — not with drunkenness but with surprising clarity. She collapsed to the floor in tears. Hannah marveled at the performance. *Wow, she just avoided Dean Feldman's office with this.*

The lunch monitor reached her, "C'mon, honey. Who's your guidance counselor?"

As Skylar limped away, Cynthia watched on with Hannah. Greg panted for breath. He shook his head at them. "I can't believe her," he whined and rubbed his forearm, "Gosh, she's so strong."

Cynthia's tone changed to disdainful, "You believe this? Anyone else would have been suspended."

"Yes, believe it. When your last name is Clarke, you don't get suspended. When your last name is Clarke, you can get away with murder," Sarah snarled at them.

Hannah retorted instinctively, "Watch your mouth, Sarah. You should be thanking Greg. Skylar was about to light you up."

Sarah put her hands on her hips and laughed. But her twisted joyful expression changed when Dean Feldman appeared at the doors of the cafeteria.

"Sarah Young, come with me."

Hannah and Skylar were early for rehearsal. Skylar had finally sobered up but spent the rest of the day snoozing in the guidance lounge. The two entered the dance studio to find Sarah Young being lectured by Mr. Samuels. *Wow, she is having crappy day. First Feldman and now Mr. Samuels is being a beast to her.*

"Oh, sorry, Mr. Samuels. We can wait outside," Hannah offered and took in the room. Just the director and Sarah. And a small pile of glitter swept to the side of the floor.

"It's fine. We were just about finishing here anyway."

Skylar and Hannah sat quietly by the mirror while Mr. Samuels finished his speech. Hannah checked Instagram while Skylar arranged her wavy hair for a selfie and texted it to Derrick.

"Now, Sarah. I need you to understand how important cleaning the stage is after 'More Than This.'"

"Oh, I know Mr. Samuels. The crew knows too. We have Greg helping us sweep while we change scenes. He didn't want to do it at first."

"Because Paige could get hurt dancing on a stage full of glitter. Ms. Panzini reminds me daily."

Sarah nodded empathically, "But it won't be. Full of glitter. I promise."

Skylar leaned into Hannah, "I hate all the glitter. Gets in my hair. I feel like a mythical creature in the shower. It's everywhere."

Hannah moved closer, "Is it in your hair downstairs?" Then she muffled a laugh.

"Oh my God. So gross, Hannah." The two giggled loudly. Just like they had at the theatre intensive over Columbus Day weekend. It felt like they hadn't stopped giggling that whole weekend in the city. *I wish we could go back to that weekend.*

Mr. Samuels shot Hannah a look and her next laugh caught in her throat. The rest of the dancers started filing in. Soon rehearsal was underway.

Later that week, the cast performed the number on stage. Samuels barked at the dancers and the crew. *Alright already with the glitter removal. Sarah seems to have it down. She's a tool but her crew moves like the gears in Skylar's Philip Patek watch.*

They scoured the stage and reset the scene pieces. Panzini timed their movements until the scene change was more precise than the choreography itself. And Sarah Young was getting it done. Every time. Her crew was impeccable.

Until they weren't.

And Paige fell.

Hannah stood off stage watching Paige finish her ballet solo. The big ending. Pristine turns that went into leap after leap. High, high, higher. Every inch of Paige's graceful legs articulated. Hannah watched in awe as she had watched Zoe. Both Kellogg sisters—natural talents.

Then Hannah spotted it. The small pool of silvery fairy dust at center stage. Right where Paige would conclude this impressive show of grace and athleticism. But she never got there. As Paige came down from her penultimate jump, Paige's ankle twisted unnaturally.

Snap.

Despite the music blasting and bustle of backstage work, everyone could hear the tiny sound that signaled the end of Paige Kellogg. She let out a yelp as she collapsed to the floor.

Paige's face was terrified. She writhed in pain. Sweet, little sophomore Paige. Paige who still wore her skirt unrolled and her uniform shirt perfectly ironed and tucked into the skirt's small waistband. She was secretary of the Young Christian Fellowship, working under her sister, the president.

"Is it broken?" Paige wailed and gripped her ankle.

Ms. Panzini held Paige's torso as Mr. Samuels tried to pry her Herculean grip from the shattered foot.

"No sweetie, it's probably just a bad sprain," Ms. Panzini perjured herself.

"I told them in the office," Sarah Young ran back to the stage.

An ambulance was on its way. So was the principal.

Mr. Samuels leered up at Sarah, "How did this happen?"

"Not now, Aaron!" Ms. Panzini spat. Another dancer came running with the ice pack and tossed it to the choreographer.

The rest of the cast had been told to keep their distance, give Paige space.

Why do we always have to give the injured person space? As if space is going to fix her ankle? As if the extra oxygen will intoxicate Paige enough where she forgets that her whole dance career is probably over. She gave up competitions this season for the musical. Shame.

Hannah continued to examine her feelings. Did she see the glitter in time to stop Paige? She saw the shiny pile before Paige fell but was it enough time? Could Hannah have prevented this? *I feel awful. But no one else here can perform Paige's features. That means...I'll get all her solos.*

In a while, the adults saw Paige safely off to the hospital. A few students watched from the windows of a nearby classroom.

With one daughter in a coma and the other never to dance again, Mrs. Kellogg looked almost catatonic when she met them in the parking lot.

"So sad. It's just too much for one family," Cynthia dabbed her wet eyes.

"I hope she's okay," even Greg's voice faltered.

Skylar came up behind them and put her arm around Hannah's shoulders. Her breathing was even. Her scent was rousing. "I guess you make out pretty well in this," she spoke softly.

The cast assembled on the stage. The crew sat on the scaffolding behind them. Mr. Samuels paced back and forth just beyond the apron. Ms. Panzini sat in the first row, head in her hands. Since the beginning of the musical season, one student had died, another lay in a coma, and now a student was on her way to an orthopedic surgeon. This production would need some luck to get through the last two weeks.

At length, their director began, "I know you love this show. And I know you are not professionals. You're just teenagers. Kids. But you're the best in Westchester county. I'd wager in you're the best in the whole state. And now it's time for you all to start acting like the professionals you hope to become. Hannah, you'll go to the dance studio ad learn all of Paige's solos. Ms. Panzini will teach them to you. Paige's foot is likely broken, and she will probably need surgery. If she's involved in our production of Stagecraft at all, it will be as an audience member."

He paused turned back to Ms. Panzini. The color drained from her face. She shook her head 'no' ever so slightly.

"Here it comes," Skylar hissed.

Mr. Samuels glared at Sarah Young, "I told you and your crew time and time again that getting the stage clear of glitter was your responsibility or Paige could get hurt."

"But I did, Mr. Samuels. It was clear. I'm always the last to check it. I don't know what happened," Sarah trailed off and the director held up his hand to make her stop.

"It was your responsibility. You didn't deliver. Now Paige is out of the show and you might be responsible for her never dancing again."

Sarah whimpered. No one looked at her. No one comforted her. Maybe some wanted to. But they didn't. *I can't believe he's doing this in front of everyone. I can't believe Sarah didn't get the glitter off the stage.* After seeing Sarah's crew execute that scene change multiple times, Hannah wracked her brain. *How did the pile get there?*

"Sarah, you're no longer student director. You're no longer part of this cast and crew."

Sarah shrieked, "What? But, Mr. Samuels, I swear I had nothing to do with it! Please don't do this."

He folded his arms, "Take your things and go. Do not come to anymore rehearsals."

He was stone, eyes black as ink.

Hannah felt hot tears on her own cheeks. She wiped them away quickly. Sarah gathered her bags and left while the cast watched in utter silence. Her shoulders rounded, Sarah walked up the long aisle. The light from the hallway peeking in and then shut out again as the door closed behind her.

Sarah has been on crew for every show at Whispering Hills since freshmen year. I can't believe she won't finish like the rest of us.

"You are all dismissed," Mr. Samuels declared.

But no one moved.

"Go!" he yelled, his voice shocking the students back to life. A few people whispered to each other. A few click clacked away on their phones. Hannah went to Ms. Panzini and waited awkwardly.

"Just go to the dance studio, Hannah. I'll be right there," the choreographer didn't even look up.

A text from Skylar on the way there.

SC: TOLD
THAT BITCH
NOT TO
FUCK WITH
ME!! LOL.

Hannah clutched her gut and cried again. *Of course, Skylar did this. But how?* She texted back.

HC: Why
would you do
something so
awful?
SC: Really
Hannah?
coming from u,
that's rich.

Hannah wrote nothing back, but Skylar wasn't finished yet.

SC: think
about it. this
benefits you
BIG TIME.
stop being a
whiny pussy.

A few more minutes.

SC: Good luck
at your Tisch
audition
tomorrow.
You'll kill it.
[knife emoji]
[heart emoji]

Chapter Twelve
Crescendo

Hannah,

I wrote out the directions to the train. I had to go to school early for a meeting. Don't worry...I'll let your teachers know that you will miss classes this morning. ☺

Train:

Take the 8: 37 am train from Pembroke Station to Grand Central.

Subway:

Take the 6 train towards "Brooklyn Bridge City Hall"

Get off at Astor Place.

Good luck today! I'll be thinking of you.

Love,

Mom

The door to her bedroom flung open! Hannah looked up from the note. Greg stood there with a bouquet of flowers, a big smile, and a Dr. Seuss hat with red and white stripes.

"Oh! The places you'll go!" he projected his voice as if from center stage.

"What's this about?" Hannah laughed. "And how did you get in my house?"

"Duh. Your mom let me in." Greg shut the door behind him. "And this was about me, but it can totally be about you." He pointed to the flowers and hat. Hannah looked at him quizzically.

"Okay," Greg sat down on the bed, "I got the lead in The Cat in the Hat! At Westchester Children's Theatre. So obvs I got myself some flowers to celebrate. And just now, I got this hat at the mall. But then your mom told me how well you did at your Tisch audition so I'm giving them to you. Not that hat. Just the flowers."

"Thank you, Greg," Hannah smiled. Greg's visit was a nice respite from calculus homework and the ever-present question of whether or not the police will discover who was actually driving that SUV.

The Tisch audition had gone well though. Made her forget about all of it— even if it was just for a few hours. Hannah nailed her performance. No more forgetting the words. Her voice filled the Farkas Auditorium. The sound expanded through the impeccably designed acoustic space. *This is it. This is my time,* she had thought. *No Skylar here to mess it up.*

Of course, it helped that Hannah already knew one of the Tisch voice teachers. Stella McKay gushed about her to the two other professors. And even in the dim light of the desk lamp that illuminated the small table they'd set up to hear auditions, Hannah could see Stella's face. Her expression gave Hannah even more confidence. *My voice sounds mature. They know I'm the real deal.* No longer a high school chorus girl doing her bit line with transparent bravado. Hannah's voice had meat on its bones. Her movement on the stage showed she was someone who would do what it takes to make it in show business, an industry that claims dreams as casualties every day.

"Hannah!" Stella called to her on the street afterward. "Hey! I thought that was you. I can't believe it's April and we are still bundled up like this." She lit a cigarette. *It would be so cool if she offered me a cigarette right now. Right here. On 1st Avenue. Stella McKay and Hannah Cross just smoking casually.*

Instead, Hannah replied with "Yes, it's still so cold. I keep hoping for some spring weather." *Don't ask how the audition went. Resist with every bone in your body.* Asking about an audition would be a major faux pas. But Hannah didn't have to ask.

"You did great!" Stella took a long drag.

Hannah smiled awkwardly, never too good at accepting compliments.

Stella spoke again, "You walking to the subway?"

"Yeah. I'll take that to Grand Central and then from there…" she trailed off. *Stop rambling. You sound like you've never been to Manhattan before.*

"I'll walk with you." Stella flicked the remaining half of her cigarette on the street and the two walked in silence for a bit.

"What part do you have in Samuels' production? He's putting up Stagecraft, right?"

"Yes, Stagecraft. I'm in the chorus. I have a few dance features."

"Wait, you don't have a role?"

Hannah broke into a cold sweat. Dreams of Tisch shriveled up. *Why would you say that? If you can't even get a high school part, how are you going to carry a show at Tisch?*

"Well, I'm the understudy for the lead. But…"

Stella scoffed, "The understudy? What's wrong with Aaron? I find it hard to believe that someone was that much better."

Hannah thought of Skylar. How she probably swayed her hips walking up to the stage. How "Aaron" was mesmerized in seconds. It's how it was with everyone at Whispering Hills.

"I think the lead will do a good job," Hannah responded with quiet diplomacy.

"But you'll be ready if she's not. That's the part of a good understudy." Stella walked with an unexpected briskness. Hannah had to jog to keep up. *This is how they walk in Manhattan. This is how people in the big city get from place to place. Walking faster than their shadows.*

Stella launched into a story about how she was finally discovered. Understudy for Idina Menzel in Wicked. Idina had a long run but when she came down with shingles, Stella was ready. Hannah should be ready too. *Anything can happen. Even in high school. Even when you only put on shows for one weekend. Saturday night and Sunday matinee. Skylar would die before missing it though.*

Hannah was thinking again of getting to take Skylar's place while Greg blathered on about The Cat in the Hat. Then she pictured her friend looking perfect in a black long sleeve turtleneck, cat make up, and the classic hat.

"I'm excited for you, Greg."

He sat at Hannah's desk and fiddled with her laptop, "Thanks, girl. Hey, by the way, you need to turn this laptop in for maintenance on Monday. That tech guy was collecting them on this morning. Something about Microsoft Office updates."

"Oh, okay."

Greg continued, "I'm super excited for you. You are so going to NYU!"

Hannah blushed and deflected the compliment, "I hope so. I won't know anyone if I do."

Greg sighed, "Yeah, no one from our group is going there. But you'll make friends. Stinks though…you know who was going to NYU? Katie Greco."

Hannah's heart quickened at the mention of Katie's name. It had been a few days since anyone mentioned her and Hannah thought the group had collectively forgot about Katie's death. But Greg rambled aimlessly, "Yeah, accepted early decision in the fall. Katie talked about the Tisch school incessantly. Like every summer. Makes me sad to think about it," he sighed and paused.

Should I say something here? Is he really going dark on me right now? I'll just wait. Greg will pop back up for air in a minute. He went on, "Yeah, here we are…living our lives and Katie won't get to go to college. I went to the funeral, y'know. What a long drive. Skylar didn't even show. So weird."

"It's so sad," Hannah's eyes were downcast and her voice low. She felt a mixture irritation and nerves. *How do I steer this conversation? I really don't want to talk about Katie.*

Greg burst out laughing, "Oh my GOD! Good try, Jennifer Lawrence! You can't fool me though." He reached over and patted Hannah's leg.

"What do you mean? It is sad!"

His eyes widened, and his tone was almost scolding, "Like you're so broken up about it. You hated Katie Greco."

Hannah began to protest, "I didn't…"

"Yes, you did. No big deal. Lots of people hated Katie. She was a snob. And when you got to camp, Katie was even worse. But—day one—you knew the game. You're savvy like that. Katie was afraid of you. Skylar would do anything for you. You kind of control Skylar sometimes. Katie saw that and…"

Hannah got upset. She gripped her bed for balance. *Why is he doing this? I didn't hate Katie Greco. Did I? And I don't control Skylar. She does that to me. I'm the victim here.* She felt scared and confused.

Greg leaned in, noticing Hannah's reaction, "Hey, are you okay? I'm just teasing."

"I didn't want anyone to die!" Hannah yelled.

A tender silence passed between them.

Hannah grabbed a tissue and dabbed her eyes. "Sorry," she whispered. Realizing his harm, Greg was next to her in an instant. Hannah's mom called from downstairs. Was everything okay? Greg called back. Everything's fine. Just running lines.

Shoot. Get a hold of yourself, Hannah. She breathed deeply, feeling her stomach fill with air, willing herself to calm door. *Stop the tears. Stop the tears.*

"Sorry, Greg. I'm just super tired. I think the audition took a lot out of me."

This answer seemed acceptable. Greg smiled and apologized again, "No, I'm sorry. I shouldn't have made fun of you. I know you're sad Katie died. That was mean of me."

"What did you mean about Skylar and me?" Hannah was unable to resist the follow up question. *Why would Greg say that? Katie wasn't afraid of me. She was afraid of Skylar. Everyone is afraid of Skylar. Who would be afraid of me? And I have zero control over Skylar. Zero.* And yet, Hannah felt perversely flattered that Greg said all that stuff.

"What about Skylar and you?" he asked.

Don't go there. Not now. The urge was so deep and hard to fight. *Why would Greg say that Hannah controlled Skylar? Everyone knew Skylar was top dog. Hannah was the lieutenant. That's how it was. That's how it worked from freshmen year.*

She forced a smile, "Nothing. Let's not talk about it anymore."

Another pause.

"So…we should celebrate your audition and my casting," Greg offered with a big smile.

Hannah smiled back, "Want to go to the diner?" *Maybe Brody will be there. He had texted more than once today. About schoolwork but still. Maybe, just like NYU, Brody is going to happen too. I've been really nice to Cynthia lately.*

All Hannah needed was an accidental-on-purpose meeting at the diner. She'd sit in a corner booth by the restrooms with Greg. Brody would look over from his Lacrosse bros table about a million times until he couldn't stand it anymore. Then he'd come over "just to say hi" and make like he had to use the restroom.

But Greg had other plans, "No, I want to get pedicures. My feet are so dry. And I want to swing by Skylar's too. Ask her to join us."

"No Cynthia?" Hannah remarked snidely. "And I'd rather just go to the diner. I'm kinda hungry."

"We'll grab some Burger King on the way over."

Hannah searched her mind for another excuse that wouldn't give away her need to see Brody Wolcott in his letter jacket and tight jeans. *I really don't want to see Skylar right now.* After the Paige incident, Hannah was keeping her distance.

Already in his coat, Greg beckoned, "Fine! We can go to the diner. But we'll get Skylar first."

"Did you tell her we were coming?"

"No! I'm going to surprise her. She's been so down since GlitterGate. I feel like Ms. Panzini blames her."

Well, Ms. Panzini has both eyes and a conscience. So, of course, she does. In fact, Jill Panzini hadn't been at rehearsal for a few days. Hannah's mom was evasive about. Just "under the weather" so Aaron told her to take time off. No one takes off this close to Hell Week. And Ms. Panzini looked just fine when she taught her dance classes during the school day. She'd even subbed for History class. Well, she popped in a History Channel DVD and then stared at her phone.

"Ms. Panzini is just upset about Paige," Hannah replied. "Skylar knows better than to take it personally."

Once in the car, Hannah continued her pleas. But Greg didn't listen.

I really don't want to be a part of this master plan to cheer up Skylar. She will hate this. I am the only person who knows her, Hannah thought pompously.

They pulled in the Clarke's long winding driveway and stopped under the portico at the side of the house. "She's probably in the kitchen," Greg said, all familiarity. Hannah detested him in that moment but quickly let it go.

Skylar is in her room. Or her mother's old boudoir. That's the only two places she ever hangs out when she's home alone. Because it's the only two places she can be sure she won't see any of the staff. And Brooks Clarke wasn't due back until tomorrow morning. Hannah thought of telling Greg they should go around the front, but his long legs had already climbed the steps of the porch. He peered in the kitchen windows. His breath fogged the glass.

"Not there?" Hannah asked, hand on her right hip. *This is amusing. Or maybe it's bemusing. I can't decide. Okay, Greg, keep playing your little game.*

Greg turned and narrowed his eyes. "Guess we'll have to go around to the front."

"Maybe she's not home."

"Well, we won't know until we ring the doorbell, will we? Sheesh. I thought you'd be happy I thought to bring Sky. We are like the perfect trio. The unholy trinity. Ha!" Greg trudged through the gravel drive, grazing the flowerbeds with his ankles as he walked. Hannah followed closely behind.

Suddenly, they heard a voice. It came from the front porch. Hannah grabbed Greg's arm.

"Shh!" She pulled his long body back. They ducked into the bleak darkness cast by the bushes onto the drive. The house was well-lit outside, but the sculptural landscaping still cast some shadows.

"What was that?" Greg whispered.

"I think it was a man's voice," Hannah replied softly. Her heart beat faster. Greg moved closer to the voices. Two voices now. Hannah begged him to stay back with furious nods and a death grip on his arm, but Greg was surprisingly strong when he wanted to be.

"C'mon. I want to see," he hissed.

The voice again. "I have to go."

A man.

Now the other voice. "Don't go yet."

Skylar.

202

Wait, Skylar? Who is she talking to? That's not Derrick's voice. What the hell is going on? Greg tiptoed through the maze of hedges and bushes and flower beds. The two were close but completely hidden by darkness. Hannah stepped on a branch and it snapped loudly.

"What was that?" the man said.

"See, I told you it's creepy out here. At least let me drive you to the train."

Then his face came into view. Aaron Samuels.

Greg turned to see Hannah's face, but it was so dark. If he could see Hannah's expression, he would have seen a girl who just got punched in the stomach and told her beloved chocolate lab got hit by a firetruck. That's the face Greg would've seen.

Hannah held on to Greg tight and this time he held her back. *I can't believe it.* She rubbed her eyes furiously...almost comically. *It can't be. But it is.* It was indeed Aaron Samuels. His face illuminated by the antique lamps outside the Clarke's entry. And then Skylar's bare arm stroked his jacketed one.

Time slowed to a stop. Like when the Film History teacher would pause Citizen Kane every other minute so that they could unpack every friggin' shot. At the time, Hannah thought it was torture. But seeing Aaron Samuels outside Skylar's door was a torture much worse.

Greg still held Hannah's arm; an electric coil buzzed between them. He sizzled with the scandal, she with rage.

"You can't drive me to the station, Skylar. You know that," Mr. Samuels growled. There was a masculine spice to his words. Like they were cologne. This was a different Aaron Samuels then Hannah saw at school. And a different one from the Aaron Samuels who dated her mother.

Skylar moved her body closer to his. She wore a thin camisole and tight leggings. Bra straps exposed, nipples hard against the night air. Her hair cascaded down her back from a loose ponytail. *If teen dream girls were my thing, well, Skylar would be it.*

"Please let me drive you," she cajoled.

Aaron licked his lips and looked around. No one there. *No one except us creepers in the bushes.* He took Skylar's face in his hands and kissed her deeply, unable to resist the beyond-her-years sexuality any longer. Greg gasped, and Hannah grabbed his arm tighter. He clasped his hand to his mouth and looked at Hannah. If he could see her face—which he still couldn't—Greg would have seen a single tear moistening each cheek.

"We have to go," Hannah whispered. The two lovers still groping and sucking and smacking. The noises churned in her stomach like that day's lunch—a sandwich from Subway and an undercooked chocolate chip cookie. Her legs quaked. Hannah worked to find her footing.

"Shh!" There was no way Greg was missing this. Then Hannah noticed something she hadn't before. Greg's phone placed high in the air. A perfect shot of this illicit affair. Hannah stepped closer. She could hear Greg's breath between his flint-locked shoulder blades.

They stayed a few more agonizing minutes. The fake breathless moans of Skylar. Sounds Hannah recognized. Like when Skylar spent seven minutes in heaven letting Jake Whaley do God-know-what to her in the tenth grade.

Greg almost inaudibly, "Oh. Em. Gee."

Finally, Mr. Samuels broke away.

Did you just figure out you're a pedophile? Or are you afraid you'll be late for the train?

He trotted down the steps without saying good-bye. And off down the long apple-blossom-lined driveway he went. Mr. Samuels would be on time for his train. No one would see him with Skylar. Well, no one except Greg and Hannah. And school and rehearsal would go on as normal. Hannah imagined him thinking how he tried to end the affair. *Self-righteous ass.* So many times — he tried. Hannah remembered the spied text messages on Skylar's phone at Easter. *Didn't he try so, so hard? But Skylar wouldn't let up. It probably happened in his last school too. Disgusting.*

Hannah watched Mr. Samuels walk until he faded into the darkness. She thought of racing to Greg's car and mowing him down the way she'd run Will Bartlett off the road. *Doesn't Aaron Samuels know what I'm capable of?* If Hannah was able to kill sweet Will and put even sweeter Zoe in a coma, imagine what she could do to the man who was cheating on her beloved mother.

This guy has no idea.

Then Hannah turned her attention back to Skylar. She shivered without her man-toy pressed up against her. Arms folded across her ample breasts. Swaying back and forth as she watched Aaron walk away. She had him. He wouldn't be done with her until she was done with him.

This was so easy for her.

Hannah imagined the smirk on Skylar's face. The same smirk she had when they sent Paige to the hospital with a broken ankle. The same smirk she had when Sarah Young left the theatre in disgrace. It was the expression of a person who could bend gravity to her will. A tyrant. An empress.

It was that moment. Well, probably that moment, that Hannah decided to take Skylar Clarke down.

They waited in the dank bushes a few minutes more. Skylar's maid called her from inside the house and Skylar scampered back in. Greg left the headlights off as he sped down Skylar's driveway. He made distasteful jokes about how crazy it would be if he were to accidentally hit a drifting Mr. Samuels on the side of the winding road.

"He's probably at the train already," Hannah said flatly.

Innocent Greg had no idea how to process what just happened. Hannah asked about the video.

"What are you going to do with it, Greg?"

He replied coyly, "With what?"

"With the freakin' TMZ video you just took. What are you going to do?"

"I'll bide my time. I'll use it at just the right moment," he postured.

You have no clue what you're talking about. Idiot.

Hannah channeled the one person who would know how to play this situation. Skylar. She summoned up some tears, "Listen, if you post that, you'll be hurting my mom."

"I would never—"

"Oh, shut up, Greg!" Hannah raised her voice. His knuckles went white on the steering wheel, "Send it to me. I have to show her privately first. She can't go on dating this—this scumbag."

Greg drove in silence for a minute. *I have him. He loves my mom.* Gillian Cross was one of the first teachers Greg came out to last year. She even let Greg dominate a whole Film Club meeting with his queer theory reading of the movie Frozen. And she stared down anyone (anyone!) who would breathe a whisper of ridicule. *Greg would never publicly humiliate her. I know it. He knows it. Just needed some reminding.*

When they stopped at a light, he picked up his phone. Click, tap, send.

And then Hannah's phone chimed with victory. There was the video.

"Thank you," she murmured.

"Your mom deserves better."

"Hey, Hannah!" Gillian Cross looked up from her chamomile and British mystery show to greet her daughter.

Hannah sat on the chair opposite the couch and stared at her mother. *I should show her. Show her right now.* Gillian's sweet face looked younger than her years in the glow from the television.

But her daughter hesitated. *No, I need to think this through. I could show Mr. Samuels tomorrow at rehearsal. Pull him aside under the guise of showing him some amazing Midwest show choir performance on YouTube. Then. Bam! Play the video.* A nefarious smile rose to Hannah's lips. But the sweet emotion that accompanies thoughts of revenge was replaced quickly but another glance at her mother.

All the control Hannah felt in the car melted away. *How does Skylar do it? She is a master of spinning these webs, of maneuvering.* Skylar knew the answers to unsolvable riddles. Skylar would set everyone off. Then she'd sit back and watch. All of them clucking like chickens. How many secrets and sins did Skylar keep locked in her heart to wield so much power over Whispering Hills Country Day?

"Oh, Skylar called the house." Gillian said as she brought her teacup to the sink. "I forgot we even had a house number," she laughed.

Hannah looked at her phone. At least ten text messages from Skylar and two missed calls as well. Hannah had ignored those bleeps and blips in the car with Greg. Too focused on working him over. She looked at the time stamps again. Immediately after Samuels left, Skylar tried to contact her. *She can't be alone in that big house for more than five minutes.*

Anger bubbled up again as Hannah thought of how much space Skylar had to herself. All that room in Clarke mansion. So spoiled. *I can't go ten feet at home without bumping into my sticky brother or an even stickier bag of recycling he forgot to take out. If I lived in Clarke mansion, I wouldn't take it for granted.* Hannah thought of reading in the sunroom, bathing in one of the home's eleven bathrooms, watching television in the home theatre, practice yoga in the fitness room. *And Skylar resents all of it.*

"Mom, there's something I need to show you," she began.

Gillian turned on her heels and walked slowly from the kitchen.

She's praying I'm not pregnant right now. Hannah tried not to roll her eyes.

"I'm not pregnant."

"Oh, I—I didn't think that. Your voice was just so solemn," Gillian laughed it off.

"Well, you can't get pregnant without having sex." Hannah thought ruefully of this fact. Her lack of sex life now seemed a failure. Hadn't everyone lost their virginity by senior year? Everyone except prudes like Zoe Kellogg. *Shoot, I'm going to go to college still carrying my V-Card.*

"You don't have to have sex, Hannah. It's fine to wait until you're ready…" Gillian kept going. The same speech she'd given Hannah before. Gillian had Hannah at 22. She fell hard for her ex. He was an adjunct professor. He seemed so capable, but he was a disappointment.

Ugh, this again.

"Aaron is cheating on you," Hannah blurted out in frustration. Her mother nearly choked on her last word.

"What?"

"He's cheating on you. You need to break it off," Hannah declared, finding her strength. *I've been right all along.*

Gillian cocked an eyebrow, "Umm, how did this become about my relationship? And you don't need to worry about me and Aaron. I know you don't like Aaron, but you don't need to make up lies. And furthermore, he introduced you to that Broadway star Starla whatever."

"Stella McKay!" Hannah cried. *Why does she never pay attention to what I like to do?*

"Yes, Stella McKay, who then got you a Tisch audition. You're likely going to NYU now precisely because of Aaron's generosity. You should think about that," Gillian rejoined.

"Mom! Listen to me!" Hannah's voice was shrill with exasperation. The tears rose to her eyes and brimmed there on the edge of her lashes.

Gillian fell silent.

Hannah took a deep breath, "I'm not lying. I'm not being ungrateful. We didn't end up going to the diner tonight. When Greg and I went to pick up Skylar, we saw Aaron and Skylar on her front porch. They were, um, kissing. And that's putting it mildly."

Now it's out. Hannah was relieved for a second. *What do I say next?*

"That's ridiculous!"

"Yes, it's ridiculous and it's disgusting," Hannah replied before her mother could say more. "But it's true. Greg was there."

"No, you must have seen wrong," Gillian shook her head wildly. She started to cry.

Hannah couldn't contain her tears after her mother started to weep. She cried, "I'm sorry, mom. I don't' want it to be true."

"Hannah, he's an adult and Skylar is a student. Maybe you didn't see it right. I know that in your heart, no one will be good enough for me. That you're worried about another man like your father. But Aaron isn't like that."

"Mom! Stop! Stop, psychoanalyzing me. This has nothing to do with dad. And speaking of dad and Aaron, I'm pretty sure dad wins in the decency category. At least dad doesn't hook up with teen girls."

"Skylar is hardly a girl," Gillian lashed out. She wished the words could be erased the moment she uttered them.

"And now you're defending this asshole?"

She's kidding right? Skylar was the devil incarnate but the accountability for this affair still fell on Aaron's manly shoulders. Now Hannah saw it clearly. *This is how your marriage was allowed to linger on so long.* Flashes of her mother rationalizing her father's bad behavior sparked in Hannah's mind. She pitied her mother. It was a weird sensation for a daughter.

The video was cued up. Hannah didn't even realize she was doing it until she was handing the phone to her mother. Pressing play. Gillian looked at her daughter suspiciously, "What? What is this?"

"Just watch it."

When the video ended, they sat in silence for what seemed like an hour. Only the sound of sniffles and the whizz of the dishwasher. Gillian still held the phone. Then she started pressing on it. Figuring something out.

"Mom, what are you doing with my phone?"

"Deleting this filth," she spat.

"Mom, don't—" Hannah jumped up from her chair but it was too late.

Gillian handed her back the phone. She got up and walked toward her bedroom, "I'll end it. But you don't need to be involved." She closed the door behind her.

Hannah ran upstairs to her room. She sat on her bed, gripping her phone, and waited until her heartbeat slowed. Yes, her mother deleted the video from the photos app. But when she opened up her messages from Greg, there it was. *Thank God adults know nothing about technology.*

From the downstairs, she could hear the muffled sounds of her mother crying and yelling on the phone. All of a sudden, Hannah was a little girl again, listening to her father and mother bickering. Hannah felt small and vulnerable. She piled blankets over her body. Earbuds in. Listening to Stella McKay's recording of "Out Tonight" from the reboot of RENT.

Just as Hannah drifted off, her phone pinged.

> BW: how was
> ur day?

Brody. I can stay awake for this.

> HC:
> interesting.
> yours?

His texts came quickly.

> BW: I'm
> exhausted.
> And I didn't get
> to see u.

Suddenly glare of her phone screen didn't bother her eyes. Another text before Hannah could craft a coy reply.

> BW: can i pick
> u up for school
> on Monday??

Hannah thought for a moment. A ride to school from Brody would definitely trump her usual transportation: her mom's beat up minivan that first drove Ricky through the carpool line at Oakbrook Middle School. But would Cynthia be in the car. She decided to make him work for it.

HC: I have to
ask my mom
but she's
asleep. Can I
text in the
morning?
BW: come on!
Cynthia and i
just got new
cars. finally
reaping the
benefits of
Dad's
dealership.

Cynthia won't be there. She'd definitely want to drive her own car to school. She wouldn't care that it's a douche move to take two coveted parking spots in the student lot when both students came from the same house, the same uterus.

HC: Wow!!
Congrats!!
Graduation
present?

BW: no, at
least not right
now. But it
might be once
my parents
see the tuition
at Hofstra.
LOL.

HC: I thought
u were playing
Lax for them

212

BW: I am. But
no scholarship
with it. That
team is
competitive.
HC: but at
least u have a
new Lex

BW: preowned

HC: OMG! ur
sooooo
spoiled

BW: LOL. I
know. Pick u
up at 7:10.

That's early, Hannah thought. She set her alarm a half
hour earlier. *Fifteen minutes for Brody's early bird pick up time
and fifteen minutes for primping. Hashtaaaaggg woke up like this!*

Chapter Thirteen
Hell Week

From: Stella McKay <smckay@yahoo.com>
To: Hannah Cross <hannah.cross@whcds.edu>
Date: Sun, Apr 19, 2018 at 2:37pm
Subject: Shh! Don't tell Aaron!

Hi there,

Can you send me the dates and times for your show? Oh, and the address of your school. I'm coming to see it! And I'm bringing Tad. Tad Conrad. But I don't want Aaron to know. So, keep it a secret between us.

Thanks! Can't wait.
Best,
SMc

Hannah waited by the window. *Five minutes until Brody will be outside. Hmmm. Let's look up Stella's boyfriend on IMDB again.*

Tad Conrad. Mostly a television director with some Broadway credits. Hannah had scoured the Internet for clues ever since the email came on Sunday afternoon.

She scrolled. *Okay, CSI, CSI: Miami, CSI something else. Ooh, and two episodes of Glee.*

A car honked outside and without even looking up, Hannah went to greet Brody. Only day three of rides to school and it was routine. Their carpool included some major make-out sessions too.

Hannah welcomed the distraction. This was Hell Week. The term, borrowed from Navy SEAL training, means rehearsal late into the night. Hannah's been known to get home after midnight. Rehearsals finish at 10 p.m. and then there's the ninety minutes of notes to sit through. The run-throughs never start on time because they are always waiting on some errant musician running late from the city.

It's an awful and wonderful week. All the kids walk around school in their cast T-shirts with the name of the show on the front and performance dates on the back. Waffle knit long sleeves from Abercrombie poking out. Leggings hugging bodies drummed tight with doing the numbers "full out." Scarfs coiled around sore throats. And Uggs. So. Many. Uggs.

Hannah's toes curled in her black cardy Uggs as Brody kissed behind her ear. He loosened the scarf on her neck. *How can I be expected to concentrate in calculus after this?* Hannah thought of the 67 she got on the latest quiz.

Brody made his way back to her mouth. Everything was warm. Even the ground outside was warmer, little purple crocuses pushing their way through hard wintered soil and spitefully blooming.

A powerful knock on the driver's side window startled them both. *If this is one of his meathead friends…* But it wasn't one of Brody's teammates. And when Hannah saw Dean Feldman's ruddy face, she wished herself invisible. "Uh, Dean Feldman," Brody quickly found the buttons to bring the window down.

I'm so screwed, Hannah thought. *God, I hope he doesn't tell my mother. Is there even a code for this behavior on our detention slips?*

Dean Feldman grimaced, "We'll have none of that. Step out of the car. The bell is about to ring." It was his disciplinarian voice, the one that spoke 'comply or your life at this school will be very different.'

They gathered their bags and began walking to the doors. But Dean Feldman seemed preoccupied. Hannah began to relax. *What's going on? Are we in trouble? I'm not going to ask but it seems like our make-out sesh isn't a top priority in the world of Pat Feldman. At least not today. Could we actually be this lucky? Usually he lives for this shit.*

"There are a few students the detectives want to meet with again. Hannah, you're one of them," then a flash of doubt, "at least I think it was you, Hannah." A hesitant hand rose to his cleanly shaven chin. "Yes, I believe it was. Come to my office during homeroom."

Then he picked up the pace leaving Hannah and Brody a few steps behind, navy Vineyard Vines wool pants swishing more intentionally. The dean looked back, "And I'm going to pretend I didn't see you two going at it. Mr. Wolcott, the student parking lot is not a place to take your dates. Ms. Cross, you should know better."

Brody nodded obediently. All of a sudden, he looked like a little boy to Hannah.

"Don't let it happen again," the dean added and trotted up the front steps of the school.

"Yes, sir."

Hannah looked at Brody. Her heart sank. *The detectives need to talk to me again. She thought of the last time and felt queasy. And Brody was no use.* He shrank in front of Dean Feldman. He would be no protection against the law. *And why would he want to protect me? If knew what really happened...*

As they walked through the halls, Hannah felt everyone's eyes on her. Comments made behind locker doors. Surreptitious glances. *Are they looking at me and Brody?* Her knees wobbled. *Was Brody seeing this?* She focused on getting to her locker. A boy leaned up against it. His back to her. Hannah's eyes narrowed. The hair was right. The silhouette. *Will? Yes, it's him. He didn't die.*

"Oh my God! Will!" Hannah ran to the boy, placing her hand on a muscled shoulder.

"What?" he jerked around. His face scrunched up with confusion and agitation. Brody stepped into the space between them.

"Hannah, are you okay?" Brody weaved his arm through hers.

The boy shook his head and scuttled away. "Drama queen," he muttered under his breath.

"I'm fine," Hannah replied. *But I'm not fine. And why is everyone looking at me?*

Cynthia ran up. Eyes big with excitement. "Did you guys hear? Samuels is out. Fired!" Her voice raced to catch her breath. "Sexual misconduct with a student!"

"Holy shit," Brody laughed uncomfortably.

Hannah's mouth wagged open. Her first thought was of her mother. She needed more information. And she needed it now. "How did you find out? Did this happen this morning? Is he here right now? What about Sky--" Hannah fired the questions stopping short of Skylar's name.

Cynthia's brow furrowed adorably. She loved being the center of attention, so she didn't catch Hannah's mention of Skylar. "Calm down, girl. I don't know much more than that. But that's what everyone is talking about."

Looking around the corridor once more, Hannah could see it. The students were abuzz with the news, the speculating. Cynthia tittered on. Her voice sounded like the jingle from a laundry detergent commercial. She always knew it. Samuels looked at her weirdly. Like he wanted something. His eyes were so beady and unnerving. She was glad she was never alone with him.

Brody interjected, "Cynthia, maybe we should stop talking about it. Hannah, I think we should get you to class."

Hannah barely noticed as Brody switched her books from her bag.

"Calc, right? Then AP Gov?"

She nodded obediently, and the couple walked to third floor for her class. All eyes gave Hannah a scan. After all, the relationship between her mother and Mr. Samuels was a known quantity at school. And students loved Gillian Cross. And Mr. Samuels was unknown at best and disliked at worst. A new teacher who didn't make a great impression. *They pity me. My single mom played by a man who liked 'em young.* Hannah's skin crawled.

Mixed with the hatred for Samuels and sympathy for her mother was an unexpected feeling of liberation. Hannah walked in the school thinking the detectives were there to arrest her, that all the students knew about Zoe and Will. But that wasn't the case. The students didn't know her dirty secret. She was safe in the eyes of her classmates, her cast, and especially Brody. Hannah spent the whole day walking by students who quieted when she appeared. And yet, she was grateful. *Dean Feldman might have been mistaken this morning. Confused me with someone else. No one knows about me and the accident. No one except me and Skylar knows.*

Later that afternoon, rehearsals plunged forward. No director? No problem. This was still Hell Week. Mr. Samuels had painstakingly put together the immaculate timepiece that was Stagecraft. All they needed to do was rehearse in costume. Besides, Ms. Panzini was back. So was Sarah Young.

Paige, giddy with hope, had news about her sister. Zoe showed signs of waking. After almost eight weeks in a coma, Zoe was going to return to the world of the conscious. At least that's what the doctors said.

"And Daddy's a doctor. And Daddy knows lots of great doctors. We're so happy," she gushed to other sophomores and a few crew members.

Hannah's bubble of reassurance burst in such slow motion she felt herself the star in a Lifetime movie. The news felt like gravel getting poured on Hannah's legs. She couldn't move. *No, this can't be happening. Zoe has to stay in a coma. She has to stay asleep.* NYU, Brody, the rest of senior year flashed before her eyes. Memories ruined before they were even made.

Hannah looked around furiously. Skylar would know what to do. Just like she knew what to do in ninth grade after Hannah let Jacob Wiseman put his balmy video game hands up her shirt at Brandi Gerard's birthday party. Jacob told everyone that would listen. That is, until Skylar put an end to it. It was then that Hannah knew Skylar would always protect her. And her gut hurt thinking of how much she loathed Skylar's entitlement. But Hannah needed Skylar's privilege and the badassery that accompanied being the richest girl in school.

Bounding Hannah's way — fast as those crutches could take her — Paige wore a smile like Christmas morning and overdosing on Halloween candy rolled into one. "Did you hear, Hannah? Zoe is getting better. We are going to see her this evening. But only for a little bit. The doctors don't want to overwhelm her either."

"That's great news," Hannah lied.

Paige held Hannah's hand for a moment. "Oh my God, did you see who's back?"

"Yeah, Ms. Panzini."

"I know! Can you believe about Mr. Samuels? Is your mom okay?" Paige asked with such sincerity Hannah felt her heart break in two.

"I'm sure she'll be fine. She's better off. Really." Hannah had been practicing these lines all day. She continued, "I mean, an affair with a student? Jeez. I think she's glad she dodged that bullet."

With the lines delivered perfectly, Hannah began to feel more comfortable. Then she spotted Sarah Young. Paige noticed immediately, "I asked Ms. Panzini to bring her back. We need her." Paige looked down at her ankle, "It wasn't her fault. Sarah is the best stage manager. Sure, she yells at us a lot but it's all out of love, right?"

Hannah tried to collect herself, "Yeah…uh, right." Sarah Young flashed Hannah a confident grin. *She knows. She's figured this out. I can't be around her.*

Spotting Skylar across the auditorium, Hannah motioned her head towards the doors. "Hey, Paige, I'll be back. I have to pee before we all sit through Panzini's notes."

"Sure, Hannah. I'll cover for you if she starts."

Once outside the auditorium, Skylar and Hannah—as if an invisible string connected them—took completely different routes to the third-floor bathroom. The one far away from the dorky Speech & Debaters in the Writing Lab. Far away from the gym where dutiful Student Council members were setting up for the Leadership Assembly, set to happen that night. Hannah thought of all the proud parents, how they would perch on their seats with haughty tallness. *A fifth of the school gets an award. That's almost a hundred kids.* Hannah got a Leadership Award when she was VP of Film Club, an organization that met once a month (if that). She did nothing. And yet, a pin with a self-important Latin adage still decorated the lapel of her dress blazer.

Then Hannah thought of the musical cast and crew. *We're the hard workers. Not these nerds getting pins.* The cast had their spray tan armor on. They wore their exhaustion proudly. Without a doubt, whoever got pinned at this Leadership Assembly was weak compared to the theatre kids.

She found Skylar in the bathroom doing a sweep. There she was—Hannah's General since the ninth grade. *Skylar will know how to handle Zoe waking. Won't she? And we should stick together. Shouldn't we? I have to put this Aaron Samuels stuff aside…for now. Be the lieutenant once more.*

The expression on Skylar's face spoke otherwise. *She doesn't have her shit together.* She didn't have a plan, Hannah could tell. Like the time Skylar cheated on a Math quiz in ninth grade. She bawled to Hannah about what her mother would say. How her sister would never do such a shameful thing, And Hannah had to console her. A reverse pieta.

With that realization, all the resentment and anger came back. *If she can't come up with a plan now, what good is she? I need Skylar to calm me down. Not the other way around.*

"I guess you heard that—" Hannah began but Skylar interrupted.

"Zoe is waking up. Yeah, I heard. I'm freaking out, Hannah. What if she wakes before the show and I lose my part? She's the only person who would remember!" Skylar paced back and forth, "Hannah, I can't lose my part because of something you did."

Is she kidding me? I don't believe this. Hannah's mouth dropped open. "You were there too! You were a maniac. Follow them. Run them off the road. It was all you. You grabbed the steering wheel. How was I supposed to drive when you were being such a beast?" Hannah shouted. Skylar stepped back. And Hannah leaned in further, unable to surpress the fury inside her. *She's broken right now. And I'm going to lay it out there. She's going to hear everything.*

Hannah remembered Greg's comment—you kind of control her. His words emboldened Hannah and she continued, "And all because Will Bartlett knew what was good for him and left you. You were a bitch to him, so he left. And you never got over it. Zoe was a better performer. And she was a better girlfriend."

"Shut up, Hannah! Just shut up!" Skylar began to cry. Hannah immediately felt vindicated and sorry at the same time. *This is her fault! Don't feel bad for her. But she looks so helpless.*

I've won something just now. I'm not sure what, but I've won. Furthermore, someone might overhear them no matter how isolated this bathroom was. Hannah went on, this time more softly, "We are both responsible. Stop trying to pin it only on me."

But Skylar never understood soft. She never respected kindness or empathy—the hallmarks of good friendship. She stood a little straighter and fired back, "No, Hannah. The driver is still responsible. You knew I was still drunk from the night before. You knew I would freak out if I saw them. You knew what you were dealing with and still you let me fly off the handle."

The words sank in for a moment. *I should have protected Will from Skylar. I should have protected Zoe. Maybe I should have protected Katie Greco too. Is this all my fault? Is she right?* Hannah shook her head. *No, this is another con. Everything with this girl is a con.*

Hannah took out her phone and quickly retrieved the detective's card from the front of her backpack. *Let's see if Skylar will call the bluff.* "I'm done, Skylar. You're right. I'm guilty. I'm going to call the police now." Instead, Hannah cued up the video, "And I'll be sure to let them know to question you too. Considering it's your car, driving from your house, and you're the type with loose morals anyway."

Hannah turned the phone around and watched Skylar's face contort and twist. It's the ugliest she'd ever been. *Check and mate.*

Skylar watched, and the moments plodded by. An aching for Skylar but aches of pleasure for Hannah. *Finally, the upper hand with the girl who terrorizes the whole school.*

"Where did you—"

Hannah interrupted right away. *No, Skylar, you don't get to ask questions.* "Doesn't matter where I got it. Doesn't matter how I know. It only matters that you're the one. The student that Mr. Samuels was sleeping with. I wish I could say I'm shocked but I'm not."

Skylar paced faster and faster, running her hands through her lovely brown hair, "You can't go to the police, Hannah. You can't do this to—"

"To you? Oh, I can. But I'm not going to the police. Listen, we both have a horse in this race, I'm going to NYU next year. Zoe isn't going to screw that up. We'll go to the hospital tonight—"

"I'm not going there! What if she wakes up and points right at us?" Skylar's mouth twisted. "You're crazy, Hannah."

Hannah put her hand up. *Stop. Now.* The roles were reversed, and Hannah enjoyed this alternate universe she'd stepped into. "You're going with me."

"I don't want to go," Skylar whined.

Then calm as a sky after a thunderstorm and clear blue too, Hannah declared, "And I don't want to have to upload this video to YouTube. But everyone is dying to know who had sex with a teacher. And we must give the people what they want."

"Fine." The word stuck in Skylar's mouth. "I'll come. Don't upload the video. I'm sorry for it. It got out-of-hand. I'm sorry about your mom."

Hannah softened at Skylar's apology. *Is the apology sincere? Maybe it did get out-of-hand. Maybe she is sorry.* Sincere or not, it was an apology. And an apology from Skylar Clarke was like spotting a unicorn dressed in a Yeti costume.

"It's done now. You did what you did. You can't take it back. You're coming with me tonight. Pick me up after rehearsal," she marched toward the door.

"Wait? What is the plan, Hannah? Are we going to kill her? Together?" Skylar smiled a little too earnestly at the thought.

"Just pick me up after rehearsal. I have a plan."

"What about us? Are we good?"

Hannah slammed the bathroom door.

Skylar arrived on time. They drove in complete silence to the hospital. Silence except Skylar's nasty cough. Too many cigarettes. Hannah wondered what thoughts swirled in Skylar's stormy mind but dared not ask. *This is poker. I need to keep a stoic face at all costs.*

When they got to the hospital, Skylar did her good girl routine and the two scooted past the nurses. They murmured about how Skylar was such a sweet friend. How you never forget the friends you made in high school. Such a special time. Such a shame about Zoe's accident.

They stood in the doorway of Zoe's room for a few heavy moments. This lovely girl whose chest rose and fell with such peace would undo both of them. Throughout these past weeks, there were times when Hannah wanted Zoe to wake up. Zoe would take control of the horrid situation, even if it meant Hannah's ruin. A catharsis at the end of a Greek tragedy. And Hannah held up as the cautionary tale. She almost craved the punishment. She knew she deserved it even though it made her tremble.

But not tonight. Zoe needed to stay in her medicine-induced dreams. And as far as Hannah was concerned, Zoe should remain there for the rest of her days. *There's just too much too lose now.*

"So…what's your big plan?" Skylar began and coughed again.

"Paige said that Zoe showed signs of waking. We are going to talk to her while she's still asleep. Remind her how we are all good friends. Tell her that she doesn't know who was driving the other car. Convince her that we had nothing to do with it. If we talk to her enough…"

Skylar violently pulled Hannah into the bathroom.

"That's the plan?" Skylar's face reddened, "God, you're an idiot. You want to talk to her? And then what, bring in a hypnotist?"

"I've heard that coma patients can hear you. I think if we talk to her…maybe come back a few times. She'll believe us…or, or, at least be confused when she gets up."

Skylar put her hands on the counter and stared in the mirror.

Hannah tried again, "It's worth a shot. According to the websites I've been reading, you're supposed to talk to loved ones, tell them about your day. Some people wake up having heard everything that happened around them while they were asleep."

"Fine," Skylar groaned and wagged her head.

Walking back out into the room, they surrounded Zoe's bed. Hannah took Zoe's limp hand. It felt old and lifeless. She looked at Zoe's blanketed body, her sunken cheeks, her pale neck.

"Zoe," Hannah began. "It's Hannah and Skylar. We are here to visit you again. We miss you so much at school." Hannah chatted without response about school, the show, Paige. *Ignore Skylar. Ignore the death in her eyes.* "She's so good, Zoe. Her ankle is healing well. I think she will be able to do some stuff in the show."

After a few minutes it didn't seem weird anymore, just like talking to a friend. Hannah even laughed at her own jokes about Cynthia and Greg. "And I need to tell you about Mr. Samuels. He got fired. So, Ms. Panzini took over for him. Teacher drama never disappoints, right?"

For a split second, Hannah could see a smirk on Zoe's face. She would never gossip about anyone but always loved hearing the "juice."

"Yeah, he was fired," Skylar chimed in, smiling coyly at Hannah. *Good she's finally talking. Maybe she agrees with me.*

But Skylar didn't agree. After a few more coughs, she frowned, "Fired for sexual misconduct. Sex with moi. And he was sleeping with Hannah's mother too. What can I say? I'm irresistible. Will knew it too. I bet you hated having my slopping seconds."

"Skylar, stop." Unknowingly Hannah gripped Zoe's hand even tighter.

"This is never going to work. We have to make sure she doesn't wake up. Like for good."

Hannah's rib cage contracted. *What did she just say? Did I hear her right?* "We can't make sure of anything. She could stay in a coma forever or wake up after we leave. That's why we have to play the long game."

"I was never one for patience," Skylar grinned.

"What are you doing?"

Skylar fiddled with wires behind the hospital bed. "Looking for where to unplug Princess Vegetable."

"What?" Hannah's voice caught in her throat and cracked when the word came out.

"You heard me. It would be a mercy."

"She could still wake up," Hannah griped. *She's just screwing around. Just messing with me.*

A head popped up from the other side of the bed, "A mercy for you. You're pathetic right now. We aren't going to come here every night and con Zoe into thinking that the crash didn't happen."

Hannah called the bluff, "You don't even know what you're doing back there. The moment you mess with anything, all these machines are going to freak out. The nurses will rush in and resuscitate her."

"Found it," Her voice was small from behind the bed, hoarse even.

Hannah rushed around to see Skylar contorted and following wires with her hands to different machines. "Found what?"

Skylar kept fiddling. Adjusting her body at different angles. The lulling beeps of the machines now sounded like ticking bombs. And Skylar was Jack Bauer from 24, diffusing the explosive that would ruin Hannah's life. Was she grateful in some dark recess of her soul?

———

227

"Found what?" Hannah repeated. *I could let her do this. Right now. I could be free of this.* The darkness like spilled wine spreading on a cream-colored duvet.

No answer still.

"Found what? Skylar, stop, or I'll go get the nurses."

Skylar lifted her body up and sighed, "You know nothing, Jon Snow." She stood, much to Hannah's relief, and dusted off her Lululemon yoga pants. At length, Skylar began, "All you have to do is unplug the ventilator. If it's unplugged, it can't beep. The patient loses oxygen and dies. That's how easy it is."

"How do you know this?" *I think I might vomit.* Hannah looked toward the bathroom. *How fast can I get to the toilet?*

"One of the perks of sitting through countless boring dinners with my dad and his friends. See, my dad is on the board of Harrison Hospital. And one time, this young doctor—another board member him brought along. I guess… for colorful conversation. Anyway, the doctor went on and on about the need to lock down the plugs. While he was in residency, a janitor unplugged a patient by accident, and they lost him. I mean, we could always go the pillow-over-the-face route. But that's pretty screwed up. Even for us."

The information sank in. *It's that easy. Terrifying but easy.* In disbelief that she was even rationalizing this proposal, Hannah applied to Skylar's logic, "If you unplug one of these machines, they will beep like crazy. Surely there is some, I don't know, mechanism, that tells the nurses in the hallway what's going on."

Skylar stepped over to one of the machines and flipped a switch. It kept doing its job of nagging the body to be alive without any sound. "Silence button," she replied flatly. Then Skylar flipped it back on and the device began its song again.

Of course. Skylar's mother. Hannah remembered how much time the Clarkes spent awaiting Mrs. Clarke's fate in hospice two years ago. Ironically, it was Trina who showed the family how to silence the machines. All those awful sounds that reminded everyone why they were gathered around the bed. Brooks Clarke heard the sounds even when he was at home. They haunted him.

Trina, already priming herself for assistant-turned-second-wife, obliged deftly, "See? They have a silence button. They go off all the time in hospice care. I remember from my grandmother." The room suddenly silent except for the lull of jazz music from the CD player Skylar's sister had placed next to the bed. Bethany Clarke had kept vigil at Mrs. Clarke's death bed. Half angel, like she was waiting to courier her mother's soul into heaven.

Skylar dutifully visited once a day. But she spent most of her time with Will. And, unable to see his wife dying or face the joy he felt with the impending freedom, Brooks Clarke barely showed his face at the hospital. But he was there that day. With Trina. And she made the beeping stop.

Skylar gestured to the device next to Zoe's head like a TV salesman. It was clear from Skylar's expression that she'd been thinking about her mom too. Hannah walked briskly to the machine and flipped the switch back on.

Looking at Zoe, Hannah began, "We can't do this. I won't let you kill her."

"She's already dead. I don't know what the hell those doctors are telling her family."

"How many coma patients do you know?" Hannah snapped.

"It's in the friggin' pamphlets out in the hall. If she didn't wake in the first month, the chances of Zoe waking up are slim."

A beat. Then Skylar was back underneath the bed.

Hannah grabbed her friend, "Skylar, no!" But Skylar swatted Hannah away and scratched her face.

"Ow!" Hannah cried. A little too loudly.

Just then, the machines around Zoe chimed with urgency. Sentient beings protecting their ward from these evil spirits around her. Zoe's eyelids fluttered. *Oh my God! She's moving. Wait, is she moving?* Hannah studied Zoe, unable to move. *No, I think she's still.*

Shouting out in the hallway. Then footsteps. With ninja quickness, Skylar grabbed Hannah's arm and pulled her back in the bathroom. Finger to mouth, Skylar motioned to be absolutely still.

The nurses rushed in. The girls stood statue-like and waited for the beeping and chiming to stop. Skylar suppressed her cough with great effort.

A voice, "The patient must have been agitated. Weren't there two girls in here?"

"No, the family left early." Nurse Amy's voice.

She covered for us, Hannah thought, realizing just how deep Skylar can tunnel into a person's mind. *She should never have let us in this late.* Hannah remembered Paige chirping away at rehearsal, *The doctors are optimistic, so we have to keep the visits short and very positive. She needs rest.*

"Good, because Dr. Rosenstein has a good feeling about this one. Could be any day now."

Hannah's heart quickened even more. She never realized this drum in her chest could beat so fast. *Zoe is going to wake up. The doctor says so. The doctors are always right. And Skylar was wrong. Zoe is going to wake up. And then they'll all know.*

More sounds from the room. Clicking and adjusting. Calling out numbers and recording data. Then Nurse Amy again, "But did he tell the family yet?"

"Let's leave that to him. It's his patient. We just need to be supportive when they find out."

"Find out what?" Hannah mouthed. Skylar shrugged.

Hannah moved toward the door, wanting more information, wanting her fate written on the walls of the dark room. The two nurses walked past the restroom. Nurse Amy spoke softly, "Poor girl. I heard she was a great singer. And now she will probably never walk or talk again. I hope Dr. Kellogg realizes it."

"He knows. But he's her father. So, he's holding out all hope. Poor man. Such a wonderful family."

"Yeah," Nurse Amy sighed. And they left the room.

A slow exhale from Hannah. Looking at Skylar, seeing only the whites of her eyes and the muffled glow of Skylar's phone in her hoodie pocket, Hannah saw something black open up inside her friend.

They stood over the bed once more. This time more careful. No holding Zoe's hand or arguing in fevered whispers.

"See?" Hannah began. "We don't have to do anything. Just short, positive visits." Flashes of voice lessons and rehearsals at NYU entered Hannah's imagination. Meeting Brody during holiday breaks. Traveling by train to see him play. Watching New York City progress through the school year in all its seasonal glory. *I can have all of that. And now I want nothing more.*

Skylar answered, "You're right. The odds of her recovering after a month are bad. This week will be eight weeks. With each passing day, she's more cucumber than human."

Hannah waited. They should leave but Skylar had this solemn expression, as if she were paying respects to the faithful departed. Skylar leaned in, "You always had the personality of a cucumber, Zoe Kellogg."

Hannah studied her friend's face. *It's like she doesn't have a heart. I'm out of here.* She walked to the door.

"We're not done here," Skylar's voice slithered to where Hannah stood. "We need to finish what we started."

The look of determination on Skylar's face was enough. She wanted Zoe gone. Only the dead can stay silent.

"I'm not doing this," Hannah blurted. "You're alone. I want no part of it."

Skylar walked to Hannah, "You want no part of it? You're the reason she's in this bed."

Hannah turned but Skylar grabbed her arm hard, "You're doing this."

Hannah yanked her arm back.

"If you leave…" Skylar's voice faltered. "If you go, you're done at school. You know that right?"

Hannah turned in the doorway and uttered with eerie calmness, "I guess it's the chance I'm willing to take."

She was halfway to the elevator and Hannah swore she could still hear Skylar breathing, seething. *Don't look back. Don't even dare look back.* She only waited a few minutes in front of the hospital. When the white Lexus RX pulled up and Brody smiled at her, Hannah swore he was wearing shiny armor and riding a white horse. *Reliable Brody.* By the time they waited at the traffic light at the exit from the hospital, Hannah felt her heart steady.

Chapter Fourteen
One Last Run Through

www.signupgenius.com

Strike the Set Party
Please RSVP below for the Strike the Set Party for Stagecraft. Also make sure you sign up for a time to work on cleaning up the stage.

And it's not on here but we are collecting money for flowers for both Paige and Zoe. You can Venmo my mom. She's @Jennifer-Young. We have to celebrate all our cast members. They are our family!

--Sarah Young, Student Director

Date: 04/26/2018 (Sun)
Time: 2:00pm EST
Location: Whispering Hills Country Day School, Clarke Theatre

Created by: Sarah Young [SY]

Available Slots:

Rice Krispies Treats 1 of 2 filled
[GT] Greg Tate

Water Bottles 3 of 4 slots filled
[SY] Sarah Young
[SY] Sarah Young
[SY] Sarah Young

Garbage bags 0 slots filled.

Starbucks Coffee 2 of 3 slots filled
[SC] Skylar Clarke
[CW] Cynthia Wolcott

Dunkin' Donuts Munchkins 0 slots filled

Hannah clicked the button for Rice Krispie treats. She and Greg would make them together. They always brought Rice Krispies treats to the Strike the Set party. Even put mini-M&Ms in them. Their friends would look for it.

Sitting at a back table in the library, Hannah scanned the area for enemies. Skylar vowed to make Hannah's life miserable at school and so far, the day had been just that—miserable.

A few girls stopped talking to Hannah altogether. Derrick spent AP Calculus glaring at her. And when Hannah had approached the lunch table, Skylar was stone. The look said it all: "Oh, you can sit here. But I'll verbally abuse you for the next 42 minutes." And Cynthia was sitting in Hannah's usual seat.

So, Hannah told the lunch monitor that she needed to study for a chem quiz. And she scarfed her ham and cheese sandwich on the way to the library. With its musty encyclopedias and old PCs, the library was the perfect hideout. Hannah sat with her phone propped up inside her binder.

> GC: What time
> is the "run
> through"?

Mom. Why is she texting me? Hannah smirked at the quotations around run through. The precise use of punctuation even in text messaging. *Ever the English teacher.*

> HC: 7 pm. we
> have to wait
> for some of the
> musicians to
> get here from
> the city

HC: I can get a
ride home.

Why does Mom want to know when the run through is?
This was Hell Week. Gillian Cross knew the deal. She barely
saw her daughter at all until she saw Hannah for two hours
straight on the Clarke Theatre stage.

GC: Ms.
Panzini says I
can come
watch.
[smiley face]

What? Mom was coming to watch the run through?
Hannah smiled involuntarily. *I'm surprised she remembers how
to get to the emojis on her keyboard. I bet one of the younger teachers
showed her,* Hannah giggled.

HC: Ok. I
guess I'll see you later then. Lol.

GC: What is
"lol" again?

Oh my God, Mom. Hopeless. Hannah texted back.

HC: nvrmnd.
i'll see u later

GC: Ok. Right.
Yes, you
shouldn't be
texting at
school.

HC: Then why
are u texting
me????

GC: I shouldn't
be. But I
couldn't find
you in the
lunchroom.

HC: I'm in the
library.

GC: Oh, okay.
Oxox.

Hannah sat gazing at chem notes for the next few minutes. *Maybe this will sink in by osmosis.* Exhausted, she put her head down and closed her eyes.

"Hannah…Hannah…" a sing-songy voice came from above Hannah's head. A light touch on her shoulder. Hannah opened her eyes and blinked rapidly. *Shit. I fell asleep.* She had that weird sensation that she'd fallen asleep for either ten minutes or 24 hours.

Still relishing her newly bestowed authority as director, Ms. Panzini smiled broadly, "This week is so taxing, I know. I hit my snooze button three times this morning."

"Yeah…Umm…what time is it? Did the bell ring?"

"You've got like eight minutes. It's still fifth period."

Thank God. And eight precious minutes to imbibe as much chemistry as possible before this quiz. But Ms. Panzini sat down across from Hannah. Her face still and serious. "I need to give you a heads up. We have one more run through tonight. Skylar needs to rest. I'm going to ask you to stand in."

"What?" Hannah's voice raised, and the librarian shot her a look. "What?" she whispered.

"You're the understudy for Aurelia. You can totally stand in tonight. Don't worry about your other features. I'll have a freshman mark them for the spotlights."

"I'm not worried about my features," Hannah raised an eyebrow. *Ms. Panzini knows. Before I'm agreeing to anything, I want to know about Skylar.*

Panzini took a deep breath, "I wanted you to be prepared. Skylar doesn't know yet. But she's been coughing for days and between you and me, she sounded awful yesterday. I want her to rest. Just for tonight."

It makes sense, I guess. Hannah took a big inhale and let the air out the side of her mouth slowly, cheek puffed like a blowfish. *And I'm already on Skylar's shit list. So why not add this to my infractions?*

"Okay. I can do it."

Panzini gave a cheesy thumbs up, "Of course you can! And I invited your mom to come watch. That way, she'll get to see you play the lead. It's a dress rehearsal so it's basically the show."

That last line stung a little. *No, it's not the show. The show is the show. It's a dress rehearsal. No audience and you yelling at us or rushing back to the lighting booth or waving your arms at the orchestra for everything to stop.*

But, of course, Hannah didn't say any of that. "Yeah, basically the show. Thanks for asking my mom. That was real nice of you."

The bell.

"You've got this, Hannah."

I've got this. I've got this. I've got this. Hannah chanted in her mind. But when she walked into Ms. Connor's AP Chemistry class, Skylar had already filled Hannah's seat with a new lab partner. Hannah padded to the back of the room as Ms. Connors handed out the quizzes.

A glance at Skylar — *still scowling at me.* A glance at the four-page booklet Ms. Connors called a quiz — *what the hell is Connors thinking?* And Hannah's chest tightened involuntarily. *Ugh. I really <u>don't</u> got this.*

The school's theatre was oddly cold. The last few days had seen the beginnings of spring in Westchester county, NY. But Clarke Theatre needed the warmth of 500 audience members to feel warm. Hannah grabbed her scarf out of her dance bag and coiled it around her neck.

Greg sat next to her, rubbing his hands together. Hannah considered him. Every action he did was performed as if he was on stage. *Does he actually feel the cold? Or does he know from all the stage experience that rubbing hands together shows the audience one of two things – you're cold or you're hatching an evil plan?*

"Here." Hannah handed him hot water with lemon and honey.

"Thanks," Greg smiled. "Phew, it's freezing in here. Spring…please awaken."

Hannah chuckled at her friend's reference to Spring Awakening. He never missed a chance to allude to a show.

Skylar walked up the aisle toward them, Cynthia with her. Hannah held her breath and waited. *Cynthia looks terrified. Finally, back where you want to be but at what cost? Please, Skylar, don't say anything to me. Silent treatment is just fine.* Hannah really didn't want to get baited into sparring with Skylar…because Hannah had a healthy sense of self-preservation.

Skylar stopped at their row and gave Greg a black look. Then she sat a few rows behind them. Cynthia held both of their Starbucks cups until Skylar was situated in her padded auditorium seat.

Greg was unphased. Hannah admired him for it. Then she remembered Greg's words that fateful night they discovered Skylar and Mr. Samuels. *Greg is sitting with me. He's choosing me. Is there something to that?*

He leaned in, "Guess I've been excommunicated as well. Team Hannah for the win."

"It's my fault. I'm sorry. You chose the losing team."

Greg scoffed, "The losing team? No, Hannah. You really have no idea, do you?"

Hannah stayed silent. *I shouldn't have made that "losing team" comment.* She felt guilty.

Greg continued, "I'm one of the only out kids at this school. You think this is first time someone has been mean to me? The only gay kid that has it worse is the Matt on the basketball team. But he never misses a three-pointer, so Matt is God's gay gift to Whispering Hills." Then a moment later, "I feel like there's a joke in there somewhere."

Hannah laughed a little too loudly.

Skylar called from behind, "What's so funny, Hannah Banana?"

Hannah Banana. Already three students had teased her this afternoon. It was the easiest nickname for anyone named Hannah. She was reminded of Katie Greco and Camp in the Round. "Every first-time camper needs a nickname! Hannah Banana!" Katie had laughed and the rest of the girls in the bunk joined the chorus.

And before that, there was what happened with Judith Stahl in the ninth grade. A nasty girl with an eraser-shaped head and acne-pocked cheeks, Judith had dared her to put the banana down there. It was her first sleepover with Whispering Hills kids. Hannah had heard stories about the rich kid school but never imagined she'd be endearing herself to her classmates by inserting fruit into her southern hemisphere. Hannah ducked into the bathroom and waited a few minutes. Waited until some pithy comeback came to her. When she emerged, Hannah began but Judith ran up and grabbed Hannah's arm. She waved it in the air triumphantly. "She did it! You nasty freak!"

Skylar knew all this, of course. Went along with the joke even. Everyone knew Hannah really didn't do...that. Still, the 'Hannah Banana' legend bled into the freshmen narrative that year. Got "out of hand" as Hannah had overheard Dean Feldman tell her mother. Dean Feldman had no power to stop the teasing though. And later that year — after the two friends had vowed to remain besties forever — Skylar put an end to Hannah Banana for good. She'd overheard a heavy-set defensive lineman taunt Hannah in the lunch line.

"Hannah Banana, Hannah Banana" he sang the words. Looking back, Hannah realized he probably had a crush and was trying to get her attention.

But Skylar wasn't suffering some football meathead taunting her girl. "Banana? Can you even find it in all that blubber?" Enough classmates were in the lunch line. From then on, no one called Hannah by that name.

Until now. Today, Hannah had been "Hannah Banana" at least three times. Her Skylar protection switched off. The whole school knew it.

As Hannah sat deciding on a retort, she was alerted to the feeling that Hannah Banana didn't bother her anymore. *So, freshman year, she thought. The name doesn't mean anything. It's just a stupid nickname. Ancient history.*

But Skylar's furious energy emanated all the way from three rows back and made Hannah spill the hot water with lemon on her leggings. She winced at the burning pain. A sense of dread washed over her. *If this was one school day without Skylar Clarke — what does the rest of senior year look like? What does prom look like? Graduation festivities?*

"Hannah Banana! What are you and Greg talking about?" Skylar shouted again.

Greg answered Skylar back, "Just three pointers and homos. That's all. Nothing you'd be interested in!"

"I didn't ask you, Greg." Skylar snapped — the edge to her voice created another fit of coughs.

240

Greg leaned in, "Don't worry. This will calm down after the show. She's on a 'diva high' right now. You know how she is. She's done it to Cynthia. And to me." He paused before adding, "Skylar's showing everyone she can do it to you too."

"Yeah, I've seen the diva before. Still, it's sucks when you're the target," Hannah sighed.

"Hmm, maybe you'll see it differently now."

The words fell on Hannah and the guilt set in. *He's right. I'm awful to him and Cynthia when Skylar wants me to be. I just take cues from her. Do her bidding.* It was a long time coming but Hannah saw how intoxicated she was by Skylar Clarke. The word "toxic" right there in the middle in all CAPS. The word "toxic" now burned in her mind.

Mercifully, Ms. Panzini called the cast together for rehearsal. Mostly notes about the "Big City Ballet" towards the end of the first Act. "We need to run the part where Aurelia gets her purse stolen and the song speeds up. Go to your places for outside Ray's Pizza joint," Panzini called over her reading glasses. The cast collectively rose and walked to their places. Hannah instinctively went to her spot with the rest of the chorus.

"Okay, from that part in the music, please."

And the conductor waved his wand. And the band played a few bars before.

"5-6-7-8!"

After two more runs from the same spot, Ms. Panzini walked up to Skylar.

Hannah strained to hear their conversation. Skylar's face reddened.

"I'm fine!" Everyone heard Skylar shout. Then she cleared her throat some more.

"Go home and rest. We need you, Skylar. We need you fresh for the actual shows."

Dismissed from rehearsal. No one had ever dismissed Skylar from a rehearsal. If Skylar cut rehearsal, well, that was one thing. She'd been known to hang out under the bleachers sipping Peach Schnapps. But she hadn't missed one second of rehearsal this year.

Skylar turned to leave the stage but after a few steps, she swiveled back around. "And who is going to play the lead tonight? Hannah? Good luck with that shit!"

"Language, Ms. Clarke!" Ms. Panzini widened her stance.

"Or what? You're going to tell me I can't play the lead tomorrow? You know that won't fly. Even if I have pneumonia, I'm getting on this stage."

Ms. Panzini stood perfectly erect; a coldness flashed in her eyes. She wasn't going to back down. But Jill Panzini wasn't an idiot either. *No way she goes toe to toe with Skylar,* Hannah thought. *She'll be fired by Monday. And we'll all get told some bullshit story about a sick family member and Panzini needing time off. Or a bogus line about her fiancé taking a job in Boston or Charlottesville.*

Tentative murmurs from backstage followed the achingly long moments of this stand-off. Skylar finally packed her things and left. Hannah imagined Skylar peeling out of the lot in her Range Rover and almost hitting Ms. Connors who invariably stayed late to grade those quizzes.

Cynthia came up behind Hannah. "Hey, congrats! You'll do great. And don't be nervous—it's just a dress rehearsal."

Despite Hannah's best efforts to be pissed at Cynthia for joining forces with Skylar all day, Hannah responded with a smile.

"Thanks, Cyn."

Greg's mouth still wagged open from the scene. He literally sashayed over to Hannah. "Ding Dong! The bitch is dead," he cackled. "Well, at least for the last run through." He trotted backstage. "You'll kill it, girl!"

The smile on Hannah's face expanded.

Yep. I've got this, Ms. Panzini.

I won't be nervous, Cynthia.

I'll kill it, Greg.

She spied her mother entering the theatre. "Mom!" Hannah ran up and gave Gillian a long embrace.

"Hey! What's that for?" Hannah's mom was knocked off balance, her bag full of student essays suddenly on the floor.

"Sorry," Hannah replied and quickly scooped up the papers.

"I just brought the papers for in between scenes. You know, when Jill is giving notes."

Hannah laughed. "I don't think you'll need something to do. Mom, if we don't have this by tonight, we might as well return the ticket money."

Greg bounced up with Cynthia trailing behind.

"Mrs. Cross!" Cynthia waved.

"Hannah's mom is here!" Greg belted out. Hannah looked at her mom proudly. *I love how much everyone loves her.*

"Hey Greg and Cynthia! So, where's a good place to sit? I'm going to watch the run through."

Greg motioned to ten rows from the front, "Best view of the stage. If you're in the first row, you miss the big picture."

"Sounds good."

In the dressing room, Hannah noticed the onslaught of messages on her phone. *Shit, these are all from Skylar. Don't look at it. Don't look.* She looked in the mirror, lightbulbs shining from the border and illuminating her face with that stage glow. *Okay, foundation first.* She began the arduous process of caking on layer after layer. Red lips. False eyelashes. Deep pink blush.

A sophomore came up behind her. "Ms. Panzini says I need to braid your hair for the wigs."

Hannah was taken aback. Still forgetting that she was indeed the lead tonight.

"Oh yeah. Of course."

The sophomore braided her hair in two tight Dutch braids then pinned the ends atop her head and applied a wig cap. Then she fitted a curly blonde bob—the one brunette Skylar had been donning—onto Hannah's head.

Hannah stared at herself in the backstage mirror. She was Aurelia. The ingénue with big dreams of leaving her current life for better future.

Yes, I am Aurelia.

"Hey, Hannah…Hannah…Hannah?" The voice sounded far away. Suddenly Hannah snapped back into her own skin.

"Sorry, Cynthia. What is it?"

Cynthia placed her hands on Hannah's shoulders—a gesture that felt both maternal and infantile. Her voice was small, "They are ready for you. For warm-ups. I brought your first costume."

"That was amazing!" Gillian Cross beamed as they drove home.

"Thanks for coming, Mom!"

Gillian's voice tilted into ecstatic, "I wouldn't miss it!"

Hannah looked at herself in the sideview mirror and sighed happily. *She finally understands why I love this so much.*

"Hannah," her mother went on, "I want you know that Ricky texted and said an envelope from NYU came for you today. A big envelope. A fat envelope."

A gasp from the passenger seat. "Really?" Big, fat envelopes only mean once thing…acceptance packet. Thin envelopes from universities mean rejections. Hannah had already received two of those.

"But—" Hannah started to ask how her mother's teacher salary would cover NYU's tuition.

Gillian interrupted, instinctively knowing where this was headed. "Don't worry about it now. You just did a beautiful job on stage. Your director was happy. The cast was happy. I was blown away!"

Then she pulled the minivan to the side of the road. "Hey," she began, "I want this for you. It's an excellent school. And you're an excellent performer. NYU is lucky to have you. I'm going to find a way to make this happen. We will apply for scholarships. We will make this work."

Tears brimmed at her mother's eyes as she spoke. Hannah couldn't help but cry too. The hugged again. Hard and long.

"Thanks mom," Hannah sniffed.

"Have fun at your last shows this weekend. Come Monday, we will start figuring this out."

Hannah laid on top of the covers, clutching the acceptance letter to her chest. Her eyes wide open to the Drake poster that hid the stain from that roof leak a few years back. She inhaled deeply as if trying to smell Union Square on the university letterhead. *I'm going there next year. I'll be a whole new Hannah Cross.*

Only Rachel Woodson and Stephen Fleischmann were going to NYU. *Neither of them is going to Tisch.* Stephen was going to the engineering school and Hannah had no idea where Rachel was going. She was a visual arts kid. They wouldn't cross paths. *There will be no one from Whispering Hills. A whole new me. And only a few more months left in high school.*

Then Hannah realized with some sadness that she wouldn't even be a blip on the Whispering Hills radar if it weren't for Skylar. Her best friend had made her life tolerable—no, fun and mostly enjoyable—at school. It was exhilarating being Sky's number two. Her loyal lieutenant.

Don't think about her right now. Hannah held the letter tighter.

Her phone vibrated. She wanted to look so badly. She was sure most of them were from her friends congratulating her on tonight's winning performance. And Hannah hoped (like she always did) that one or two were from Brody. *Now, I kind of want to text Brody. See if he's still up.*

Screw it. I'm looking. Just going to delete any of Skylar's madness. She pressed the home button on her phone and unlocked it. *47 messages. Okay, deep breath.* Skylar's name was close to the top. And the first few words of her text were definitely cuss words. *Let's save that for later…or never.*

One from Greg came in just a minute ago.

> GT: just
> wanted to tell
> u that u were
> FAB! such a
> good job. so
> proud of you.

Hannah grinned. It was gummy and toothy and cheesy all at once. *My adoring fans,* she laughed to herself.

> HC: thx. love
> you to pieces.
> Oxox

Greg's reply came swiftly.

> GT:
> oxoxoxoxoxox
> oxoxoxoxoxo

Hannah covered her mouth and tried not to laugh too loudly. A few from Cynthia.

> CW: Girl, you
> rocked it
> tonite.

CW: i heard
Panzini
singing ur
praises. and 1
of the guys in
the band
asked about u.

CW: i was all
like—she's
taken! By my
twin brother!
LMAO.

These are probably the nicest texts I've ever gotten from Cynthia Wolcott. And still she can't avoid making her weird affection for her brother apparent.

HC: Thx! And
yes, I'm totes
taken! LMAO.

Just use the same stupid lingo. No, I'm not laughing my ass off. But whatevs. Another ding. And a WhatsApp banner dropped down. *Brody. Hmm. Delicious Brody.* She opened the app right away. Fingers flying across the screen.

BW: Hey! u
still up????
can I come
over??? JK.
but not really
kidding…if the
answer is yes.

Hannah's knees weakened at the thought of Brody driving to her house this late at night. If Skylar could do this stuff, why couldn't she? It was a few tries before she actually hit send.

HC: yes, come
over.

No. Too sterile.

HC: i'm up, I'd
love to see u.

Ugh. Too mature.

HC: I wish but
my mom is still
up grading
papers.

What the hell is wrong with me? Why would I ever mention my mom? Talk about a boner killer. Finally, Hannah figured out what to send.

HC: i'm up.
And i wish u
could come
over. But i've
got to get to
sleep.
Showtime
tmrw.

Brody responded even quicker than Greg.

BW: worth a
shot

Hannah wrote back.

HC: Lol. I'll
see u tmrw
night after the
show. u
coming to the
diner with us?

BW: Yep.
Boyfriend duty.
Be at the
show. Flowers.
And diner
afterward with
the theatre
kidz. Lol.

Boyfriend. Without realizing it Hannah dropped the
NYU letter to the floor and flipped over onto her belly.
Boyfriend. She wracked her brain. *No, that's definitely the first
time he's said that.*

HC: just the
perks of
having a
girlfriend in the
show

*You said boyfriend first. So there, I said girlfriend. We're
like, together.*

BW: [smiley
emoji]
[laughing
emoji] Perks.
Don't tell
anyone but I
kinda like the
show. Lol.

Could Brody be more perfect? Hannah didn't think so. They chatted for a while more. Hannah fighting the burn in her eyes, her body screaming out for sleep. Hannah remembered the first time she met Brody Wolcott. Two days into freshmen year. She stood on the winding line of newbies waiting to get their ID pictures taken. Right behind Elisa Crane, who, like her namesake, had a long and elegant neck. Hannah was worried about her forehead zit she'd impulsively picked the night before.

Brody walked up to Elisa and inserted himself between them.

"Can I back cut?" he flashed those lightning white teeth.

Hannah thought he was the most beautiful boy she'd ever seen. Immediate forgiveness for the use of the "back cut" excuse. Fresh out of public school, Hannah would've skewered some dork for trying to "back cut." *That's bull. Back cut is still cutting the rest of the line.*

But not Brody Wolcott. Hannah didn't realize it then, but Brody her at the "hello" he didn't even offer. In fact, Brody immediately turned to Elisa and started chatting it up. Same country club. Father owns the Lexus dealership. Twin sister named Cynthia. Yes, they came from St. John's. No, their family doesn't do the Hamptons over the summer. His mother just finished remodeling their place in the Berkshires. Hannah was entranced by it all.

It wasn't until later that month that Skylar explained how the Wolcotts had a place in the Berkshires because they couldn't afford South Hampton or Amagansett.

"No, we don't have a house Upstate," Greg had chimed in too. Cynthia was getting a diet soda from the vending machines. He'd looked over his shoulder then back at Skylar, "My family has a house in Sag Harbor. And we ski in Vail. There's never a reason for the Berkshits."

Hannah never realized there were levels to being rich. Brody and Cynthia had two houses. Hannah's mother rented one. And while Hannah imbibed all this intel like a good proselyte of the wealthy, it didn't change her perception of Brody. He was gorgeous. He was athletic. He was rich.

And Brody Wolcott was totally out of her league. So, she spent the next three years admiring him from afar. Dating stupid boys and hooking up with other less-thans. Giving her first kiss to some eager stagehand. Letting an ambitious Speech and Debater touch her nonexistent breasts.

"Just two bee stings," she'd heard he told his friends.

"Speech and Debate jerks. Thinking their hotshots because they go to tourneys at Princeton," Skylar had boiled.

Skylar got back at the Speech and Debate kid. She let the air out of his bicycle tires one day after school. "No one makes fun of your boobies," she laughed maniacally. "Those are my bee stings!" She hunched over and stabbed the rear tire with a small Japanese paring knife she'd stolen from her chef.

When Skylar stood up, she brushed her uniform skirt off and laced her arm through Hannah's, "Besides eight grand and a good plastics guy can fix them."

Hannah realized — laying there in her bed — that all the while, when she hooked up with guys, she pictured Brody's face. One big rehearsal for the actual performance. Now it was Brody's mouth she kissed, his muscled forearms around her, his hot hands hiking her uniform skirt up.

Inexplicably, Hannah opened the messages from Skylar. *Should I look at them or delete? Delete them*, the sensible voice in Hannah's head asserted. *Look at them*, Hannah's heart rejoined.

Finger across the screen once more and the messages were laid bare. Pandora's box and all its chaos unleashed onto Hannah's eyes right before bed. *What an idiot I am.* Paying attention to the time stamps, she began scrolling.

SC: did u know about this crap? I know Panzini and ur mom are tight. **6:07pm**

SC: u fucking bitch. u totally knew. and u don't answer ur messages now?!? too important for me? too busy getting ready for your big shot? **6:10pm**

SC: ur going to blow it anyway. auditions ring a bell, HANNAH BANANA!!!! **6:22pm**

answer my texts, goddammnitt! U think this is a game, bitch? life as u know it is over. **6:24pm**

SC: u used
me. u became
such a bitch
after ur stupid
NYU audition.
Ur still going to
be a sewer rat
from oakbrook.
OakBROKE!
Fancy NYU
ain't gonna
change that.
6:29pm

SC: how's the
run through?
still sucking!?
tell everyone
I'll be there
tmrw to nail it.
not to worry,
minions!!!
7:12pm

SC: I know u
have seen
these by now.
answer my
texts u
coward.
9:01pm

SC: hannah, u
had better fall
in line. See
how fast ppl
changed at
school? want
to lose Brody
too? I just
have to shake
my hips and
wink at him
and it's done.
DONE! He'll
drop u so fast
to be at the
top. Just
remember that
next time u get
the courage to
fuck w me.
Nighty-night.
10:41pm

The last one stabbed Hannah in the gut. The little girl inside her, the one who stood in line waiting for her ID picture, was back. *He would break up with me in a heartbeat to date Skylar. Wouldn't he?*

No, he wouldn't. Hannah pushed the thought from her head. She spent a few long minutes wishing she had access to Skylar's vast supply of Clonopin so she could go to sleep.

Then one more text from Skylar. The chime even sounded evil now. A photo this time. A screen shot of Skylar's texts. First it read, "look at what you do to me." Then a dick pic. Veiny and erect and surrounded by hair. Hannah sneered, disgusted by the genitals flashing on her phone. She threw her phone on the floor.

God, she's an animal. Wait. Whose penis is that? Hannah scrambled to grab her phone. Out of battery. *Shit!* She quickly found the plug and waited what seemed like an hour for it to power up. Fingers flying on the screen, Hannah found the appalling picture again.

Oh my God! The name in the screenshot was Aaron. *Mr. Samuels was sexting her?* Hannah ran to the bathroom thinking she might retch. But nothing came up. Just her gut contracting hard as Hannah bent over taking in the smell of toilet water, cold and foul.

Her phone vibrated on the bathroom tile floor again.

> SC: that's from
> months ago.
> I'm sending
> this to ur mom
> now, btw. K.
> love u. bye.

Chapter Fifteen
Curtain Call

Whispering Hills Country Day School
presents

The Whispers in

STAGECRAFT

Saturday April 25th at 8 p.m.
Sunday April 26th at 2 p.m.
The Clarke Theatre

Reserved Seating $25
General Admission $15

With Special Thanks to the Board of WHCDS, Clarke Capital, and Wolcott Lexus

Questions? Email Jill Panzini at jill.panzini@whisperinghillscds.org

Hell Week was over. Now it was showtime. Classes passed in a blur on Friday. Skylar continued to ignore or torment Hannah. In math class, a lacrosse player with a scallop of sweat staining his Hollister t-shirt leaned over and whispered, "Hannah Banana." When she looked, he'd gestured down at his pants. Hannah shuddered and tried in vain to concentrate on calculus.

And Cynthia — basking in Skylar's glow — only acknowledged Hannah when the queen wasn't around. And Greg still standing his ground. Hannah was proud of him, even took his invitation to sit with them at lunch again.

"You've been sitting with us since like week two of freshmen year," Greg had argued, and Hannah abided.

Needless to say, Skylar wasn't happy about Hannah's return. But when she started to quip, Greg interrupted, "Sky, I'm one of two out kids at our school. You think you can do worse than the football team? You think you can do worse the Christian Fellowship group inviting me to 'Pray the Gay Away' class?"

Skylar was silent for a moment and all Hannah heard was Greg crumpling the package from his protein bar. Then Skylar laughed. The lump in Hannah's throat receded back down to her gut. Momentary relief. *She's not going to fight today. She's too pumped about this weekend.* For once, Hannah was grateful for Skylar's being the lead in Stagecraft.

Soon the Saturday evening performance was done — successful and even euphoric at times. And just like that, this chapter in Hannah's life was fast coming to a close. It was the Sunday matinee and Hannah's last performance on the Clarke Theatre stage.

The cast and crew were milling around backstage, readying themselves. *The moment we've all been waiting for. It's kind of cliché. But it's true. And that makes this energy even more cliché,* Hannah thought to herself as she dabbed foundation under her eyes, hiding the dark circles.

Earbuds in, Cynthia propped her left leg up on the radiator, foot pointed perfectly. She mimicked a ballerina at the barre and stretched her torso back and forth.

Sarah Young picked through the costume rack, found what she was looking for, and shoved the hanger into a little freshman's chest. "I told you it was here. Bring it to the Prop Master. It shouldn't be with the costumes," Sarah growled in a lovable way. As Hannah took it all in and she smiled despite herself. *Sarah's in her element right now.*

"Where's Paige!?" Greg busted through the dressing room door.

"Female dressing room, Greg!" Sarah hollered.

"Like I care about anything in here! Where's Paige? Panzini is freaking out."

Sarah looked around once, paused dramatically, then took another scan. Her brown eyes darted, met Cynthia's dead gaze, Hannah's disinterested eyes, and then went back to Greg.

"I don't see her. Surely, Paige signed in," Sarah whipped through the pages of her clipboard. "Everyone had to sign in!" Then Sarah yelled at everyone, "Everyone should sign in!"

"She's not here either?" Greg shouted back. "She's in so much trouble."

Sarah brushed past Greg and he whirled around. Then he sauntered over to Hannah and leaned up against the make-up table.

"Drama!" Hannah sang operatically as she etched red pigment onto her lips.

"I know! Of course, Paige is here. Everyone's just totes nervous."

Just then, Skylar started singing her vocal warm-ups. Humming with her rose gold Beats headphones on. Her low voice sounded sexy and full.

Hannah's heart sank. *She'll be amazing. Maybe this will be enough for her. Maybe she'll be satisfied now. Then things can go back to normal.*

"Don't let her bother you," Greg patted Hannah's shoulder. Hannah was grateful for the empathy, but she felt vulnerable too. *Am I really that transparent?* Hannah needed to hide her hurt better. *Girl fights are sophomore bullshit. I'm about to go to college in Manhattan – away from this suffocating, small town. I'll be at Tisch and Skylar will probably never perform again.* Hannah had found out a few days ago that Skylar took the scholarship from UConn. She'd be playing softball in the fall.

And then, Skylar's voice cracked. *It cracked. She cracked.* Hannah looked at Skylar in the mirror's reflection. Their eyes met. Skylar's eyes like black holes. Shivering, Hannah looked away immediately.

But her voice cracked. *And it wasn't even that high. Not even the high E she has trouble with sometimes.* Skylar strutted past Hannah and knocked her water off the table.

"Clean it up, Banana!" she snickered. Cast members tried not to stare but the drama was too good. A queen and her courtier at odds.

Hannah bent down to wipe up the spilled water. Then she used a hairdryer to dry her stockings and leotard. *Of course, the crotch of my costume is wet.* Hannah rolled her eyes. *It looks like I peed myself. But...I'm not angry. Weird.* Hannah almost laughed. *Why am I not pissed off?*

Hannah quickly realized why. *She cracked. I can't believe it. She sounds awful. It's going to take some serious warm-ups now. Maybe she is really too sick to be here. Maybe last night was a fluke.* The fantasies of taking Skylar's place took over Hannah's mind.

"Hannah...Hannah," Cynthia chirped.

Drunk on desire, Hannah didn't quite catch that Cynthia had been standing there with a new bottle of water.

"Here," Cynthia spoke softly, ensuring Skylar was out of the room.

"Thanks."

"My brother is outside the stage door by the way. You two are so gross. But whatever…I'm over it," she giggled.

Hannah's heart felt a little lighter and right then, just right then, Hannah didn't care if Skylar was the lead tonight. *This is the first of many times Brody would wait for me by the stage door. Except next year, he'll be waiting downtown at an NYU venue or some cool blackbox theatre in the Village.*

But before Hannah could reach her Romeo, she met a frantic Mrs. Panzini.

"Have you seen Paige? Paige Kellogg?"

As if there's another Paige in the show? Hannah almost rolled her eyes.

"I think I did. Earlier."

Ms. Panzini huffed, "Well, I can't find her, and I have her tap shoes!"

Hannah shrugged. The frazzled choreographer moved on so quickly it was as if she vaporized.

Showtime drew nearer. Everyone in costume. The last of the wigs fitted over thick Dutch braids. Sound checks. Body mics attached. Body mics removed then reattached the correct way by Sarah. Hannah never got to the stage door, so she hid in a stairwell and texted Brody.

While she hovered in the shadows, Hannah overheard adult voices. Whispers echoing around empty cement steps.

"I never say this about a student. But what a bitch. What an awful child."

Mom? Hannah felt anxiety sweep through her like fever. *Why wasn't she seated already?* Hannah listened more closely.

"Skylar Clarke has always been awful. And she's no child," Ms. Panzini answered.

"Ever since her mother died —"

Ms. Panzini broke in, "Yes, she's been worse since her mother died. But she's always been a spoiled little bitch. Her sister was too. Remember how bad Bethany was? How Feldman looked the other way even though she damn near started a riot in the cafeteria? I mean, we have a no fight rule. Does it even apply when your last name is Clarke?"

Gillian sobbed softly, "Sometimes I wonder if sending Hannah here was the right choice."

"Let me see it," Ms. Panzini ventured tenuously.

"Here."

What are they looking at? Hannah peered around the corner and saw the light from a phone.

Ms. Panzini's face, lit by the fluorescent light, looked like she just tasted a lemon, "Appalling. I can't believe him. Aaron friggin' Samuels. He had me fooled."

Gillian cried harder, "I thought he was the one. I know it's cliché but...after my ex left, I just..."

"Oh, Gill!" Ms. Panzini hugged her friend.

She sent it. I really didn't think she would. That bitch! Skylar's menacing barrage of texts flooded Hannah's brain. And the threat to send that screenshot, the one of Skylar and Mr. Samuels' illicit exchanges. *I never thought she'd do it. All the times my mom helped her. The hours my mom spent working through her college essay. That sob story Skylar wrote! 'My mommy made me a sociopath and now she's dead and I'm sad. And all the money in the world can't bring her back. And I'd give it up everything to have my mommy back for just a day.'* Skylar had sat with her mother for hours on a Sunday afternoon revising that essay.

The taste in Hannah's mouth was metallic and sour.

"We're five minutes to places people!!" Sarah's voice bellowed from elsewhere backstage. Hannah waited a beat then looked around the corner again. Ms. Panzini and her mom were gone.

Hannah's heart felt hard and heavy — no kid should have to see their mom cry like that. She blinked her eyes hard in an attempt to erase the image. Two women hiding in a dark hallway, gossiping and crying. Like schoolgirls. Like vulnerable schoolgirls.

"Places!" Sarah almost knocked Hannah over. "Why are you here? Shouldn't you be backstage?! Let's go, Hannah."

She raced to her spot onstage. A few feet behind a poised and gorgeous Skylar Clarke. Hannah leered at her — imagining her hands around Skylar's tanned neck. The amber skin turning white as life drained out. Her wig dislodging as she tried to pry Hannah's grip away from her throat. *I hate her. God, how I hate her.*

The hostility only grew throughout the first act. And Hannah didn't notice that Paige was still a no show. And of course, Skylar nailed it. Not one crack. Not one waver.

By intermission, Hannah was fed up. *It's time. How could she send that picture to my mom? How could Skylar be so awful?* Hannah stood next to Skylar and looked in the mirror with her.

"Are you going to congratulate me, Hannah Banana?"

Hannah smirked, "On what? Giving a blow job to a pedo and getting the lead in the school play?"

Skylar parried, "Uh, Hannah, you idiot. I got the part then I gave the blowies. And we had a connection." She took a deep breath in like she was smelling Mr. Samuels' cologne, "A real connection. He's meeting me after this, y'know."

"Bullshit!"

Skylar shrugged, "Okay, ya caught me. He's not meeting me." A big pause and then, "Brody is."

Suddenly, Hannah felt her cheeks dimple. She was smiling. *I'm ready. I'm done with you. Done with being your bestie. Your lieutenant. Your whatever. You're nothing to me.*

She spoke slowly and methodically. She hit Skylar where it would hurt the most. "There's about as much chance of Brody Wolcott meeting you as there is your dead mother rising from the grave to see this piece of shit show."

Skylar's eyes narrowed. A small cough rose in her throat and her cheeks blushed. She tried to repress the coughs. Then she whispered, "What the fuck did you just say?"

"I think you heard me. Better than you can hear the notes in 'More Than This.' No matter how much you want that note to be A sharp, it will be always be an A natural. Takes you a solid eight bars to get back on track." Hannah knew Skylar rehearsed that one phrase again and again. Because, as understudy, Hannah had to sit through Skylar screwing it up…again and again.

By this time, Greg and Cynthia had appeared. Cynthia was only half-costumed for the second act.

"How dare you! How dare you mention her!" Of course, Skylar meant her mother. But Hannah pretended not to remember.

"Her who? Zoe? The person who should have this role," Hannah began to shout, and the cast gathered around them. Sarah Young, who was close by rehanging a vest, positioned herself a little closer to the impending explosion. Terror and glee all over everyone's faces.

Hannah hollered, "The girl who you called Princess Vegetable! She should be here right now! This is her night and you stole it! You evil whore!"

Skylar lunged, "Shut up, Hannah!" She grabbed the back of Hannah's head and threw her into the portable costume rack. Immediately, Hannah remembered the time Skylar had threw her up against the wall in her bedroom. *This is worse. Where does she get this Herculean strength?*

Hannah writhed on the floor and made attempts at rising, but Skylar was too quick. Suddenly, she was on top of Hannah and throwing punches. Hannah's hands waved and pushed and dodged. *Please don't let these punches land. Why is no one pulling her off?*

A few blows landed. Right, left, right. The side of Hannah's head screamed in agony and she cried out. She tangled her arms with Skylar's and tried to scratch, to pull, to jab. But the scene just kept getting blurrier, the figure above her more obscure.

Was it Greg Tate or Dean Feldman who pulled Skylar off? Was it Tim from the crew? Panzini? Hannah still couldn't say. The next thing Hannah remembered was leaning against Cynthia. And Sarah Young on the ground, a gash in her head from a hanger. The costume rack must have gone flying into Sarah. There were garments everywhere. Colors and scarves and hats strewn all over.

It felt like hours before Hannah heard Dean Feldman's booming administrative voice quell the din of student squeals and gasps and screams. But it wasn't hours. Only a few short minutes had passed.

"You are done here, Skylar Clarke!" Dean Feldman blasted.

"Did you even hear what she said to me?" Skylar shrieked. "My mother! She said my mother—"

Feldman wasn't having it. Hannah thought of her mother and Panzini in the stairwell—Bethany Clarke and that lunchroom brawl she started. *Feldman has been waiting for this forever. A disciplinary wet dream.* All professionalism thrown aside, as Dean Feldman yelled back, "Shut up! I don't care what she said! Fighting is strictly prohibited on school grounds. You're expelled. Immediately!"

"You can't expel me!"

Ms. Panzini butted in, "We're in the middle of the show!" But Dean Feldman glared at her and Panzini shrank back, regretting her words. *Stay in your lane, Ms. Panzini.*

"You can't expel me!" Skylar repeated. Tears now replaced by the terrible anger only Skylar could conjure. The scene like a witch and a boiling cauldron and lightning crashing in the distance.

Skylar spoke with an eerie softness, "That's my father's name on the theatre. You can't expel me! I'm Skylar fucking Clarke."

"Frankly, Skylar, I don't give a damn."

Wait. What? Did Dean Feldman just reference Gone with the Wind in the middle of expelling someone? Was this amazing or ridiculous? I think Pat Feldman is my hero.

He went on, "What you are, my dear, is spoiled little brat. And you will not be getting your diploma from Whispering Hills Country Day School. I don't care how much money daddy has donated. You will not return to school on Monday. And you will certainly not finish this show!"

Skylar stood there. She wasn't going anywhere.

And then the most incredible thing happened.

"Get out, Skylar!" Greg yelled. Cynthia stood stone-faced behind him. A few "yeahs" and "get outs" rippled through the crowd. Other seniors chimed in. Hannah's eyes darted around. All she could see were students who had endured Skylar's torture finally having their moment of rebellion. A fiefdom crumbling before Hannah's eyes.

"Yeah, get the hell out!" Sarah Young held an ice pack to her head and propped herself up.

"It's time to go, Skylar." Ms. Panzini tried to play the teacher, the adult. But she was enjoying this too much. "Don't worry. Hannah can finish the show for you."

And just like that, the black mamba was defanged. Eyes brimming with tears, Skylar grabbed her bag and her phone and met the school security guard at the backstage door.

She was gone.

Cynthia's eyes twinkled toward Hannah. Then she knowingly hummed a little tune from *Wicked*.

This was it. Anticipation swept through Hannah like a fever. She stood behind the curtain at center stage and waited for Sarah's cue. It was just the second act. But it was Hannah's.

This is where Skylar stood. This is where Zoe stood last year. Did they feel this nervous? No, I'm not nervous. I'm ready. I'm going to NYU next year. I'm going to...

An announcement from the front of the house. Ms. Panzini's shaky voice apologizing for the delay. *What will she say about me taking over for Skylar?* Suddenly, the stress of this transition fell hard on Hannah's chest. *No, don't worry about that.*

What if people think I suck? They're getting gipped. I'm just the understudy.

"I'm sorry for the delay, everyone. Thank you for waiting. Unfortunately, one of our cast members got sick and had to go home."

The audience gasped. Someone went home during a performance?

"I know this is highly unusual. But Skylar Clarke won't be finishing the show."

Another gasp. This time louder.

Hannah rocked back and forth. *Maybe I shouldn't listen to this?* She hummed the first song softly. But blocking Ms. Panzini out was impossible.

Skylar was so good. And now there's going to be a comparison. Shit. Hannah bit her lip hard — stopping short of breaking the chapped skin.

"However, because Whispering Hills is full of talented students, we have an amazing cast member who will step up and take her place. For our second act, may I present Hannah Cross!"

The audience clapped. And the applause got louder as the din of the "Entre Act" played in the orchestra pit.

Suddenly, two arms wrapped around Hannah's shoulders.

Greg.

"Knock 'em dead. This should've been yours anyway."

Hannah smiled and wiped a tear from her cheek.

A murmur of "good lucks" and "break and legs" from behind her. And a few sniffles.

Cynthia ran to her spot next to Hannah. "Do great, Hannah. Do it for Zoe."

"I will," Hannah whispered back, forgetting that she herself was responsible for putting Zoe in a hospital bed.

The curtain opened. Spotlight shone in Hannah's eyes. The music led her in and the song came naturally, beautifully even.

Just like the run through.

A few scenes in, Hannah was on the wrong side of the stage but played it off. The dancers adjusted seamlessly. 'We got you' their faces seemed to say. When the song ended, the audience applauded, and Hannah's heart soared. *I love this. I love this. I'm meant for this.*

Hannah danced and sang and delivered an emotional monologue. She owned every scene. In the middle of it all, she abandoned any thoughts of the accident. About what she'd done to Zoe. To Will. *Everything is good and right.* The feeling took over Hannah's body and mind at a cellular level. Like the accident didn't even happen. Like she and Skylar never ran the silver Prius off the road. Like there was no police investigation. Like Will and Zoe just never existed.

This feeling was probably why Hannah missed Sarah Young sobbing in the wings as she exited stage right. And this absolute elation (the only feeling that can come with a superb performance) was why Hannah missed a few of the sophomores hugging it out backstage.

Because Paige still wasn't there.

Because by now, everyone knew why. Everyone except Hannah.

Paige missed the performance because the doctors had called her parents. Zoe wasn't looking good. It was time. The family spent the afternoon unplugging their daughter from the life-giving machines. The family prayed for her passing. For her peace. And in the early evening hours—when the cast was readying themselves to shine bright on that Clarke Theatre stage—the Kellogg family was watching their daughter's bright light extinguish.

Because of Skylar.

Because of Hannah too.

When the last song came, Hannah felt a pang of sadness. The opening chords squeezing her heart just a little. Just enough to make her really present for this last ballad. The lyrics and notes raised up in her throat like pure color. Hannah sang the best she'd ever sung. Better than the NYU audition. And when Hannah held that last note just a touch longer than the orchestra, the crowd roared approval.

There is nothing like applause. And there's really nothing like a standing ovation.

Audience members slowly rose to their feet. The faces surged, a few at a time then almost in unison. Their hands clapping proudly. Their smiles wide. Their eyes even wider.

It was intoxicating. Hannah didn't have to pretend anymore. At this point, Zoe and Will were just old memories. She left behind any recollection of her wrongdoing. Hannah was drunk on the admiration of an audience.

The curtain closed—its corners crashing into each other and folding back on themselves like ocean waves. The cast rallied around Hannah. All the yipping and squealing and Hannah heard nothing in particular. A sea of adoration from her peers. Her body felt weak from the joy.

The cast assembled for bows and the curtains revealed the audience again. Still standing. Still clapping. They all bowed together. Then Hannah stepped forward to take her final bow. Her torso folded down then became arrow straight. Shoulders back. Chest held high. Chin higher.

Against the bright lights, Hannah could make out a few figures at the back of the theatre. *Maybe a woman and a man. Must be Stella McKay and her boyfriend.* Stella had texted earlier that she was running late. They made it. *Oh good. I hope they saw me throughout the whole second act.* The figures moved, and a spotlight caught Hannah's eyes.

She squinted harder and spotted the figures again. *Just two dads. Not Stella*, Hannah thought forlornly. The dads opened the doors at the back and Hannah saw the light from the lobby. *Just like dads. Can't wait to leave.*

The panels of the ruby-colored velvet curtain crashed together. This time, for good. The cast and crew rushed from all parts of the stage and wings. Greg climbed up onto a set piece and said, "That was our last show, seniors!" A few cast members clapped and a few hooted. The group was a blur of faces—delighted and teary at the same time. Hannah drank in the exhilaration of a job well done. *I'll slowly make my way through the crowd. Don't go too fast. They'll want to stop and congratulate me.*

And sure enough, a little freshman stopped Hannah to compliment some little detail. "OMG! Hannah! I didn't know you could hit a double pirouette and sing at the same time. Hashtag goals!"

Hannah smiled with gratification. The faces and praises kept coming. Everyone was so happy. But some seniors were crying. Wickedly, Hannah thought, *Senior year and you never got to play a lead.*

Sarah Young came up, "You did great, Hannah. And you stood up to Skylar. I…uh…I was wrong about you." She paused a long few seconds, "Zoe would have been—" She sobbed and shook her head like 'I can't even right now.'

What is going on? Why are they still mentioning Zoe? She had nothing to do with this performance. I rocked it. Not her. Hannah took a deep inhale. Not the time. Not the time to be mad at Sarah Young.

A few more sophomore dancers approached. More 'Congratulations.' More 'I can't believe it's.' No Paige in the group. These were her girls too. *Was she still not here? Did I miss her altogether? No, surely that was her on stage behind me in that last tap number.*

Like getting hit with an unexpected wave as you're exiting the ocean, Hannah was knocked off her post-performance high. *Oh God. I have to get out of here.* She made her way to the wings, nearly knocking over some scaffolding. The dots were connecting.

Cynthia blocked her, "Hannah!! You were so great!"

She kept gushing and Hannah interrupted, "Cynthia! Why is everyone crying? Did something happen to Zoe?"

I have to know. I have to know right now.

"You didn't hear? Paige didn't come this afternoon because Zoe passed away." The last two words caught in Cynthia's throat. Hannah almost shoved her out of the way.

The two figures.

They're not dads. They're the detectives.

The polyester costume stuck to Hannah's torso as sweat beaded all over her body. She felt hot and chilled at the same time. *I need to find my mom. I need to get the hell out of this theatre.*

Hannah weaved through more students and parents. The scent of congratulatory bouquets registered as nauseating. At one point, she tangled herself in a few balloons an eager freshmen mom was holding. "You were so good! How awesome you were able to go on like that!" she twinkled.

Hannah untangled her limbs, curling ribbon slowly detaching from her amber arms. "Thanks!"

"My Misty always talks about you! How nice you are," the mom smiled, looking to continue the conversation. As Hannah dashed away, she added, "Oh go! I'm holding you up. Congrats again!"

Hannah could see the backstage doors. *Just gather your stuff. Text mom to meet you in the parking lot. It's all good. You just need a plan. Get out of here and make a plan. Skylar would have a plan. It will be fine. It was just an accident.*

But at the backstage doors, there they were. Not the detectives but worse. Stella McKay and her Broadway director boyfriend.

"Hannah!" Stella sang.

"Hi!" Hannah drew the word out awkwardly, eyes darting around them. *They're totally blocking the doors.*

"I want to introduce you to my boyfriend, Tad Conrad. He's directing the reboot of 42nd Street right now."

"Nice to meet you," Hannah nodded a little too hard.

"You were great!" Tad looked at Stella, "I don't think I've ever been to a performance where the lead left mid-show." He laughed uncomfortably then turned back to Hannah, "You were superb though. I hope the other girl is okay."

Hannah looked behind her. Still no one but parents and students milling around. "Oh, I'm sure Skylar will be just fine." *She always is*, Hannah thought resentfully.

Stella jumped in, "We don't want to keep you. Tad just had to meet you though. And I wanted to say 'hi.' Girl, you've got some big things ahead of you."

Tad rejoined, "Yes, we should let you get changed. I'll have Stella set it up, but you need to watch a 42nd Street rehearsal."

"Yes, I would love that!"

The two moved away from the doors and Hannah returned to flight mode. She shoved clothes and bobby pins and make up in her bag. An eyeshadow palette crashed the floor. She grabbed the big pieces and swept the rest under the table. Hannah took one last look at herself in the dressing room mirror. *It's going to be okay.* She texted her mom.

HC: meet me
by the stage
doors

GC: I'm
already on my
way. You were
FANTASTIC!
I'm so proud.

Her mother's words plucked at her heart. *She's so proud of me. I need to tell her about the accident. She'll forgive me. Right? Of course, she will. I think.*

Her mother would be devastated.

When she reached the outside of the theatre, Hannah saw her mom waving excitedly. Brody was next to her, big grin and even bigger bouquet of roses. Her heart quickened and so did her pace. A few other families milled around. Hannah walked toward her mother and Brody. A twang of guilt in her chest mixed with the joy of seeing her two favorite people. Just as she reached them, Detectives Jones and Barry met her. The scene played out in slow motion. Hannah's surroundings began to spin slowly. The ground felt like a waterbed.

"Hannah Cross?" Detective Jones began.

"Yes," she said meekly.

"You're under arrest for the murder of Will Bartlett and Zoe Kellogg and for obstruction of justice."

"What?" Gillian Cross stepped in. "Are those necessary?" She looked incredulously at the handcuffs. "Hannah, what is he talking about?"

Stunned into silence, Brody's mouth hung open. *I wish he wasn't here. He can't save me from this.* A peculiarly horrible feeling of letting Brody down and simultaneously being mad at him spread across Hannah's heart.

"You have to come with us," Detective Jones ignored Gillian who cried and ranted.

A crowd gathered. Detective Barry addressed them, "Move out of the way, people. Nothing to see."

Detective Jones put the hand cuffs on Hannah. Tight. Too tight. Hannah winced as the steel bracelets clicked into place and pinched her skin. Hot tears rolled down her cheeks. Everything flashed in her mind. The accident. Will at her locker. Kissing Brody. Singing on stage. The standing ovation. Zoe's sweet smile. Skylar's wicked one.

Thoughts of the future flickered. NYU. The 42nd Street rehearsal. Hanging out with Stella. All gone. Just like that. *It was everything I've ever wanted, and I'll have none of it. It was all over.*

"I'm sorry, Mom." Hannah's voice — the one that had bounded through the Clarke Theatre just moments ago, the voice that had roused a crowd to their excited feet — that voice was small.

Her voice was nothing.

Epilogue
Lakeside Police Station

After basking in the glow of the impeccably designed stage lights, the long fluorescent bulbs appeared greenish and sickly. Hannah tried to convince herself that the feeling in her stomach was caused by the awful taxpayer lights penetrating her eyes, not the reason she was at the police station in the first place.

The detectives walked her through a room of desks, most of them empty. Coffee rings staining surfaces. Waste bins overfull with crumpled papers and sandwich wrappers. A few uniforms checked Hannah out. *I must look ridiculous.* Her face all caked and glittery. Her hair plastered to her scalp with Dippity Doo gel.

Hannah put on her best walk. A proud one, almost a march. *It was just an accident right. I'll tell the truth. This will get sorted. I didn't do anything wrong.* She repeated it over and over. A mantra.

It lasted about twenty seconds. They turned the corner toward the interrogation rooms and there she was. *Skylar. Of course. She came right here after the fight. She would ruin me if it's the last thing she did.* Skylar leaned back in the chair and nodded at Hannah. *Why isn't she in handcuffs? Wait, a minute.* Hannah turned her body to see more, absorb more details. *I need info. What is going on with her? She told them, but she was in the car too. How would she know the story? They have to know Skylar was involved. Don't they?*

"Wait, I..." Hannah tried to stop the perp walk.

But Detective Jones jostled her arm. "Keep walking, Hannah." His voice like ice and stone.

"But Skylar..." the words stuck in her mouth. *Skylar did this! Whatever she's telling you — it's a lie.* The words articulated themselves so well in her mind. The whole morning rushing back. Skylar was responsible.

274

"Keep moving," Detective Jones rejoined.

Is that Derrick? Hannah peered into an office at the back of the station. Likely the captain's office. It had store-front windows and blinds. She looked closer and tried to slow down again. There were two men standing with Derrick. It looked as though they were saying their goodbyes. A man in a suit with a slippery smile talked. The captain sat stoically behind his desk. *Looks like someone got a lawyer. I'll ask for a lawyer.* Hannah tried in vain to remember all she could from AP Gov class. *I have rights. I know I have rights. This is America.* But all she could think of was the project she did with Cynthia on Brown vs. Board of Ed. Another man in a gray mechanic's jumpsuit put a leathered hand on Derrick's shoulder. *That must be his dad.*

Detective Barry piped up, "Get in the room."

"Have a seat," Detective Jones deposited Hannah in the metal chair. The room was exactly like the TV shows. Stark, gray. Just a steel table and two metal chairs. An invisible chessboard between the adversaries. A one-way mirror. And a red light from a camera—the lens awaiting a confession. Who know how many stories of crimes and mistakes that glass eye has recorded?

Detective Jones sat down. Detective Barry lurked behind him, never taking his eyes of Hannah.

"I want a lawyer," Hannah blurted—tears surging, face hot.

Detective Jones scoffed, nearly smiling. "You'll want to hear what we have to say." He paused. A few well-timed breaths and strategic looks at Hannah, his partner, and the camera. *This is torture. Is he going to talk or what? Feels like I've been here for hours.*

"Hannah, we know that on March 7th you were involved in the hit and run accident that killed Will Bartlett and…as we just learned this afternoon…the accident that killed Zoe Kellogg too. We know you were driving a midnight blue Range Rover, owned by Skylar Clarke, and that you deliberately side-swiped Bartlett's silver Prius. And we know that because of your reckless driving—perhaps even drunk driving—the Prius went tumbling down a hill off Lakeside Road."

"I didn't do it on purpose!" Hannah cried. Hearing her sins spoken aloud—in Detective Jones' sterile voice—was too much to bear. Her heart nearly burst. The tears flowed more rapidly now. She looked for a box of tissues in vain. But Hannah would get no comforts in this room.

"I swear! I didn't do it on purpose. I would never hurt—"

But Detective Jones slammed his hand on the metal desk, "It doesn't matter now. You lied to us, Hannah. You were reckless and two young people are dead!"

"But I didn't mean to…It was just an accident." Hannah's chest heaved with sobs.

Detective Barry chimed in, "If it was an accident, why did you lie? You know how that looks right?"

Hannah cried more—half because she couldn't regain control and half because she wanted them to have mercy on her.

"I'm sure you noticed your friend in our captain's office. Derrick is 18. He'll be tried as an adult," Detective Jones' mouth was grim.

I'm 18 too. I'm going to be tried as an adult. Absurdly, Hannah's mind thought of scenes from Orange is the New Black—her latest Netflix binge. She almost laughed.

"Where you there when Derrick fixed the Range Rover?" Detective Barry asked. Without waiting for an answer, he continued, "See, the navy-blue auto paint you buy at Home Depot is actually different than the midnight blue Range Rover uses. Luxury cars, you know? Not the best weapon for committing murder. Can't really cover it up."

Detective Jones looked back at his partner and smirked.

Weapon? Murder? Hannah gripped the seat of her metal chair in an effort to steady herself. "I didn't try to cover anything up."

"Your DNA was found in Derrick's truck."

"I've never even been in Derrick's truck!" Hannah shouted back. Then the puzzle pieces started arranging in her head. She saw the auto spray paint in Derrick's flat bed. She saw the light in Skylar's bedroom. She remembered her ponytail getting caught on the truck. *My DNA. In Derrick's truck. Shit.*

Detective Barry spoke from behind Hannah, "Here's a piece of advice. When you cover up a crime, best not to leave the receipts from Home Depot and the spray bottles at your own house."

Hannah turned, "My house?"

Detective Jones explained, "We found receipts and empty auto paint cans at your home, Hannah. In the garbage pails."

I'm going to faint. Hannah couldn't feel her feet on the floor. Her limbs like a sparrow's. *They framed me.*

"We already have a signed statement from Skylar Clarke." Detective Jones slid a piece of paper toward Hannah.

She read it. Concentrating hard. Skylar's flourish of a signature at the bottom. And there, several times, was Hannah's name. It looked so different than how her name looked on the NYU acceptance letter.

Hannah shook her head, "She told you I stole the Rover? That's a lie!"

Detective Jones took the paper back and read the highlights aloud. The party. Too much alcohol. Maybe some weed too. Skylar worried about Hannah getting home. Hannah sleeping over. Then Hannah waking up early the next morning, fixing herself a drink, and taking the keys. Never waking Skylar. Thinking if Skylar was late to auditions, Hannah would have a better chance at impressing the director. Hannah drove so recklessly that she ran Will off the road.

"It's lies! I promise. I would never hurt Will or Zoe. Why would I do that?" Hannah had finally composed herself. She was ready to argue. *I'm not letting Skylar get away with this. I'll own my part. But she's not getting off.*

Detective Barry answered from the corner of the room, "A poor kid in a rich school. Zoe's understudy the year before in your precious performing arts program. Will's locker next to yours. Maybe unrequited love? Maybe jealousy? Sounds like a decent motive to me. With a motive like that, the DA can push for murder one."

Hannah put her head down on the metal table. The tears and heat from her face against the cold steel. *Is this it? Is everything I've worked for gone? Skylar won. Like she always does. She even said so. God, I hate her.* Hannah recognized this feeling from so many times before. The feeling that no matter what, Skylar and her money would win. In the past, she fell in line behind the queen. But now, she'd be the one taking the fall for her.

They said nothing. Suddenly, as if the clouds opened up and the God she wasn't sure existed spoke directly to her, Hannah saw the glaring error in Skylar's statement. She gripped the edge of the table. *That's it! And the police know it too.*

Hannah rallied, voice growing stronger, "Her statement is a lie. You know it too. She doesn't mention the truck driver." The Detectives both leaned in closer and Hannah continued, "Skylar ranted and cursed at Will and Zoe. Then she grabbed the wheel and made me speed up to get around them. But then I saw the truck. And I had to get out of the way. It really was an accident. I didn't mean for this to happen. I'm…I'm sorry."

The corners of Detective Jones' mouth perked up, "Yes, the truck driver."

They know Skylar is lying. They know it was a terrible accident. The information rushed through Hannah. *They know everything.* Images of Skylar and Derrick flashed in Hannah's mind. The accident replayed. The sign-in sheet. Ms. Panzini seeing Hannah upset. Sarah Young's super-sleuth voice echoed in Hannah's head.

Of course, they know everything. Then Hannah smiled too. She thought of Skylar sitting so smugly in that police station chair. *But Skylar doesn't realize it yet.*

"Hannah," Detective Jones began, "We have someone else you need to talk to."

Another man entered the room. 40s. Sharply dressed on a cop's salary. Gold badge on his belt catching the light.

"This is Detective Will Santos. He's from Connecticut."

Detective Jones spoke more gently now, "We know exactly what went down on Lakeside Road. We know you were involved." He pushed a yellow legal pad across the table and took a pen from his shirt pocket. "We need you to tell us everything. But we need you start back in August. We need to start at Camp in the Round."

Detective Santos pulled a chair up and sat beside Detective Jones. He placed a manila folder on the table. Hannah read the writing on the table and recognized the name right away.

Katie Greco.

Oh my God. Skylar's the cyber bully. She's the one everyone was talking about on the Facebook page.

Detective Jones laced his fingers, "Hannah, tell us everything you know about Skylar Clarke."

So, Hannah began to write.

Made in the USA
Coppell, TX
24 April 2020